Praise for the Books of

Books by Betty Hechtman

Crochet Mysteries

Hooked on Murder
Dead Men Don't Crochet
By Hook or By Crook
A Stitch in Crime
You Better Knot Die
Behind the Seams
If Hooks Could Kill
For Better or Worsted
Knot Guilty
Seams Like Murder
Hooking for Trouble
On the Hook
Hooks Can Be Deceiving
One for the Hooks
Killer Hooks
Murder by the Hook

More Books by Betty Hechtman

Yarn Retreat Mysteries

Yarn to Go
Silence of the Lamb's Wool
Wound up in Murder
Gone with the Wool
A Tangled Yarn
Inherit the Wool
Knot on Your Life
But Knot for Me
Knot a Game
Knot Dead Again

Writer for Hire Mysteries

Murder Ink
Writing a Wrong
Making It Write
Sentenced to Death

Crochet and Crumpets Mysteries

Death Among the Stitches

Murder by the Hook

BETTY HECHTMAN

Murder by the Hook
Betty Hechtman
Copyright © 2025 by Betty Hechtman

Beyond the Page Books
are published by
Beyond the Page Publishing
www.beyondthepagepub.com

ISBN: 978-1-966322-07-8

Acknowledgments

Thank you to Bill Harris for another great editing job. Jessica Faust keeps making things happen for me.

Thank you to my loyal blog commenters Linda Osborn, Patty Jenkins, Sally Morrison, Miss Merry and Miriam Lubet. And top fans Valley Weaver, Melissa Phillips Cook and Catherine Guerin.

Dru's Musings blog, *Kings River Life* magazine, and the Facebook groups Cozy Mystery Lovers/Meg's Cozy Corner and Cozies, Conversation and More have done a great job of creating a community of mystery readers and writers.

Thanks to Max and Jakey for all the trips to Ojai. And thanks to Burl for being the cake tester and giving it his stamp of approval.

Chapter 1

I chuckled to myself as I walked into the lobby of the Century City office building. It was lunchtime and people were flooding out of the elevators, and I was sure that none of them would guess why I was there. Not that they even noticed me. They were like a bunch of zombies staring at their phones and bumping into each other as they made their way to the doors leading out. It was lucky that the glass doors opened automatically or they probably would have walked right into them.

It was my own little secret why I was there and I loved it. I was leading a double life. No one would think it by looking at me. I was a fifty-something woman dressed in khaki pants, an untucked white shirt with a black pullover sweater on top, which was perfect for my job as assistant manager/event coordinator at Shedd & Royal Books and More, but hardly something Mata Hari would wear.

Another elevator arrived and as more zombies got out, one person was actually looking up at the crowd in the lobby. There was no mistaking the broad face with the lock of salt-and-pepper hair on his forehead. I lifted my hand with a discreet wave to make sure he saw me without anyone else picking up on our connection. Mason Fields was a high-powered attorney with a lot of celebrity clients. He never dressed casually for work, even when he was in his corner office for the whole day. I didn't know what the color of his suit would be called. It was a blend of beige tones with some yellow and dark threads woven in. From a distance it appeared as a warm neutral. I couldn't see below his shoulders, but I knew it was custom-tailored with a perfect drape. His shirt was off-white and had a silky sheen from the high thread count. He wore no tie and the collar was open.

His expression was a pleasant enough smile, but nothing close to the reaction I used to get when he saw me. I let out a heavy sigh. It was all my fault. I had been a runaway bride. Well, not exactly. We didn't get as far as an actual wedding, just planning to get married. Now I was merely an employee. I ordered myself to snap out of it and to be grateful that he had been able to set aside our past and appreciate my skills enough to have me work for him. I had come up with my title. I saw myself as his private private investigator. My assignments weren't things like infiltrating a biker gang or anything really dangerous. I went undercover and did things like pretending to be part of a cleaning crew to get a discarded plastic champagne flute with a DNA sample, or hanging out at a playground to see if a nanny was breaking her nondisclosure agreement and gossiping with the other nannies about the embarrassing habits of her celebrity employers.

My last job had been to work as a mobile drink and snack server at the local country club. While I was whipping up some smoothies on the trailer attached to a golf cart, I took in a golf foursome's conversation about setting up one of Mason's clients so he could be ousted as CEO. The group of them ignored me, and if they noticed anything, it was probably that I was taking a very long time to make their drinks. They never guessed that my phone recorded their conversation as an audio file.

Mason walked past me and discreetly gestured for me to follow him. He eyed the new group of zombies going through the lobby, concerned someone might notice if it appeared as if we were together. No one was supposed to know I was working for him.

The only person who had any idea what I was doing was my older son, Peter. It was ironic because Peter was so embarrassed about my amateur sleuthing, and yet he had been instrumental in me going pro. It still made me laugh to think that Peter had asked me to help him check up on some investors in his new venture. I had done a good job if I said so myself and saved my son from a lot of trouble.

Peter had stayed connected to Mason, despite our breakup. It was a long story, but Peter's production company had imploded and Mason, with all of his entertainment business connections, was helping my son make a new start.

My success at using my sleuthing skills to help my son had gotten back to Mason, which made him think about hiring me. Mason had felt an obligation to tell my son about our arrangement, though I was pretty sure Peter had done his best to forget all about it. He had enough on his own plate with his new production company, a baby with a hostile woman who would have divorced him if they had gotten married, along with using my converted garage as his office.

Once the grief of losing my husband, Charlie, had gotten manageable, I had begun a whole new chapter in my life that had started with getting the job at Shedd & Royal as the event coordinator. One of the events I coordinated were the meet-ups of the Tarzana Hookers for social crocheting. They offered friendship and a way to keep my hands busy. I was spending too much time eating homemade caramel popcorn. My life kept expanding from there. I looked at my working as a private private investigator as the cherry on the sundae.

I knew I was supposed to not tell anyone about my side gig, but I didn't think telling my best friend, Dinah Lyons, about it counted. We had no secrets. Besides, she would have figured out that something weird was going on when I suddenly had the temporary odd jobs like working at that golf course.

I followed Mason outside the tall building and waited while he looked for someplace private to conduct the rest of our business. Once part of the Twentieth Century Fox Studios, Century City was now an enclave of high-rise office buildings with fabulous views, luxury residential units, a hotel and a high-end outdoor shopping mall. It was considered a posh area, but to me it seemed like a lot of concrete that felt stark and impersonal.

The morning clouds were just beginning to melt. The weather people called it June gloom and made it seem like news even though it happened every year. The mornings were cool and gray before the sun came out and made the afternoons hot. I was glad for the sweater but knew I would be taking it off soon. We moved away from the entrance. Since I had already given him a report on my last job, this meeting was just to pay me. He handed me an envelope containing cash so there would be no paper trail.

"That should keep you in yarn for a while," Mason said, glancing at the envelope in my hand. He knew all about the Tarzana Hookers and that the group met in the bookstore's yarn department. I always felt the need to explain why a bookstore had a yarn department. These days the more things to draw in customers, the better. Once I had learned how to crochet, it hadn't taken long for me to fall in love with yarn and buy way too much of it. Honestly, I had enough of a stash to last me for the rest of my life. I had discovered the hard way that it was a lot faster to buy yarn than it was to make something with it.

I nodded at Mason as if what he paid me was like my mad money. Actually, I would have done it for nothing, though the cash was coming in handy. I had my late husband's insurance money and what I earned at the bookstore, but, well, I had a whole menagerie of dogs and cats who cost a bunch in food, vet bills and toys. Both of my sons had sort of moved back home. Samuel was a budding musician with a job at a coffee place. It didn't pay enough for him to afford his own place. Peter had taken over the former garage and there was the matter of his daughter, Marlowe. She was a toddler now, and since both of her parents had careers that took up all their time, she spent a lot of her time at my house. And she needed all kinds of stuff. No more babies sleeping in an empty drawer and having fun playing with an empty box. Maybe she didn't absolutely need all of it, but after having two sons, it was fun to buy things for a girl. I was sure that someday she would appreciate all those dolls I had been amassing. In the meantime, I was enjoying them. Who knew there was a Barbie detective?

I couldn't really say that my mother and her singing group, the She La Las, added any expenses. They were working again and had put together an oldies show. They performed their one hit and did covers of other songs from the time. The big news was they were being featured on an upcoming PBS special dedicated to Girl Groups Over the Years. I was sure by now they could do their dance moves in their sleep, but they were insistent on practicing to the extreme. My parents lived in a retirement complex that didn't have a place for them to work on their act, so they used my living room. It came in handy that the "girls" and my father were at my place a lot, as they looked after Marlowe when I was at work.

And I felt bad about screwing up the name of their hit. It was "My Man Dan." What had I been thinking calling it "My Guy Bill"?

My house had been too quiet after Charlie died and now it was the opposite, but I liked that it was filled with life and even the commotion. I was glad to be able to take care of everything and everyone, even if it had altered my plan for a new chapter in my life that had included living alone.

I still laughed when I remembered how Peter had hounded me to downsize after Charlie died. He kept pushing the idea of my selling the house and moving into a condo. It was lucky for him and all of them that I hadn't listened.

"Thanks," I said, putting the envelope in my bag. I wondered if I should tell him how much I loved feeling like a woman of mystery, but it seemed better to keep anything personal out of it.

I was glad I hadn't said anything when Mason acted as if it was all business. "You really have been a help with oddball things that no one else could handle." His tone was impersonal and I started to move away, thinking we were done, but he stopped me. "There's something else. I have a new assignment for you." He looked around the walkway that led to the Century City Mall. It was barren except for some concrete planters filled with succulents. "I thought we could talk about it over lunch," he said. I knew that he didn't want anyone in his office to know about me. They had an investigative staff who took care of the firm's regular needs.

My mind went back to the old days when he would spirit me away from the bookstore and we would go somewhere wonderful for a long lunch. There was that restaurant in Topanga Canyon that had most of the tables outside overlooking a creek. And then there had been that picnic at the bluff in Malibu where we watched a pod of dolphins play. I was thinking over some of the other atmospheric places we had gone when he threw cold water on the image and suggested a fast casual place in the outdoor mall. But then it was a business lunch and he was now my boss.

Mason had been full of romantic gestures, like ordering a bunch of dishes that we would share. There was none of that this time. I stood with him in line and looked over the offerings of Mexican dishes and chose a tostada salad. I was about to add that I wanted it without the shell and with rice instead of beans, but he did it before I could.

"Thank you. I'm surprised you remembered," I said as we moved down the line.

He looked at me with an inscrutable expression. "Habit," he said with a shrug. "We had a lot of meals together." He left it at that and we went outside to find a table. We took one shaded by a rainbow-colored umbrella that was far enough away from the others that no one would overhear.

I looked at the pager on the table as it slowly blinked, ready to change into quick flashes when our food was ready. "Do you want to talk about it now or wait until we get the food?" I said.

"We might as well get to it," he said. His manner was crisp and professional. "This job is a little different. It's not local and would require an overnight stay. And you would be working with me directly."

My mind was already whirring. Up until now, I had taken care of my assignments on my own and then just handed over a report and whatever evidence I had to Mason in a meeting like this. I wasn't sure how it would be dealing with him *directly*, as he put it. I considered stopping him right there and turning it down, but then I ordered myself to get it together. If he could be all impersonal, so could I.

"Then you would be there overnight as well?" I said. "I would need to know where and when."

"Don't worry. This would not require us to act like a couple. You would be introduced as my cousin." He looked at me and I nodded. "As for where, it's the Ojai Valley, actually a town called Pixie." He couldn't help but smile at the name. "It's named for the mandarins that grow there." Then he hesitated. "There's something else. It came up at the last minute," he said and then explained it was in two days.

"That is last-minute." I took a moment to absorb what he'd said and check the calendar on my phone. "But lucky for you it actually could work for me," I said. "The Hookers are having a getaway trip to Ojai, leaving on Wednesday." I glanced across the table at him. "Once I'm done with the job for you, I could join them for the rest of the weekend." I took a sip of water. "What exactly do you want me to do?"

The pager went into a flurry of flashing red lights and he got up to get the food. When he returned, he set the plates on the table. I took one look at the salad and felt my stomach clench. There was too much going on in my mind, and I knew the food would taste like cardboard.

It was confusing to me that he could be so matter-of-fact and I was feeling a flurry of emotions connected to our past. He picked up his soft taco, managing to take a bite without any of the filling falling out. When he had put it back on the plate, he looked at me. "I'll tell you all about it on the ride up there. This assignment is very confidential." He looked at me squarely and I knew that he had figured out that Dinah knew I was working for him.

"You mean I would be riding up there with you?" I said, and he nodded. I wasn't sure about taking a road trip with Mason even if it was only around an hour away. I'd be a captive audience, stuck in the car with him. It already felt awkward having lunch with him. We had never really talked about our breakup. If anything, he had acted pretty cool about the whole thing. But then, even though I'd done a number of jobs for him, I hadn't spent much time with him. And when I did, they were just brief impersonal encounters where he seemed eerily distant. It was almost as if he had erased our whole relationship from his mind.

7

"Was there something wrong with it?" he asked, indicating my salad. I had pushed it around on the plate and only taken a bite or two. It seemed unprofessional to admit that the whole situation from having lunch with him to the assignment he had offered had left me feeling unnerved. "I'm not really hungry," I said and pushed the plate away. I was not going to let on how ruffled I felt.

We walked back to his building and he said he would pick me up on Wednesday. Just before we parted, I asked him how I should dress for the mystery assignment and he gave me my first clue.

"You'll be attending a party. I would suggest something that is casually elegant," he said before he went inside and I rushed back to my car.

• • •

My challenge now was to get to the other side of the hill before the freeway became like a parking lot. The so-called hill was actually the Santa Monica mountains. The whole area on both sides was technically Los Angeles, but the San Fernando Valley was like a different world. The weather was more extreme and the vibe more casual. It was definitely a lot lower on the snob scale than places on the city side like Beverly Hills and Brentwood.

But we had this magnificent view. I never got tired of that moment when the 405 cleared the Sepulveda Pass, and I got that glimpse of the whole valley framed by mountains in the distance. It was even more magical at night with all the twinkling lights. Once I got through the interchange with the 101, I zoomed past the open green space of the Sepulveda Dam area before the freeway became bordered by apartment buildings and businesses.

I was back to thinking about my meeting with Mason as I pulled into the parking lot off Ventura Boulevard in Tarzana. It was one of the communities that hugged the main thoroughfare that ran along the base of the Santa Monica Mountains. Part of the appeal of the area was that one minute you could be shopping at Gelson's and just a few minutes later be up walking in the mountains on Dirt Mulholland, where you had to be on the lookout for rattlesnakes and mountain lions.

I put it all on hold until I could spill the whole situation to Dinah. I knew she would understand my confused emotions and I was going to need her help dealing with the weekend, starting with telling the Hookers why I wasn't going to be there for the first night.

And now it was back to my day job. I took a deep breath and walked into Shedd & Royal Books and More, knowing the usual peace had been upended. The store was open and there were a few customers, but the whole place was unsettled in preparation for the mini remodel. Not only was it being painted and recarpeted, but parts of the interior were going to be rearranged. Times had changed and the video and music room was obsolete, and the plan was to make it into a craft area. The yarn department was to be moved from the back of the store and incorporated into an area that had kids' classes with glue and paint. It was going to change everything. For now, the cubbies filled with colorful yarn, the comfortable chairs, and the wood table felt like a peaceful enclave for the yarn group to meet in, or for errant crocheters or knitters to relax and work on a project, or try out some yarn. I pictured rowdy kids playing keep-away with balls of yarn while the crochet group tried to talk.

I nodded a greeting at Mrs. Shedd as I passed on my way to my "office," which was the information booth. She was talking to a man in jeans and work boots who I assumed was the contractor. I was always amazed how my boss never changed. Her honey blond hair didn't have a thread of gray and her classic skirt and blouse were timeless.

The bookstore was going to shut down while the major work was done and Mrs. Shedd had suggested the getaway for the Hookers since their hangout spot was going to be off-limits. As the assistant manager and event coordinator, I was loosely in charge and the plans were still coming together even though the trip was imminent.

Mr. Royal caught up with me and saw me staring at the alcove that had been devoted to CDs, vinyl records and DVDs. It had already been cleared out and was a big empty space. He had a wiry build and longish dark hair with some strands of silver. He was about the same age as Mrs. Shedd, but something about him made him seem younger. "It's time to give the bookstore a rebirth," he said. "We want to include more crafts groups, have classes for all ages and sell the necessary supplies. We're starting up the writers' group again and we want to host more book clubs."

With all the rearranging starting in a couple of days, I realized it might be my last chance to make my pitch, and I told Mr. Royal my concerns about mixing up the yarn crafters with impatient kids waving glue guns. He smiled, instantly understanding. "That would have been me in my younger days," he said with a chuckle as he mimicked holding a glue gun. "You gave me an idea. It's not exactly a craft, more like a skill. We could have juggling lessons," he said enthusiastically. "We could make it a craft by having the students make their own objects."

He grabbed some stress balls from a display and started juggling with them. He wanted me to have a try, but I politely refused and went back to my concerns. He lost his concentration and the balls fell to the ground. He shrugged off his failure and went to retrieve them. "I'll do what I can to save the back area," he said, giving juggling another try, this time with four balls. He kept his eyes on the balls as he talked to me. "But no guarantees. Pamela has this vision how the place should be." He was keeping all the balls in the air and had a confident smile. "Did Pamela give you all the info about the house in Pixie?"

"All I know is that the house belongs to a friend of hers and they offer it as a short-term rental when they're not using it," I said.

"I wish I was going up there with you. The whole vibe of the place is perfect for a relaxed stay. You can just kick back and do your yarn thing in a calm and peaceful atmosphere. No ripples in the pond."

I felt myself smiling. Maybe all that would be true for the others, but I had my secret assignment. I was sorry I couldn't tell Mr. Royal about it. He had traveled the world doing all sorts of odd jobs and I knew he would appreciate my side job.

Now that he had shown off his skill, Mr. Royal tired of juggling and put the balls back in the display. He went to join his wife and the contractor, while I made a detour to the café. At their suggestion, I had tried calling them Pamela and Joshua, but it felt too strange. They would always be Mrs. Shedd and Mr. Royal to me. The funny thing is that their last names weren't correct anymore, at least hers. After years of having a working and private relationship, they had finally gotten married. I could definitely relate that going through a name change at their age was awkward, particularly considering the name of the bookstore.

It was a relief to walk into the connected café. It was not being redone and had a nice feeling of normalcy. The café wasn't even going to close during the remodel since it had its own outside entrance.

Bob was the main barista and was leaning on the counter, reading. He looked up and smiled when I came in. "The usual?" he said and I nodded.

The usual was a red-eye, and I suddenly wondered how all the caffeine of a shot of espresso in a cup of coffee would be on an empty stomach since I hadn't eaten my lunch. A sweet buttery smell was coming from a tray of freshly baked cookie bars sitting on top of the glass. "You better add a couple of those," I said. I looked over the rest of the snack offerings and picked up a bag of almonds to go with them.

He put everything into one of the cardboard carriers and I went back into the bookstore. When I got to my cubicle, I realized I had forgotten napkins. I left the carrier and started to retrace my steps. As I passed the entrance to the children's department, I heard moaning and groaning along with some loud muttering.

I had a pretty good idea who was making all the noise and wanted to ignore it, but what if customers heard her, or worse, someone brought their children into the kids' department just then. I felt an obligation to the bookstore to fix the situation. Ha! As if anyone could fix Adele Abrams Humphries.

It was hard to define our relationship. We were fellow crocheters and coworkers, though she still felt miffed that I'd been hired to be the event coordinator instead of her being promoted to the position. Being in charge of the kids' department was supposed to be a consolation prize. It might have worked if Adele liked kids, which she didn't. But somehow the kids loved her. Her story times were always at capacity and full of drama and wild costumes. Even when it wasn't story time, she tended to dress as though every day was Halloween. I knew I would probably regret it, but I crossed onto the dark blue carpet that featured cows jumping over the moon and lots of stars. I was glad the new carpeting was going to be the same design.

Adele was a tall woman with an ample build, kind of like Julia Child. She dominated the space as she paced back and forth, muttering to herself. She was dressed all in black and so wrapped up in herself that she didn't see me. "Mother Humphries is crazy. Not doing my wifely duties, ha! What is she from, the Dark Ages? I am woman, hear me roar. So what if Eric has to pick up pizzas a lot. Why can't she do her mother-in-law duties and butt out. He should be honored by what I made for him and wear it proudly." She let out a heavy moan. "What am I going to do?" She began to pace again, holding the back of her hand to her forehead in a melodramatic pose out of a silent movie.

She still hadn't noticed me as she continued. "Well, I'm out of there. I can't take any more of their criticism." The moans had made me think she might be injured, but after hearing her soliloquy, I realized it was all mental and personal and I tried to slip out unnoticed. But just then her long vest made out of granny squares caught on one of the kid-sized chairs, causing her to look up. She jumped when she saw me.

"You startled me, Pink," she said, furrowing her brow. "You should have said something when you walked in." Adele was the only one who called me by my last name, though lately she had actually begun to sometimes call me Molly. She knew it annoyed me to be called by my last name and I thought it was connected to me getting the job she wanted, though by now I wondered if she even remembered why she did it. The only way to deal with her was to shrug it all off and let it go.

"Sorry," I said, putting up my hands in apology as I started to back away. I had discovered that saying I was sorry even when I wasn't even involved went a long way to keeping the peace.

She reached out to stop me. "Don't go. I need to talk." As I paused, she continued. "I just don't know what I'm going to do."

Along with being a fellow crocheter and bookstore coworker, there was something else. Adele often seemed hostile to me, but at the same time, more than once she had told me I was her best friend in the world. It seemed like she was having one of those moments because she abruptly and rather awkwardly hugged me.

It was against my better judgment, but I couldn't keep myself from doing it and asked her what was wrong. "I can't take it anymore," she wailed. "Eric chose Mother Humphries over me again. He refuses to see that she doesn't like me and keeps starting trouble."

Was there any point in mentioning again that calling her mother-in-law Mother Humphries might be part of the problem? Probably not, so I let it go. I considered asking her what had happened to make her feel that way, but I figured it would be opening a can of worms and kept quiet.

"I need to get away to think," she said, putting her hand back on her forehead. "Thank heavens we have our trip." She looked at me. "Then maybe I can stay at your place. Didn't you turn your garage into a guest house?"

I took a politician's way out and didn't answer, and instead talked about something else entirely. "What's with all the hearts?" I asked, looking at the array of crocheted hearts in shades of red and pink on the table in front of her. Most of them were small, but there was one that was larger and had been doubled and stuffed. All of them had strips of paper attached with writing on them. I picked one up and read the banner attached to it. *Dream Big!*

I was relieved when the distraction worked and Adele's whole demeanor changed. "Nice, huh," Adele said. "I'm trying to decide which pattern to use. One of the bookstore customers saw me crocheting and hired me to make hearts with inspirational messages for a luncheon she's hosting." She poked through the different versions. "I like this big stuffed one the best, but the smaller flat ones are quicker to make." She started to gather them up and put them into a tote bag. "I need to finish them over the weekend. I'm sure everybody will want to pitch in and help. I tried working on them at home and Mother Humphries fussed that I was leaving strands of yarn all over. She hates crochet. You should have seen how she reacted when I showed Eric something I made for him. I'm sure he would have loved it if it wasn't for her." Adele made a *grrr* sound and grabbed a heart. "I should make one of these for her with a note that says *Butt Out and Move Out.*"

Accepting that the distraction had only been temporary, I let out a sigh. Not only was she back on Eric's mother, but I got the drift that Adele was going to keep things stirred up during the getaway. We would be hearing her woes about Eric and his mother the whole time while she pestered everyone to help her make the hearts. And who knew what else she would come up with. I would have to make sure that she didn't find out about my job for Mason. Even though letting her know I was now a professional sleuth might get her to stop calling me Tarzana's Nancy Drew.

Chapter 2

It was late afternoon and I was back in the yarn department waiting for the Hookers' meetup. They didn't know about the plans to move the yarn department. Not even Adele knew. Mrs. Shedd had only told her about what was being done to the kids' area, which was probably a smart move. I wasn't about to enlighten them either. I was holding out hope that Mr. Royal would get Mrs. Shedd to reconsider.

For now, it just looked like the yarn was being packed up in plastic bins to make it moveable and safe from getting paint spattered on it. The bins had been left spread haphazardly around the back area. The first thing I did was straighten and stack them. The little move did a lot to give the space a sense of order.

I mentally went over the things the group needed to talk about regarding the trip. One thing I knew for sure was that I was leaving it up to Adele to tell them she expected them to help with the hearts. Why should I be the heavy.

My thought drifted back to my secret mission. Mason had said my job was at a party and I wondered where it would be and who would be there. Why did I have to stay overnight? What did he want me to do this time? And what was casual elegant?

"Oh, what chaos, dear," CeeCee Collins said, looking around as she came into the yarn area. "The whole store feels like it's upside down." She put her tote bag on the table. "I hope it's all fixed by the time we get back. You never really said what's going to change. It would be nice if this area was a little bigger." She looked at the carousel of hooks and needles and thought over what she had said. "Unless having a bigger space means adding a knitting group to meet here." She rocked her head in dismay. "You know who would have a fit about that. And we'd all have to listen to her." On top of all her other issues, Adele went crazy when it came to knitters.

"We can cross that bridge when we have to," I said. "But if a group of knitters want to hang out, we'll have to let them." I didn't want to mention what I was more concerned about. If Mr. Royal failed to get the yarn department to stay put, we were going to have to deal with a lot worse than hearing Adele throw a fit about knitters.

"Adele really needs to understand there is more to yarn craft than crochet. But I guess that's a hopeless cause, just the way she refuses to acknowledge that I am supposed to be the leader of our group," she said. As usual, CeeCee appeared put together and ready to meet the public, her public. She had kept the same blondish hairstyle she'd had since the days of *The CeeCee Collins Show*, which gave her a timeless look. Her long career had had plenty of ups and downs. Being nominated for an Academy Award recently had done a lot to keep her on the radar, though she was still referred to as a veteran actor.

I liked how she handled her celebrity status. It had never gone to her head and she had a friendly relationship with her fans. She graciously posed for selfies and gave out autographs whenever she was asked. CeeCee was the original leader of the crochet group, though Adele had gotten it into her head that she really was the chief Hooker. The solution had been to seat them at opposite heads of the table.

"I'm really looking forward to our trip. Getting away from pressure will be great." She let out a heavy breath. "It's exhausting taping three shows in a day." CeeCee was benefiting from the abundance of game shows on broadcast TV now. She had been hired as the host of *Try to Fool Me.* I didn't understand exactly how the game worked, but there was a big wheel that got spun, something about guessing who the masked celebrity was, and finally, picking a door to get the prizes behind it. She paused for a moment and let out a sigh. "I'm waiting to hear about something else. Something really big. The waiting is killing me and I need to get my mind off of it."

She asked me about our accommodations and what the plans were.

"It's going to be a serendipity kind of weekend," I said, and then I thought of what Mr. Royal had said about the area. "We'll kick back and enjoy the vibe. Just let the weekend happen."

"I didn't realize you were so New Agey, dear," CeeCee said and took out the baby blanket she was making to donate to a shelter.

More of the group filtered in and then Adele made a grand entrance. She poured the hearts on the table with a flourish. "I have the group project for our trip," she said, before explaining that she needed thirty of them to fill the order she had.

"I don't know about that," CeeCee said. "Why should we do a group project to help you with a job you took on and are getting paid for."

Adele began to pout. "But I thought we were one for all and all for one. I'm under a lot of pressure here. I promised to have them done next week."

"We're not the Three Musketeers," CeeCee said. She looked over the group. "Or the Six Musketeers. You shouldn't take on jobs that you can't do yourself, Adele. We should really talk about carpooling and who is going."

"I can't go," Sheila Altman said in a plaintive tone. "Now that I'm the manager of Luxe, I can't just take off time." Luxe was a lifestyle store down the street from the bookstore. Sheila was the youngest member of the group and had really wanted to work on costumes in the entertainment business. The job at Luxe had been meant to be temporary until she got a chance at her dream job. But now that she was the manager, she was all about the bird in the hand.

"I really hoped I could work it out," she said. "But we're having a sale." We all knew the store's owner had moved on to something else but still dictated things like when they would have sales. "I thought I might be able to make it up there for one night," she said and then shook her head. "I'm sorry. I'm really sorry. I hope it doesn't mess anything up." Her voice was becoming more high-pitched and tense as she spun out. Rhoda Klein was sitting next to her and recognized what was happening to Sheila and pushed a ball of ecru yarn and a J sized hook toward her. Sheila glanced down for a moment and then, as if in a trance, picked up the hook and began to make a long strand of chain stitches. By the time she was going back over the chain stitches with single crochets, it was like a miracle. Her furrowed brow relaxed and the pinched look about her face went away. Even her breathing changed from hyperventilating to smooth and even.

She gave Rhoda a thank-you hug before showing the rest of us that she had her emergency kit of some string and a hook in her pocket. "But I was too wound up to remember that I had it."

"You better count me out, too," Eduardo Linnares said. He was the only man in our group and I wasn't too surprised he wasn't coming. Though he liked to crochet with us, he didn't do much hanging out beyond the group's meetups. He was still incredibly handsome, but his angular face had matured since the days when he was a pirate or the Duke of Somewhere-shire and graced the covers of romance novels. The long mane of dark hair was cut into a shaggy style now. He was more than a pretty face and had become a celebrity, often appearing on talk shows. He had an engaging personality and a sense of humor about his cover model days and was quick to make fun of the billowing shirts open to his belt buckle or the ones that appeared to have been ripped off.

He continued to crochet an elaborate doily with fine white thread as he explained why he couldn't come. It always amazed me to see how he could make such delicate stitches with his large hands, but it was second nature to him. His Irish grandmother on his mother's side, having no granddaughters to teach, had taught him how to crochet lace.

"It's hard when you're a business owner," he said. He had opened the Apothecary, which was a high-end shop in Encino that sold drugs and sundries. His latest endeavor was a restaurant. It turned out that he was a great cook.

"I was looking forward to you making that French toast you're always talking about," Elise Belmont said. She had a birdlike voice and looked as if a strong gust of wind could carry her away. But her personality was nothing like her looks. While she appeared kind of scattered, she had an iron core and was like a terrier on a pant leg when she focused on anything, whether it was her infatuation with vampires or selling real estate. "But don't worry. I'm definitely coming. I wouldn't miss the chance to get a look at the real estate market in Pixie and the Ojai Valley. It's become a real magnet for celebrity types who want to get away from LA, but not too far. You know, Johnny Cash lived in the area for a long time." She looked over the group. "And of course, I want to spend time with all of you and our hooks."

"Count me in as a definite yes," Rhoda Klein said. "I already left dinners packed for Hal in the freezer." She addressed the group. "He's not happy that I'm going and freaking out that he's going to starve while I'm gone." Even after years of living in Southern California, Rhoda still had a strong New York accent. She had a blunt personality and just said what she had to with no filters. Like now when she looked at Adele. "What's with the black clothes? You look like you're in mourning."

Adele jumped on the comment and stood up, striking a melodramatic pose. "I am in mourning—for my marriage. After this weekend, I'll be living at Molly's."

All heads turned to me and I shook my head. "Nobody agreed to that," I said.

Dinah had come in just as Adele made her announcement and I gave my answer. My best friend looked at me and rolled her eyes as our gazes met.

"What about you? Are you backing out too?" Rhoda asked, looking at Dinah. "And what's with the pants suit?" My friend had come from her teaching job at the local community college. It was her last day of the semester and she was worn out from teaching freshman English to a bunch of Generation Alphas. She had stopped wearing her long scarves after one got caught in her car door and almost strangled her. She took off the jacket of her gray pants suit and hung it on the back of her chair.

"I'm done with dressing to look approachable." She touched her short salt-and-pepper hair that seemed extra spiky. "No more trying to be their friends," Dinah said. She showed off her black chunky heels. "No more remote classes either. When they hear me walk in that classroom, I want them to know that I'm in charge." She sat down and heaved a tired sigh. "And I'm a definite yes for the long weekend. I need a change before I have to deal with summer school."

"What's the plan for the weekend?" Rhoda said. I tried to give the same answer I had given CeeCee, but she didn't take it as well as CeeCee had and pushed for details that I didn't have. I promised to get them the location and said that we could figure out how to deal with meals when we got there.

"I've been to Ojai and there are lots of cute shops and plenty of cafés and restaurants. This is supposed to be time off for all of us," Elise said. "Why should we bother with cooking?"

Just then a customer came into the yarn department. She looked at the long table with the group spread around it and then at the colorful cubbies of yarn. "Does anyone work her?" She glanced back into the bookstore and then at the group. "I could use some help figuring out how much yarn I need for a pattern."

Adele had already gotten up and volunteered her services when the woman held up the pattern and said it was for a knit shawl.

There was a moment when all of us sucked in our breath, knowing what was about to happen. There was no way the customer could know that she had used the verboten *K* word to Adele.

CeeCee got up and tried to intervene, but it was too late. Adele had pulled herself up to her full height and glared at the woman. "No needle stuff here. We're hookers. Crochet only," she said in a voice that sounded like it came out of the *Godfather*.

I think we were all surprised when Sheila got in the middle of it and acted as the hero. She stepped in front of Adele, blocking her with her arms, and moved the woman away, saying that she would be glad to help her.

Adele did one of her melodramatic numbers and sat down in a huff and went on with her stock speech that crochet was the royalty of yarn craft and needle heads were missing out. When Sheila finally returned to the table, everyone but Adele gave her a round of applause.

Dinah stayed behind when the group broke up. "Just another afternoon with the Hookers," she said, looking at the empty table when they were gone. "At least we got the carpooling worked out. CeeCee is used to being taken around, and Elise likes to be in control." Dinah smiled. "I don't envy Rhoda driving Adele." She turned to me. "What about us?"

"There's something I have to tell you," I said.

Chapter 3

"Wow," Dinah said after I got finished telling her about my lunch with Mason and my new assignment. "How exciting and mysterious. I miss being part of the sleuthing now that you've gone professional, but I'll be glad to cover for you. Just make sure I have whatever you want me to take up there. And the location and how to get in. I'll just tell them you had something come up at the last minute and you'll be joining us later." She laughed as she continued. "I'll make sure we share a room and I'll put pillows in your bed so it looks like you're sleeping." We had adjourned to her house, which was around the corner from the bookstore. I was finished for the day and it was much better to talk there and not have to worry about someone overhearing us.

We had gone into the room Dinah called her she-cave. The space had been added on to the compact house and was probably meant to be a den. There had been lots of compromises when she married Commander Blaine and he moved in. But this room had stayed totally hers. While we talked, he was off in the kitchen putting together a special dinner to celebrate the end of the semester. The she-cave was soundproof and we couldn't even hear the classical music he was listening to as he cooked.

"I don't know if you have to go so far as stuffing my bed. It's not like anyone is going to be checking up on me," I said.

"Don't be so sure. Adele is nuts and I could picture Rhoda coming in looking for you. It would be a lot easier if I pointed to the bed and said you were sleeping."

"Okay," I said, laughing. Then it faded as I went back to talking about working for Mason. "I hope taking this job isn't a mistake. It feels strange to go into something with so little information. I don't know anything about the party or who is giving it. Why do I have to stay overnight?"

"Couldn't you just have asked him?" my friend said.

"You would think so, but he insisted on not giving me any more details until the ride up there. He said it was essential that it stayed secret," I said. "How long will it take him to tell me the details, and then what? What if he starts talking about what happened? What if he corners me and starts to cross-examine me. He is a trial lawyer."

"He's probably afraid you would tell me," she said. "If he hasn't cornered you before this, I think that means he's past it."

"Yes, but we haven't really been alone for more than a few minutes. This is going to be an hour plus." She was the only one who knew that I was working for Mason and the state of our relationship, or more correctly, lack of. She knew all about the mistake I had made blowing everything with Mason when I went off with Barry Greenberg.

Just thinking about Barry made me shake my head. What had I been thinking? That what hadn't worked before was suddenly going to be okay now? He was still a homicide detective and no matter what, the job always came first. Once he got called on a murder—which by the way never happened at a convenient time—he was gone for days with barely any word. There had been the steamy two weeks in Hawaii. But as soon as we came back it was back to the way it was. It had taken barely a month before I realized my mistake and it blew up with Barry. Dinah had been the one to point out that there might have been more to it. That I might have been Mason's runaway fiancée because I didn't really want to get married again.

I was sure Dinah was right. I had been married to Charlie for a long time before he died and I wasn't sure I wanted all that again. Okay, I knew I didn't want that again. I couldn't even figure out where we would live. Would I move with all my animals to his house, where his dog Spike might feel outnumbered? I couldn't imagine him moving to my house with all the stuff going on with my family. And if we didn't live together, why even get married? And what would my name even have been, Molly Pink Fields?

"I like my life as it is—my job, my friends and even all that's going on at my house," I said. "It's not as if I could drop everything and everyone to start a new life with someone. And I don't want to."

"Tell me about it," Dinah said with a knowing laugh. She had gone through a lot of adjustments when she married Commander Blaine. But she had less baggage than I did. There had been issues when Commander moved into her place. Their taste in furniture was different and they had very different schedules, and his daughter was a problem. They had compromised on the furniture and she'd moved the chartreuse couch into her she-cave. Having the separate space helped with their different hours. He could go to bed early and she could stay up late without being worried about waking him.

Dealing with his daughter was a work in progress that Dinah knew would never be settled. They had become flexible about meal times and didn't always eat together. He continued putting on social events for his Mail It center clients and doing his volunteering at the retirement home without her always having to take part.

"Mason will probably be fine on the ride. If he was so upset with you, he never would have hired you to work for him," Dinah said. The she-cave was pretty soundproof, but the smell of Commander's cooking came right in. Dinah saw me sniffing the air. "He's making mushroom stroganoff and that salad I love."

"It sounds great. We better finish up," I said. "But back to Mason. It's almost unnerving, the way he acts. It's like he has amnesia or something. It's not quite that way for me."

"You mean you still feel something?" she said.

I nodded with a sad expression and told her how I'd been thinking about all the romantic lunches Mason and I had had. "But now it's just fast casual Mexican and all business."

I changed the subject and went back to the plans for the Hookers' trip. "I guess you'll have to figure out dinner the first night. Someone said there are lots of cafés." I thought for a moment. "I can send up bins of yarn with you in case they want to do a group project."

"I'm sure it will all work out," Dinah said. She gave me a supportive hug and I left to deal with the chaos I claimed to love so much.

• • •

I pulled in to the end of my long driveway and stopped next to the structure that had been the garage. The big door was gone, replaced by three French doors. The blinds on the glass were open and I could see Peter hovering over his computer. Light streamed in through the window we'd added when the space transitioned from a place for cars and junk to what we called the studio. It was perfect for his office, and I pictured his expression if Adele showed up with her suitcase and said she was moving in. Peter really needed more of a sense of humor.

My house was a white stucco ranch-style that had a classic design that never looked dated. The back of the house was all windows with a view of the yard, which still had a line of orange trees left from the time when citrus groves covered the area. It felt like a private space thanks to the tall redwood trees and Torrey pines that ran along the back fence and almost totally blotted out the huge two-story house in the yard behind.

I could already hear the music as I walked across the gray stone patio to my kitchen door. I recognized the She La Las' new song. It was a whole new world where they didn't need a record company to get their music out there. It was called "Second Chances." I had heard it so many times I practically heard the lyrics in my sleep. *"We're not finished. Just redefined. It's another chance, and it's all on the line."*

My greeting committee was waiting and jostling for position to be in front when I opened the door. A whirl of gray wiry fur flew past me as Felix took off out into the yard. It was hard to tell which end was up, as Cosmo rushed behind him. His long black fur gave him the appearance of a mop with feet. He was truly mine now that Barry had relinquished ownership when we broke up the last time. He and his son had adopted the dog, and viewed him as their pet even though the dog stayed at my house. A white puff of fur barreled out after them. Princess was tiny and a poodle mix. I'd taken her in when her owner died. I shut the door just in time to stop the cats from exiting. It didn't matter what their real names were, the two cats Samuel had brought home were known as Mr. Kitty and Cat Woman. He was black and white with a crooked mustache and she was an odd grayish color and looked like she was wearing a skirt of mottled orange and gray. The third cat, Buttercup, watched it all from a perch on the kitchen table. She had long hair and was butterscotch and white. Her owner was deceased as well.

I knew I would find the last dog in her chair in my room. I thought of Blondie as the Greta Garbo of canines since she seemed most content to be alone, away from everyone. She was my first dog and I had adopted her right after Charlie died. She was a terrier mix with a very un-terrier aloof personality who had been at a private shelter for a very long time. I was pretty sure she had been adopted once and returned, probably when they realized she was never going to really bond with them. I felt for her. We were both feeling abandoned. I accepted her reclusive personality and she seemed to accept all the other animals and people that kept moving in.

The kitchen was full of cooking smells. A salad bowl was on the turquoise tiled counter with a pile of vegetables next to it. My father walked in just as I was about to check the oven. "I put in the pan of lasagna you left," he said. He was a retired dermatologist who was now devoting himself to supporting my mother in the resurgence of her singing career. Among other things, he had taken on the job of making sure there was always food and lots of it.

In the beginning, he had brought in such an array of takeout that my refrigerator seemed like the United Nations of leftovers. But recently I had gone back to cooking. I would leave things like the pan of lasagna that was heating or homemade soup with sourdough bread and hunks of sharp cheddar cheese. There were fixings for salad, or bowls of coleslaw that I'd made up. Occasionally I made a cake or a batch of cookies. My dad took care of the serving and the cleanup.

Someone yelled "cut" from the living room.

"What's that about?" I asked.

"Samuel thought we should put some video clips on the website of the She La Las practicing for the PBS special." He chuckled. "It's been a problem keeping Marlowe out of it. I think she's going to be a dancer."

I left my father to his salad duty and walked through the living room to get to the other side of the house. I got a greeting from everybody, including a guy about Samuel's age who had a handheld camera. Marlowe toddled over to me and hugged my leg.

"Maybe she'll go with you," my mother said. "At least for a few minutes so we can get done with this."

Just then Peter came in to say he was leaving for a dinner meeting. Before he could escape, I pulled him aside in the den. "I wanted to remind you that I'm going to be gone and you need to make sure Marlowe's care is covered." The little girl had followed us in there.

"That's right," he said. "You said you were going to Ojai with those crochet friends of yours." He asked me how long I was going to be gone. "That's okay, Marlowe will be with her mom and Mumsy," he said, rolling his eyes at Marlowe's other grandmother's nickname.

"Don't be surprised if you run into Mason," my son said. "He's going up there for Kirkland Rush's wedding." My son looked at me. "You do know who Kirkland Rush is?"

"I know who he is," I said, shaking my head at how out of touch my son thought I was. Kirkland had started out as a TV news reporter but become something more. He was like a news personality. He fancied himself as being a crusading journalist who would go wherever to get a story. His presence became part of the story. He tried to appear fearless and heartfelt at the same time. He had gone to war-torn areas and comforted refugees as he handed out bottles of water and food. Through it all, he always managed to have his best side to the camera and to keep a macho stance. Though actually as I thought about it, I hadn't seen as much of him lately.

"Well, I'm sure I will run into Mason since I'm going to be working for him," I said.

Peter's face clouded. "I didn't realize you were still doing things for him."

Peter cringed when I said that I had done a number of jobs for Mason. "Well, at least you seem to have kept quiet about it," my son said. "What are you going to do for him now?"

"Mason hasn't told me yet. It's usually to get some kind of information that I hand over to him."

"Good. Then you aren't going to be confronting people and falling in tanks of electric eels."

"They weren't actually eels. They're called knife fish, but I'm sure it's not going to be anything like that."

"Please don't mess things up with Mason," he said. "I don't want to ruin my relationship with him. He has been great to me. He helped me make a new start when everything fell apart despite what you did." Peter shook his head with disapproval. There was nothing like being scolded by your son. I could have said a few choice things about the way he was conducting his life, but I chose to let it be.

Marlowe toddled over to us. Peter gave her a quick kiss and headed for the door in the den that led to the yard. As he went out, the three dogs tumbled inside, still in play mode. They followed as I picked up Marlowe and entered my wing of the house. Once I had shut the door to the den, I could barely hear the She La Las as they started up again. The parade of dogs rushed down the hall past me and went on into my bedroom.

Whoever had designed this house must have seen into my future and realized that with all the people hanging out here, I would need someplace to get away from them all. The bathroom was large with a view of a private garden and enough counter space that I had a coffee setup. My craft room had been turned into Marlowe's space and I'd had to move all the stuff into my bedroom. There was plenty of room for cubbies of yarn and a small worktable, along with a love seat and chairs. Even with her own room, there was a chest of Marlowe's things in there too. Along with my bed, there was a portable one for her.

As expected, Blondie was in her chair and only looked up when Princess jumped up next to her.

I gave Marlowe some toys to play with while I went back into the dressing area to check my closet for the weekend's clothes, wondering what I had that counted as casual elegant.

Chapter 4

At midday on Wednesday, I pulled my suitcase outside to the street end of my driveway to wait for Mason. Everything seemed in order. The bookstore had closed and would stay that way while the mini remodel was done. Mr. Royal hadn't said anything, but I had my fingers crossed about keeping the yarn area where it was. Marlowe was already with her mother. Samuel would take care of the animals, and the She La Las were planning to rehearse practically nonstop since the PBS Girl Groups special was taping soon. All any of them knew was that I going up to the Ojai area for a trip with my crochet group and I was riding up there with someone.

Dinah had already left to drive up. She had the bins of yarn and would make excuses for my absence when she met up with the group. We had decided to leave it vague and have her say that something had come up and I wouldn't be joining them until really late.

Even with all that had been taken care of, I felt uneasy. There were so many unknowns and reasons to feel tense. Not having any idea of what Mason wanted me to do was only part of it. It was bound to feel awkward in the car with him. I took a deep breath and reminded myself that I was not a teenager riding with her ex-boyfriend. I was a professional investigator meeting with my employer. Then I chuckled at taking myself so seriously.

And then it was showtime. The black Mercedes SUV pulled to the curb and the hatchback opened. I had my bag stowed before Mason got out of the car to help. I was surprised at how he was dressed. "You changed your look," I said. The words were out of my mouth before I could stop myself.

Mason's casual look had been mostly Hawaiian shirts and jeans, but he was wearing taupe-colored jean-style pants with a black collarless short-sleeved shirt. He looked down at his clothes. "Times change," he said with a shrug. He glanced back at my house. The gyrations of the She La Las were clearly visible through the big living room window. He stopped to watch for a moment and I wondered if it was like a fond memory, or if he felt relief that he was done with me and all of that.

"Is that everything?" he said. When I nodded, he went around to the driver's side and got in while I opened the passenger door. He seemed completely neutral, just the way he had at our lunch. I, on the other hand, was so nervous and fidgety that I had trouble with the seat belt. Mason even asked if I needed help with it.

"Got it," I said. I turned to check out the backseat and noted the empty car seat. "Where's Spike?" I asked. "Is he all right?" The toy fox terrier usually went everywhere with Mason.

"He's fine. I thought he was better off with the pet sitter." As he pulled away from the curb, he pointed to the drink holder, which held two lidded paper cups. There was a white paper bag next to them. "I brought you a red-eye for the road and a snack." I looked inside the bag and saw a spinach empanada and a muffin.

Just as I was thinking what a thoughtful gesture it was, he said, "We don't have time to stop on the way and I can't have my employee drowsy and hungry."

He got onto the 101 and headed north. I tried to settle in and suddenly didn't know what to do with my hands or where I should look. As a result, I kept folding my hands and then holding my elbows and my head seemed to be connected to a swivel mechanism on repeat. I looked out the side window and then through the windshield and back to the side window. It was the first time I had been in the car with him in a long time. It was confusing how it was familiar and strange at the same time. Should I make conversation? The silence was making it worse.

"Are you going to tell me about the job?" I asked when I couldn't take the tension anymore.

"There's no rush," he said. "Have your coffee before it gets cold."

We passed through Calabasas and were going through the area of toast-colored hills dotted with California oaks. I took a few sips of the coffee, but my mouth was so dry that I thought I would choke on the empanada. Finally, I couldn't take the quiet anymore. "Can we just talk about the elephant in the room," I said.

Mason chuckled and glanced around the interior. "It must be invisible, because I don't see it."

"You know what I mean," I said. I had decided not to wait for him to bring it up. Instead of waiting for the shoe to drop, I would throw it on the floor myself. "We have never talked about what happened—well, what I did. If you're holding in some anger at me, could you just let it out and get it over with."

He let my words hang in the air a moment before he answered. "Is that why you seem so nervous," he said.

"What do you mean?" I said, forcing myself to sit still.

"All the fidgeting, like you don't know what to do with yourself," he said, glancing at my hands, which I was forcing to keep folded together. "You can relax. Whatever I might have felt is all gone." He took a sip of his coffee and replaced the cup. "I have moved on and I'm seeing someone else." He gestured to his outfit. "It was her suggestion."

"Oh," I said, feeling strangely deflated.

"She thought this look was more contemporary," he said. What he said should have calmed me, but it didn't. It was like he was saying that everything between us was just water under the bridge that had moved out to sea and I was just his employee now.

It bugged me that he seemed so at ease about the whole situation. I didn't mean for it to happen, but the words tumbled out in a torrent. "How can you be so cool about everything? Aren't you even a little upset with me? I expected at least a flicker of something. I don't understand how you could go from us being about to get married and all that it meant, to seeming so indifferent."

"I see we're getting right into the heavy stuff," he said. "I'm a pragmatist. I accepted that it was not meant to be and decided there was no use wasting energy being upset about it. Ironically, Tiffany wants to get married and now I don't. My life is good the way it is."

"Is she going to be there this weekend?" I asked. I wanted to appear as collected as he was, but I wasn't succeeding. I tried to cover myself by saying that it was no problem for me if she was. And then I stopped myself in mid-sentence. "Forget I asked that. Forget everything that I said that was personal. This is supposed to be business and I thought the point of us riding together was so you could tell me what you want me to do." I turned to look at him. "Does it have anything to do with Kirkland Rush's wedding?"

Mason seemed surprised. "Good for you doing some advance investigating. And don't worry, there won't be any awkward moments with Tiffany. She handles travel arrangements for musicians on tour, and she's tied up with work. If she manages to make it up there, it will be after you're done." He took another sip of his coffee. "And you're right, we should be talking about your upcoming job."

I think we were both glad to get off the personal stuff. I chided myself for what I had done. After being so worried about him putting me in a corner, I was the one who had done it to him.

I needed to do what he had managed. Accept that it was never meant to be for us and then let it go. I wasn't sure how the mechanism worked to dial down my feelings to indifference, but I needed to learn.

"The job is only remotely connected with the wedding and you'll be long finished and back with the Hookers by the time Kirkland ties the knot." We had begun the steep climb to the short pass through the range of mountains that marked the end of the Conejo Valley. The mountains on either side of the road were barren except for some scrubby-looking plants. "The wedding is being hosted by Kirkland's manager, Jerry Rayner, though everybody calls him Jerry R. He manages the bride-to-be as well. He's been a longtime client of the law firm along with being a friend. He asked me to help him with something." Mason did a quick glance at me. "That's where you come in." He took a moment to concentrate on the road as it began the steep descent into Camarillo and beyond. It was suddenly cooler and cloudy with a glimmer of the ocean in the distance.

"Jerry R and his wife Lisa R love to entertain and are known for throwing parties for every holiday or event. Recently, they noticed something of sentimental value had disappeared after one of their get-togethers, and then when they thought about it realized that some other trivial things had gone missing in the recent past. Since the items weren't worth much, they had written them off as lost."

"So, they think one of their guests is a kleptomaniac?" I said and Mason nodded.

"They have a suspect list made up of the people who have been at all of the recent events. It has to be handled very delicately since there are some very well-known people on the list. Jerry R doesn't want to confront anyone unless he's sure it's the right person. He'd like to get back the item with sentimental value and to get the person some help."

"I'm guessing they're having a party tonight and you want me to find the kleptomaniac."

Mason nodded in answer. "That's the overview of it, but Jerry R and Lisa R will give you more details." We were passing through fields of strawberries as the freeway wound through Oxnard. The side of the road was dotted with fruit stands marked with big signs with paintings of the red fruit.

"They requested that you spend the night so your findings could be dealt with in the morning. Then you'll be done." He switched lanes and went around a truck carrying a load of tomatoes. "I'll be staying on for the wedding and the festivities connected to it." I was letting what he had said sink in as he continued. "After all that, the Rayners are still having their usual soiree celebrating the summer solstice on Monday."

"They must really like to entertain," I said.

"Don't worry, they have lots of help. But what do you think about the job?"

The freeway had turned and ran close to the ocean as we went through Ventura. We passed under a railroad bridge as a train crossed it. I usually loved the view, but I barely noticed it as I thought over what he wanted me to do.

"I need more information and to see what I'm dealing with and who," I said.

"You'll know a lot more when you meet the Rayners and see their place. I did a whole number on them about how good you were for something like this," Mason said. I got it: if I didn't perform, he would look bad.

Up ahead, a sign marked the turnoff for Ojai. As we left the 101 behind, the view of the ocean disappeared and there were steep green mountainsides softened with a touch of haze.

It was all beginning to make sense. Mason was a high-profile attorney and his law firm represented a lot of celebrity clients. He had described Jerry R as being a friend, but I knew it was really a mixture of social and business. I understood that from all the years I'd worked with Charlie and his PR firm.

The mood in the SUV was smooth now that we had left the personal stuff behind. I had just one last moment when I felt a pang of regret that he was so over me before I made myself let it go. It was all about the job now.

Mason gave me more background on the Rayners. "Jerry R has the perfect personality to be a talent manager. He's like a big papa. It's his nature to look after people and arrange things," Mason said. "Lisa R complements him. She loves having people over. It's usually very casual, but then the whole area is. She runs a Persian cat rescue."

"I like them already," I said.

As we traveled inland, both sides of the road were dotted by oil well pumps doing their rhythmic rocking dance. Enough moisture from the ocean blew in to keep the mountains on either side a soft green. He told me more about the setup.

"Some of the guests for tonight's party have seen me with Tiffany. I don't know if any of them would really care, but just in case you'll be introduced as my cousin who had done me a favor and acted as my plus-one."

"I get it. You don't want anyone to think you're cheating on your lady friend," I said. "Don't worry, I'll make sure nobody thinks we're together." I tried to sound light about the whole thing, but the mention of her name had churned up my emotions again. I fought it, but finally admitted the truth to myself. I was jealous. It didn't help that I was unattached and didn't have a man friend to flaunt. I did my best to convince myself that now that I had admitted how I felt, I could let it go. It wasn't as if I was even going to meet her or see them together. I was there on a job.

"We'll be staying in a guest house on their ranch," Mason said.

"'We'll' as in you and me?" I said. I hadn't even considered where I would be spending the night.

"Yes, I did mean you and me, but not together. It's a big place and you'll have your own room."

"It's a lot to take in," I said. "I'm your cousin staying overnight on a ranch in a guest house with you so I can attend a celebrity-filled party with a kleptomaniac on the loose." I turned to Mason, wide-eyed. "And how am I supposed to catch them?"

Mason smiled. "You're the detective. That's for you to figure out."

Chapter 5

As we got closer to Ojai, I got a view of horses lounging in corrals, campgrounds, private boarding schools and just open fields. The sky was blue and a soft mist hung over the Topatopa Mountains that hugged the valley. The area had been nicknamed Shangri-La, both because it was the stand-in for the mythical Tibetan earthly paradise in the movie version of *Lost Horizons* and because it really had a reputation of being a refuge with a mystical, harmonious atmosphere. A lot of people thought it was an energy vortex.

I had been to Ojai before and saw that nothing seemed to have changed. The main part of town was still populated with stucco buildings that had a similar design. It was hard to see the actual shops in the Arcade Plaza due to the overhang that shaded the walkway. Mason had turned into a travel guide and described the buildings as Mission-style. As we passed the bell tower, he said it resembled the campanile of a cathedral in Havana, Cuba.

I was more interested in Libby Park. There was a plaza in front with a playground just behind and then a green expanse beyond. "Marlowe would love that," I said as I caught a glimpse of the interesting design of the play area. Then I caught myself. "Sorry for bringing up something not related to the job. That's what happens when you're a grandmother."

"That's okay," he said with a chuckle. "I know you're more than just a detective. I was going to tell you about the pink moment and that you ought to make sure your crochet pals experience it." Mason described a brief time just as the sun was setting and the mountains turned pink.

Despite my best intentions, I imagined him sharing it with Tiffany, the way he'd done things like that with me. My imagination went wild and I made her into a fussy shrew who complained that she was hot or cold or bugs were biting her instead of enjoying the magic. Then I ordered myself to close the curtain on the mental image.

Pixie seemed to be a continuation of Ojai with a similar look. I checked out the passing shops and restaurants, thinking of them as places for the Hookers. Mason turned off the main road and suddenly we were out in the country. We passed hillsides with neat rows of trees and Mason said aside from growing pixie mandarins, the area was known for avocados and olives. He turned off the roadway and we passed under an arch with a sign that announced Rayner Ranch.

Trees shaded the long driveway, but I could see through to the open meadows on either side. I got my first glimpse of the house when he pulled into the parking area. A tall, very old olive tree shaded the walkway to the massive one-story ranch house. The walls were cream-colored stucco with a terra-cotta roof. A covered porch ran along the front of it. I was just thinking that it looked vintage when Mason read my thoughts.

"It's an old house that used to be a lot smaller," he said. He cut the motor and said we'd drop off our bags later. As we walked to the house, Mason explained that it had started out as a getaway place for them, but they spent more time here and kept adding on more space. "They got caught up in the lifestyle and vibe up here. They still have their place in LA, and he goes into town when he has meetings or there's something going on with any of his clients, but most of their time is spent here now."

I was surprised when Mason just opened the front door and ushered me in with him. The entrance hall had a bench, and a coatrack hanging on the wall. A rug with southwestern colors covered a portion of the brick-red tiled floor. Mason called out some hellos and had his phone in his hand to send a text when a tall man came in. He was dressed in jeans meant for work and a denim shirt with the sleeves rolled up. He had even features and longish hair that was tinged with gray. He gave off a friendly vibe and shook hands with Mason that morphed into a hug. His gaze drifted to me and Mason did the introduction.

"Ah, the *cousin*." He winked at Mason and then turned back to me.

"Mason speaks highly of your skills. You're perfect for the job. Nobody would guess you're a detective."

"Thank you, I guess," I said.

"I meant it as a compliment," he said quickly. "You will blend right in with our guests. Mason told me about your background. I dealt with your husband's PR firm. He was a good man." A woman joined us. She was tall and slender, wearing khaki pants and a T-shirt.

"Lisa R," she said, holding out her hand. And you must be our special investigator." She looked at the group of us. "C'mon in and make yourselves comfortable."

We went into a large room dominated by a stone fireplace. The furniture looked like people actually sat on it and there were some books and magazines scattered on a coffee table. It was an eclectic mix of styles. Lisa R noticed me looking around. "We just get what we like and hope it gets along with the rest of our stuff." At the side of the room, archways led to what appeared to have been a covered porch that was now enclosed. I moved closer to have a better look. It was almost all windows that looked out on a grassy area and a pool with a waterfall. A box truck was parked on the side and a white tent was being erected. A woman seemed to be supervising.

"That's the tent for the wedding. Thank heavens for Julie, the wedding planner," Lisa R said. She gestured toward the area beyond. "Behind all that is the real ranch area. There's a barn and horse corrals." She pointed to a distant hillside. "And those are our beloved olive trees." The rows of trees were just visible above the foliage that bordered the grassy expanse. "We bottle our own olive oil."

She glanced toward the wedding prep and I tried to make conversation. "I know Kirkland Rush is the groom," I said. "Who is the bride?"

"It's Zoe McKenna," Lisa R said, as if the name should mean something to me.

"She's a celebrity in her own right. She does the eleven o'clock weather on channel three," Jerry R said, joining the conversation. "It's the primo spot for a weather person and she really kills it."

Lisa R let out a little laugh. "You probably guessed that she's one of Jerry R's clients."

A large white Persian cat had joined us, swirling around Lisa R's leg. "That's Jasmine. She's part of my Persian rescue. They have their own cat house, but they all get a chance to be in the house for some people time." She shook her head as she looked down at the cat, who had moved on to me. As she touched my ankles, she left a souvenir of her long fur on my leggings. Lisa R rushed to hand me a lint remover. "I'm sorry. I keep them all brushed, but it's never enough."

"No problem," I said. "I have a whole menagerie of dogs and cats. I'm used to living with extra fur." I leaned down to stroke the cat to show that I didn't mind.

I continued to look around and was mesmerized by the place. The house was huge but at the same time felt inviting and comfortable. The Rayners were totally not pretentious and so hospitable that I already felt at home.

"Why are we still all standing," Jerry R said. "Let's get some drinks and relax." He led the way to a side room and told us to help ourselves. "We have people over all the time and it's always help-yourself kind of casual. This is the drink room." There was a red cooler that had a Coca-Cola logo on the side. It was the kind of cooler gas stations and stores used to have. There was a whole selection of nostalgic sodas along with flavored soda water. "There's coffee," he said, pointing to a setup with a selection of single-cup coffee makers, including one that made espresso drinks. "And if you'd like something stronger," Jerry R said, stepping away so we could see a bar area with a selection of wine and harder stuff. "Help yourself to snacks," he said. There was a display with bags of chips. A group of tall jars had a selection of snack mixes, nuts, and candy.

"That's an amazing setup," I said. "Something for everybody."

"We like everyone to feel welcome and fed," Jerry R said. Mason and I grabbed a couple bottles of sparkling mineral water and we went back to the living room. We all sat in chairs facing the fireplace.

"I gave her the overview, but I left it to you to tell her the details," Mason said.

Jerry R nodded and began. "Discretion is the key here. The caterers will be here soon and I don't want to chance that they hear anything." He paused as if to make sure that there were no early arrivals. "As I said, we love to entertain. If there's a holiday, no matter how slight, we'll have a gathering to celebrate it. When Kirkland and Zoe announced they were getting married, there was no question but to have it here. That's just background to give you an idea of how often we have people over. Your only concern is the party tonight. It's a kickoff to the weekend's events. The wedding is Sunday." Jerry R let out an amused laugh. "Then, believe it or not, we're having our usual celebration of the summer solstice on Monday."

"You can guess the local caterers love us," Lisa R said. "We keep them in business."

"Now, down to the nitty-gritty," Jerry R began. "There's a glass case in the room we call the library that has odds and ends I regard as personal treasures. Nothing of real value. After our last party, I noticed a set of car keys were missing from there," Jerry R said.

"Why don't we show her the scene of the crime," Lisa R said before he could go on.

"That makes sense, hon." The manager smiled at his wife. He got up and we moved en masse to the room he was talking about. It lived up to its name, with walls covered with books and a ladder to reach the high shelves. I was admiring the comfortable seating as Jerry R pointed out the glass display case. He opened the top, explaining they never bothered using the lock. "It's an assortment of things that are connected to pivotal moments in my life. They all mean a lot to me, but nothing to anybody else." He pointed to an empty spot. "That's where the keys used to be. They're from my first Mercedes back when they had actual keys." He laughed. "It was the smallest, cheapest Mercedes but to me it was the first time I felt like a success. Whenever

I felt down, I would look at those keys and remember how charged up I was about getting that car. I'm sure it sounds kind of shallow but I really want to get them back."

Lisa R patted his hand and took over. "After we noticed that the keys were missing, we started talking about other small items that had disappeared over past parties." She smiled and put up her hands. "It's the silliest thing, but I had these embroidery scissors shaped like a stork that I kept in my embroidery basket." She pointed to the round basket with a work in progress in an embroidery hoop and explained she liked to listen to books on audio while she worked on her stitchery. "When they went missing the first time, I figured they fell behind something and just replaced them. I thought it was my carelessness when I couldn't find the new pair. After the keys went missing, I brought up the scissors and we realized other trinkets had disappeared. We rethought the whole thing," Lisa R said.

"And I did some research on kleptomania and it seems they often take things that have little value, so it seems that's what we're dealing with," Jerry R said. "I'd really like to get those keys back, but even more important is to get the person help before they get in more trouble or it goes public." He took a heavy breath. "The group of suspects we came up with includes some very famous people who also happen to be my clients." He looked to see if I understood and I nodded.

"Mason said this is the kind of thing you excel at. I need to have absolute proof before I confront anyone," Jerry R said. "Needless to say, we took everything we cared about out of the display case. Since it seems that the stork scissors are irresistible, we placed another pair in there along with some sparkly things." I glanced over the contents of the glass case and saw a pen, some shiny beads and a ring that looked like something you'd win at a carnival.

I asked how they had come up with the list of suspects. "We have a guest book that everyone signs when they come in. We went through it and made a list of who had been at all of the parties when something went missing." Jerry R had a piece of paper that he held close to him and then went to hand it to me. "Keep this to yourself. As you will see there are some big names on there. Once you're done with your job, you'll delete any photos, destroy any papers and forget any of this happened." He looked at me directly and I nodded.

"If you don't mind my asking, why not just set up some cameras?" I asked.

"As much as I want to find the person, I don't like the idea of cameras in the house, or outside either, for that matter. We came here to get away from that sort of life. And then we would have to worry about the cameras getting hacked and have things about our guests show up on social media. I don't want to embarrass anyone, even the guilty party. That's why we're relying on you."

"It sounds like you want me to catch the person in the act," I said.

"Yes," Jerry R said. "But don't confront them. A photo on your phone would be good or just your eyewitness account. The plan is for you to give me what you have in the morning and then I'll take it from there."

"I actually have a pair of those scissors you were talking about," I said. I looked at my side, expecting my tote bag with my crochet stuff to be with me, but I had left it in the car with my suitcase. Lisa smiled at the mention of the scissors and we made some small talk about crafts.

There was a lull in the conversation and I had a chance to think over what had been put in my lap. What seemed like a perfect way to handle it popped into my mind. "How about this?" All eyes turned to me as I continued. "You know how that Agatha Christie character used knitting as a cover when she was eavesdropping or observing characters up to no good? Well, I could do a Miss Marple, only with crocheting." I told them about my plans for the rest of the weekend. It was really extraneous information, but I thought it made me sound more like an expert.

Jerry R chuckled at the idea and shrugged. "You're the detective, so whatever you think will work."

• • •

When we were done, Mason and I went back to his car and he drove down a road to the guest house. It was in a similar style to the main house and bigger than I would have expected for guest quarters. We unloaded the bags and brought them inside.

"Other than checking the list Jerry R gave you and committing it to memory, there isn't anything you have to do before the party. You can go hang out with the Hookers and get a dose of whatever Adele is up to now," he said. His face softened into the old Mason and I told him about the latest that was up with Adele.

"Maybe then you just want to hang out in the guest house," he joked, shaking his head. His expression went back to professional as he gave me details of when to be back and explained that he had to talk over some business stuff with Jerry R. I was feeling more comfortable with the new way of dealing with Mason. At least he wasn't giving me the death stare as he had in the past.

With Mason gone, I took a moment to decompress and looked around at our accommodations. When we were together this would have seemed like a romantic spot for a weekend. The main room had comfortable furniture and lots of windows that looked out onto a garden with flowering bushes. There was an efficient kitchen set up with a sink, refrigerator, stove and microwave. The cabinets were stocked with dishes and everything for coffee and tea. It all seemed perfect except the coffee maker. I was sure that Mason would not be happy with the single-cup maker. At the very least, he would want one that made espresso, so he could create his cappuccinos. The whole setup seemed like a cozied version of a hotel.

I arbitrarily picked one of the two bedrooms. It had an en suite bathroom stocked with lots of fluffy towels and nice toiletries. The shower was tiled in cobalt blue and matched the sink of the same color. There was no reason to unpack my things as I was only going to be there the one night, and I went back into the main room to study for my mission. I looked over the list Jerry R had given me and wondered if it would do a *Mission: Impossible* and self-destruct after I read it. He was definitely right about most of the people being well-known and I understood that the media would go crazy if it got out that they were even just possible kleptomaniacs.

Kirkland Rush, Zoe McKenna, Tom Kelter and his wife Rory Bijorn, Heddy Mariano, and Verona Gilroy were all people I'd heard of and would be easy to recognize at the party. It was only the last couple who were unknown to me. All I knew about Ash and Bayleigh Selinger was that they weren't famous and I would have to find a way to pick them out of the crowd.

The paper didn't disappear in a puff of smoke and I set it aside. I took out my phone to call Dinah. I wanted to check how it was going with the Hookers now that they had arrived. Despite what Mason suggested, I planned to stay put instead of joining them since I wasn't sure how I could explain why I had to leave. It was better to stay with the story that I would be arriving late. But when Dinah said she was there alone and was willing to pick me up, I changed my mind. I was curious to see the mystery house where the group was staying.

I quickly took out my "casual elegant" outfit and hung up the cream-colored long silk shirt and black slacks before walking up to the entrance to the ranch where Dinah was picking me up.

"Wow, that's some spread," my friend said, glancing back at the grounds as I got in the car. "Lucky I had GPS or I never would have found the place. I didn't even need an address. All I had to do was put in *Rayner Ranch* and the directions came up." She drove off the dirt shoulder back onto the road. "And now to find our way back to the Hookers' house," she said with a laugh. "You better believe we need the address."

"I thought it was right in downtown Pixie," I said and Dinah shook her head.

"It's like the ranch, out in the country. When you finally see the Hookers, you'll probably get an earful about how they thought we'd be able to just walk to cafés and the shops."

"Oh," I said with a sinking feeling. "It's not like we had a choice or that it was even on me. The place came gratis from Mrs. Shedd's friend."

"They'll get over it. So, they have to drive a little to get into town." She said they were out shopping for some groceries and looking around. "Tell me, how was the ride with Mason? Did he corner you like you feared or did you have a picnic on the way?" Dinah asked with a smile.

"No picnic," I said. "He did bring me a red-eye and a spinach and feta empanada from Porto's. And a muffin. He said something about wanting his employee alert and not hungry. It didn't seem like he was joking."

"At least he has good taste," she said, meaning the beloved Cuban bakery. "Then what?"

"He was fine. I was the one who brought up the past. And then he just said that he'd moved on and met someone else named Tiffany." It was hard to keep my tone even when I said her name. "I sounded jealous, didn't I?"

Dinah nodded and reached over, patting my hand, and I groaned. "It's just so frustrating that he's so fine with everything."

"I get it," Dinah said. "There was a quote one of my students used in a paper. I remember because it was so rare that any of them quoted a person. Elie Wiesel said something like the opposite of love wasn't hate, it was indifference."

"Well, that's certainly where he is." I felt my shoulders slump. "I don't like it one bit how I feel. I don't want to be jealous of this Tiffany person. I want to be just like him, blah about the whole thing. It was easy before when I just saw him in passing when he gave me an assignment or I gave him a report. But all that time in the car reminded me of how things used to be. And now we're sharing a guest house."

"What?" Dinah said.

"It's a big place and there are two bedrooms and it's only for one night. I still can't wait for it to be over."

"What about the job he gave you?" she asked.

"Thanks for asking. I need to focus on that and not on him." I told her all about the missing trinkets taken by one of their well-known party guests.

"A celebrity kleptomaniac with a preference for shiny things," Dinah said with a chuckle. "It's certainly not hunting down a murderer. It sounds like this Jerry R's intentions are good and it's not just getting back his car keys. The party sounds interesting."

Dinah just followed the robot voice telling her where to turn while we were talking. I hadn't been aware of the surroundings until the voice announced we had arrived and she pulled into a driveway. The house was set back from the street and surrounded by trees. "Where's the next-door neighbor?" I asked, looking around.

"Somewhere over there," Dinah said, making an arc with her arm. "You know Elise. Ms. Real Estate Expert pulled up something on her computer. She showed it to me and pointed out that the property behind this is like a farm and belongs to someone famous. There's a creek and I think a hot springs."

As we walked up to the house, all I saw in the surrounding area was a lot of trees and hills with rocky slopes in the distance. It certainly wasn't within walking distance to a café or anything.

The house itself was stucco with a tiled roof. She took me inside and I saw that it was C-shaped and had French doors opening onto a patio at the back. There was already crochet residue in the main room. Works in progress were laying around on the side tables on either side of the couch.

A selection of crocheted hearts were scattered on the coffee table in front of the couch. They were the same ones that Adele had shown the group before we left. Dinah saw me looking at them. "Yes, Adele is already trying to get everyone to help her make them. She's really pushing for the stuffed one."

I picked up the puffy heart and looked it over. "That's ridiculous. They would take too long to make. Leave it to Adele to want to impress her customer with us doing the work. She'll be lucky if she gets help with the little ones."

"She's lucky we put up with her," Dinah said, shaking her head before she continued. "I know what you're going to say—that the Hookers are like family, which means we accept each other warts and all." Dinah shook her head again. "I can't believe I used that, well, overused phrase when there are so many other ways to describe Adele's faults."

She waved me on to follow her and gave me a tour of the rest of the place, including the room we were going to share. When we got back to the communal area, I opened one of the French doors and went out onto the back patio. It was paved with large red tiles softened with age and had chairs around a long glass table. Strings of lights hung over it. "It must be nice at night," I said, imagining the LED bulbs giving off a warm glow. I looked beyond the patio and there were just trees and wild growth. "I wonder what's back there?"

"Probably a fence and then that farm. Elise said something about growing avocados. She said there's another property next to it that is being developed as a spa. There seem to be a lot of them up here. CeeCee said she wished we were staying at one."

We went back inside and I looked over the projects everyone had brought. There was something finished hanging on the arm of a chair. When I picked it up, Dinah groaned.

"Don't let Adele get started on that." I held it up and saw that it was a tie made out of granny squares on the front and a plain-colored tail. The granny squares were dark green and pale blue and the tail was the same dark green. "She made it for Eric and his mother dissed it and said it was stupid-looking and her son should not wear it."

I looked it over some more. "I wouldn't call it stupid-looking," I said. "It's meant for a man with a sense of fun. Mrs. Humphries probably didn't understand that." As I was saying it, I was thinking of my sons. No way would Peter wear something like that, but Samuel might see the quirkiness of it.

"Tell that to Adele. She's upset that Eric went along with his mother and said it wasn't for him."

Dinah made us each a cup of coffee and I barely had time to drink it before I needed to head back to the ranch.

"Did Elise say who the famous person was who owned the farm you mentioned?" I asked when we were on the way back.

"Remember that pop star who walked out in the middle of her show in Vegas?" Dinah said.

I remembered the story. She had a breakdown and left her backup singers and dancers to finish the show without her.

"You mean it belongs to Heddy Mariano?" I looked at Dinah and she nodded. "That's sure a coincidence. She's one of my suspects."

Chapter 6

I had been gone longer than I had expected. When Dinah dropped me off at the entrance to Rayner Ranch, I saw there were already cars parked along the driveway. I was late and the guests had already begun to arrive.

I sprinted back to the guest house to change. It was empty and Mason's suitcase was no longer in the entranceway, which meant he had come back there probably to change. I was glad that I had hung up my outfit and the wrinkles had disappeared. I slipped into the silk shirt and pants, put on some makeup and brushed my hair before grabbing my crochet supplies in a cloth tote, and hurried back to the big house.

I had my fingers crossed that somebody hadn't already lifted the stork scissors that had been left as the most likely plant in the glass case. I joined a couple who were walking in. There was no one acting as greeter in the entrance hall. The couple stopped to sign in and I kept moving inside.

I passed through the living room. Jerry R was talking to a couple and Mason was off in a corner talking to someone else. It was irrelevant to everything, but I checked out what Mason was wearing. He had changed into a raw silk long-sleeve untucked shirt. I had a passing thought that Tiffany had probably picked out the peacock blue shirt. I fought the thought, but I actually liked the shirt and thought the color looked good on him. I caught his eye and pointed toward the library and he gave me a subtle nod.

I kept my eye on the prize and didn't even check out the side rooms, other than to note the smell of food coming from somewhere. I was relieved to see the book-lined room was empty. And more relieved when I checked the glass case and saw that the gold-tipped bird-shaped scissors along with the other things were still there. I realized I had been holding my breath and inhaled deeply as I tried to recover from my worry. How bad would I have looked if I had missed catching the thief because I was late. Even with the deep breath, my heart was doing a pitter pat and I needed to calm myself. I looked at the cloth tote bag and thought how crocheting would be doing double duty. It would be both my cover and a way to get my heartbeat back to normal.

I looked around the room for a spot where I might not be seen. A beige fabric-covered chair was partially hidden by a potted ficus tree and seemed perfect. I patted myself on the back for the choice of the flowing ecru silk shirt as it was almost the same color as the upholstery.

I started to unload the bag. I took a page from my fellow Hooker Sheila's playbook. We all knew that she carried emergency crochet supplies to help her deal when she felt the kind of tension I was facing. It was more than being late. The whole setup, seeing Mason, and the pressure of the job had me feeling almost dizzy. I hoped the rhythmic movement of my hook would work the same magic for me that it did for Sheila. This was not the time to work on a real project where I would have to be concerned about keeping to the pattern. It was just about the repetitive movement.

I took out a big ball of white cotton yarn and a J sized hook. I made a slipknot and went on automatic pilot as I started making a long chain of foundation stitches. Even if I encountered someone familiar with crochet, it would just appear that I was working on something like a scarf the long way rather than by the width. I didn't bother to count the chain stitches and just kept making them until it seemed long enough. My shoulders were starting to decompress as I went to turn the long strand. I was beginning to go back over the chains with single crochets when I heard someone come in the room and all the relaxed feeling vanished.

I recognized Kirkland Rush right away. I had never noticed when I'd seen him on TV, but seeing him in person, I saw that his head was very large and seemed out of proportion to his body. It looked good on camera but a little top-heavy in real life. His thick dark hair was on the longish side and I judged his looks as more distinctive than handsome. He always seemed dramatic and passionate on TV, but he must have been saving it for when he had an audience. He seemed more ordinary than charismatic at the moment.

I assumed the woman with him was his fiancée, Zoe. She had long blond hair that caressed her upper arms with perfect arc shapes. She was wearing a sheath dress and stiletto heels. Just as I was thinking it didn't seem like casual elegant, I realized the why of her clothes. Jerry R had said she was the weather girl from one of the LA stations. It seemed like a throwback to the past, but the females who reported on the highs and lows and incoming storms were expected to dress like eye candy. The men who did the weather mostly wore plain suits, but women were always dressed in tight dresses with belts and heels so high it made my feet cringe to look at them.

She went to grab Kirkland's arm, but he put up his hand to stop her. "Not now," he said. He glanced around the book-filled room and obviously didn't see me.

"Jerry R said not to worry. You don't have to be concerned about finding a great story right now. We're going to be the hot news right now," Zoe said. "This is our wedding weekend, can't you just let it go."

"Honey, don't be stupid. No matter what anybody says, it's always up to you to take care of your own career. I am always on the hunt for the next big story."

They hadn't noticed me and I leaned back in the chair, hoping to keep it that way. They were both on my list of possible kleptomaniacs. Neither of them even seemed to notice the glass case. Somehow, I couldn't picture Kirkland going after the delicate scissors. Would his big thumbs even fit in the round part? On the other hand, it could be her. But I wondered if she would do anything in front of him.

I waited to see if they would leave the room, but he started looking at a shelf of books and she went to look out the window and said something about the tent in the back. Because I hadn't made my presence known at the beginning, it would be very awkward if they saw me now. They both seemed otherwise occupied at the moment and

I thought I could slip out of the room unnoticed. I slumped down and backed to the doorway. I was intent on not being seen by them and had no sense of what was behind me until I felt something soft and heard an *oof* sound. I snuck a look and saw I had walked into a tall man who had put out his arms to catch me.

"Well, hi there," he said. "Does this count as one of those meet-cute scenarios in romantic comedies?" He had an amused grin as he let go of me. He peeked into the room I had just come out of. "Trying to sneak away from those two." He did an eye roll. "I can't say I blame you." He held out his hand. "Bennett Edwards," he said by way of introducing himself. He moved us away from the doorway into a hall. "I'm his field producer. It's my job to get film on the whole weekend and then create pieces for the media with blurbs like wishing them good news and sunny skies." He did another eye roll and smiled at me. "And you are?" he asked.

I hadn't considered having to introduce myself to anyone and I floundered for a moment. He smiled and wiggled his eyebrows. "What is it? Are you a woman of mystery and trying to come up with a story? This is seeming more and more like a cute meet by the second."

"No, I'm not really a woman of mystery," I said, trying to laugh off how close to the truth it was. "I'm here with my cousin. He needed a plus-one and his girlfriend couldn't make it so he talked me into coming."

"Who's your cousin?" he asked, looking back to the main room.

"Mason Fields," I said. I was about to explain who he was, but Bennett already knew.

"He's a great guy and very powerful. What about you? Do you have some kind of exciting career?"

The truth about my day job didn't interfere with my story, so I told him about the bookstore and he laughed. "No wonder you were hanging out in the library. Familiar territory."

Kirkland and Zoe exited the room and instantly went through a change in their demeanor. They were arm in arm, giving each other adoring glances as they moved past us. Kirkland gave Bennett a nudge as he passed, which seemed to be meant as a greeting.

I wanted to get back to my task, though I was rethinking whether staying in the library was the best plan. I might be seen and it would keep the thief from striking.

I scanned the area where we were standing. It was not just a connection between the library and the living room and seemed more like an alcove than a hall. I noted seating and some potted trees along with a glass door that led outside. The sound of a woman's voice cut through the din of conversation coming from the large room. Both Bennett and I turned in reaction.

There was no doubting who she was or why her voice had risen above the others. Being a singer, projecting her voice was second nature. Heddy Mariano had an indignant pose as she stood next to Jerry R. "It's not my imagination," she said in an angry tone. "I'm sorry I don't have pictures, but I'm telling you those space aliens were on my property again last night."

Jerry R was trying to calm her and get her to quiet her tone. "I'm sure you are right about what you saw, but it's another reason why you should live somewhere else. I can help you sell the place and find something in town where you can actually see the house next door."

"No way," she said. "I'm staying." Her stubborn demeanor seemed at odds with her elfin appearance. She was petite with shaggy golden-colored hair and wore black capri pants and a tank top. She was sliding out of her sandals and seemed more comfortable with bare feet. She handed a net bag with some green pear-shaped things to Jerry R. "I am not leaving my avocado trees. We are like kindred spirits. I sing to them every night at sundown and they give me these." She began to sing one of her hit songs as he took the net bag of green fruit. "You know they will make the best guacamole you've had in your life. And I'm certainly not abandoning the coffee plants that grow like their siblings just as they're about to offer their first crop." Jerry R glanced around, realizing their conversation had been overheard.

He put a protective arm around Heddy. "Let's take these to the caterer and you can tell them what to put in that guacamole."

As he tried to lead her away, Heddy turned back to address the rest of the guests who had overheard. "Don't worry, folks. I'm not crazy. I really have had space visitors. And I know what they're after." Then she let him escort her out of the room.

"That was interesting," Bennett said as we traded glances. "So this is where Heddy's been hiding out since she ran off the stage mid-show. She seems like she's gone off the deep end."

I nodded, thinking that Heddy had just moved to the top of the list as far as I was concerned. If I was going to cast the part of a troubled person who had turned to taking things, it would be her. But I would still need to catch her at it and have proof.

"I was going to get some food," Bennett said. "Since you clearly have been abandoned by your escort and I'm here alone, why not join me."

I was torn. It was probably good for me to appear social, but I was worried about leaving my post. While I was struggling for an answer, we were joined by a woman and a boy of about ten. She had wiry dark hair and an air of confidence. The kid looked as if he wanted to be anywhere but there.

She hugged Bennett as a greeting as I slipped into the background, where I could be an observer.

"It's good to see you, Meg," he said.

"Likewise. I wasn't sure about finding a friendly face here," she said. "This weekend can't be over with fast enough." She glanced at the boy. "Kirkland has been mostly an absentee father, but what could I do when he insisted that his son be his best boy-man for the wedding to what's-her-name—Sunny Delight or something?"

"It's Zoe," Bennett said. He ruffled the kid's hair in a sympathetic gesture.

"That's right," she said. "Of course, I know that. I helped put together the prenup for them." He asked her where she was staying and she explained that Jerry R had arranged for rooms at the Ojai Inn. It was also where Kirkland and Zoe were staying. She made a joke about how old-fashioned the couple was being. They were staying in separate rooms.

Bennett shrugged it off and said it was always the talent who got the posh places. He was staying at a motel where the amenity was an ice machine. She looked through the doorway into the library and said something about how it might be a nice place for them to hide out. I held back a groan. I was sure that she wasn't on the list and her presence in the room might keep the thief from acting. I was glad when Bennett came to my rescue without realizing it.

He addressed the boy. "I have a better idea. Have you seen the game room, Harrison? They have all kinds of arcade games, both old and new. I bet you'd love to play Donkey Kong." He turned to the woman. "You can watch him play or pick something for yourself. These people know how to entertain in a town where everything closes by eight." He reached out to the boy. "C'mon, I'll show you the way."

He turned back, looking for me, and in an Arnold Schwarzenegger impression said, "I'll be bock."

Chapter 7

I watched Bennett take Meg and Harrison across the main room. She wasn't on my list of suspects, but I was still curious about her. She was obviously Kirkland's ex-wife. But what was she doing being involved with a prenup for his new wife? I assumed Bennett would know and I would be sure to ask him if and when he returned. For now, it was back to my job.

I decided to set up in the open space outside the library. The wicker settee had a clear view of the doorway to the library and was partially hidden by a leafy potted cat palm. If anyone went into the room, I could be in the doorway with a few steps and watch what they did. If they went to the glass case all I would have to do was grab some photos on my phone.

I went back to crocheting the long strip of stitches and despite relaxing a little, stayed on the lookout. I was keeping an open mind about who would show up, even though I really expected to see Heddy Mariano. All that talk about space visitors was crazy and certainly some sort of hallucination. I thought about the fact that it was going on right behind where the Hookers were staying. I wondered if I should be concerned. There wasn't any way that it wasn't her imagination. But then the area was supposedly an energy vortex, and didn't that sound like something that would attract space beings? My imagination took off and I thought about the beings deciding to check out the neighborhood. What if they wandered into the Hookers' yard? I laughed to myself, picturing Adele trying to show some weird creatures with hands that were all thumbs how to use a crochet hook.

I got bored thinking about Adele and started considering ways I could have told Bennett what I was really doing there. I thought that introducing myself as Molly Pink, Girl Detective sounded better than Molly Pink, Lady Detective. But calling myself a girl seemed silly considering my age. All of it was swept out of my mind when I heard voices and snapped to attention.

"I spent an hour forest bathing," a woman said. "It would be transformational if we added some ethereal sounds. The same for the pink salt cave."

"That can wait. We need to keep our eyes on the prize. It's the only thing we still need before we open," a man said. "I hate to have to keep pushing back the date to the people who have already reserved."

"It'll be fine," the woman said.

I was trying to stay in the background while I attempted to get a better look at them and dropped my crochet hook in the process. When it pinged on the ground, the man turned in my direction and peeked past the potted plant. "Oh," he said, sounding surprised, "I didn't know anybody was here."

"Just me," I said meekly as I created a story about my presence on the spot. "I'm not really a party person. It seems like a sea of strangers and I was kind of hiding out." I picked up the fallen hook and stuck it back into a loop. "Just give me a hook and some yarn and I'm happy."

"Sorry if we bothered you," the man said. "Just so you don't think of us as strangers, I'm Ash Selinger and this is my wife, Bayleigh." They both smiled at me and moved closer.

"I'm Molly," I said, deliberately leaving off my last name. "I'm just a stand-in for Mason Fields's girl—I mean lady friend." All the conjecturing about how to refer to myself made calling Tiffany a girl just as absurd. "I'm his cousin." I waited to see if Mason's name meant anything to them as it had to Bennett. They both had blank looks and I explained that he was a big-time attorney in the entertainment world.

"That explains it," Ash said. "We're from the tech world. Silicon Valley." He waited until I nodded with recognition, not realizing I had recognized more than where they were from. They were the couple on my list that I was worried about finding. I looked them over with new interest. He was tall with light brown hair, in a style I would call contrived shaggy. He was wearing loose linen pants and a tunic top with a colorful scarf. Bayleigh wore a colorful gauzy long skirt with a white peasant-style top, and big dangle earrings.

I asked how they knew the hosts. Ash looked toward the living room filled with guests. "The Rayners are great to newcomers. They started including us in their parties right after we met them at the farmers' market."

"We love the quiet up here, but it's still great to have a social life," Bayleigh chimed in.

"What's that called?" Ash had stepped next to me and touched the trail of stitches.

"It's crochet," I said. "It's a great way to relax."

"Really?" he said. "Is it hard?"

I offered to let him have a try, glad that I had found a way to have some time with them. I was pretty sold on Heddy, but I thought I should still consider everyone on the list. Ash seemed hesitant about taking the hook and yarn at first. "I wouldn't want to ruin what you're making."

"Don't worry about it. One of the great things about crochet is how easy it is to fix mistakes." I offered him the spot next to me and said I would direct him just like it was yoga. Their outfits made me think they knew how yoga classes were conducted and would understand. Just to be sure I explained that I would tell them move by move what to do with the hook and the yarn.

He followed my directions perfectly and then began to make single crochet stitches on his own. He seemed delighted when he looked at the stitches he had made. Then he glanced up at his wife. "This could be something for our place." He turned back to me. "We went through a whole metamorphosis when we came here and we decided to share it. We're about to open Haven—that's what we're calling our healing resort. It's more than massages and yoga classes. We're going to offer an immersive experience surrounded by the natural world. Someplace specifically aimed at burned-out high-level people where they can come to regenerate." I nodded and smiled, but what I was thinking was that it sounded like a lot of verbiage to describe a fancy-schmancy place that cost a fortune to sit out in the woods. But I guessed that their clientele would feel it was a more healing experience if it cost a lot.

They went back to talking about having a handicraft option at their resort. "It would be cool if they made something to take home with them," Bayleigh said. "Something to show off to their friends and make them want to come to our place, too."

"We'll have to look into that," Ash said. "But right now, I want to hit the food." He turned back to me. "You ought to come out of your corner and check out the eats. It's always the best."

I was already counting both of them out as the kleptomaniac. If he was the one, I was sure he would go for something bigger than scissors shaped like a bird. And I tested her by showing the pair I had to see her reaction. Either she was the greatest actor of all time or they meant nothing to her.

After they were gone, no one else wandered my way and I thought about checking to see if the other people on the list were even there. I moved into the large living room and checked out the crowd. Mostly I was interested in their clothes. Apparently they had a different idea of casual elegant than Mason or I did. They had more of a bohemian, hippie sort of vibe. There were a lot of men wearing light fabric scarves wrapped loosely around their necks, as Ash was wearing. The women wore things like harem pants and colorful dresses.

I recognized Verona Gilroy right away. She was a comedic actress with a girl-next-door kind of vibe who always seemed to be smiling. The best words to describe her were *perky* and *cute*. She was in the middle of a group of people and there seemed to be a lot of laughing, as if they were all having a good time. Lisa R came over to her and the two of them separated themselves from the crowd. I moved closer to see if I could hear their conversation. I was stunned when I heard what they were talking about. Verona was asking for a recipe for olive oil cake.

"I'll text you my fav," Lisa R said.

"Perfect. That's what I love about living up here," Verona said. "We do stuff like share recipes."

"That's the way Jerry R and I feel too. You can always let us know if you need anything," Lisa R said.

"I'm good for now," the actress said, beaming her signature smile. "Or I will be after some time shooting baskets in the game room." She did a mock throw and laughed. I couldn't tell if it was about having fun or burning off some tension.

I trailed behind her, curious to see the room Bennett had talked about. It lived up to his hype and more. It seemed like a paradise of fun. The walls were lined with arcade games. There was a pool table and one set up for table tennis. Small tables with chairs were scattered around the large room with setups for chess and checkers. A shelf even held a stack of board games. It was noisier and more congested than the living room and I was sure that Bennett and Harrison were in there somewhere. Verona surveyed the area and grabbed a drink from the stocked cooler before heading to a game surrounded by netting with a hoop. I watched as she took her first shot and missed. She just laughed and waited for the ball to come back and took another try. This one was successful and she jumped, giving herself a high five in triumph. She began to shoot baskets in quick repetition after that and didn't seem to be going anywhere soon.

I went back into the main room and surveyed the crowd for the last couple on the list. Tom Kelter and Rory Bijorn were easy to pick out of the crowd. He was tall with quirky features that had lent themselves well to the comedy parts he was known for. Until someone got the idea of making him into an action star. He had bulked up and the quirky features seemed more brooding now. He was standing in the middle of a crowd as they hung on his every word. Rory Bijorn was sitting on a couch just outside the circle around her husband. She was described as someone who could play any sort of character. She had played a troll that turned into a princess in a fairy-tale and a high-powered fashion magazine editor who got attention by banging the heel of her designer stilettos on her desk. In person, she seemed rather plain and was wearing glasses. She was eyeing the plate of food in her hand as if debating something. I gathered that it had to do with eating because she brought a forkful of something to her mouth and then seemed distressed.

She managed to catch Tom's eye and he pulled himself out of the crowd and flopped down next to her. I edged in, curious about their conversation. I told myself that I wasn't being nosy. They were on the list, which made it part of my job to eavesdrop. I was expecting something exciting or dramatic, but it was completely mundane.

"We have to make plans for the kids' summer camp," she said.

"What do they need to go to summer camp for?" Tom said. "I thought that's why we moved up here, so they could have a garden and maybe a lemonade stand. You're not going to be working. You can supervise."

"It figures you would say that. You're going to be on location all summer," Rory said with a groan. "I was thinking of doing some stuff on my own. Maybe learn pottery or something." Everything about her from what she said to the way she said it made her sound discontented. She put her plate down, commenting that she had eaten too much.

"Just eat less tomorrow," he said. "By the way, Kirkland said we ought to talk to our business manager about how they're investing our money."

She gave out an annoyed groan. "Isn't that why we have a business manager, so we don't have to think about it?" She got up and patted her stomach. "I have to move. It'll make me feel like I'm walking off some of that." She gave a disdainful look at her plate where she had set it on the table.

I watched for a moment, and as soon as I saw her heading in the direction of the library, I was out of my seat tailing her. I had my phone out ready to take a picture if she made a grab for anything. Jerry R had been very specific that I was not to confront the person. She was in the area where I had been sitting before. The glass door leading outside was in one direction and the library in the other. I was waiting for her to commit to one or the other, but she suddenly turned around and stared at me. "I know you're following me. What is it? Do you want an autograph? Or to tell me how much you loved me in your favorite movie?"

I had to think fast. "It's the autograph," I said. I couldn't think of anything else to use, so I held out the tote bag and handed her a marker. She scribbled her name and then went off without so much as a goodbye. I heard the door to the outside open and close as I looked down at the autographed bag and chuckled to myself. So I was down to playing a crazed fan. Peter would be so embarrassed.

After a quick check of the library and seeing that all was still in place, I went back to the wicker settee and set myself up again to keep watch. I felt a crescendo of tension knowing the thief would have to make their move soon. My crocheting was all on autopilot now and I kept my eyes peeled.

The sound of the door to the outside opening put me on high alert. Rory had returned from her walk. She was too self-absorbed to notice me and was muttering to herself about something. She neared the doorway to the library and I was half out of my seat with my heart rate rising. But then she turned and went back into the living room, telling her husband it was time to go. He didn't seem to be in a hurry to leave and I heard him say something about wanting to spend some time in the game room, but she wasn't having any of it and told him to say his good nights. He might play an action hero, but it seemed like she was the one who called the shots.

I had seemed so sure she was headed for the library that I wondered if she had diverted at the last minute. Maybe she saw me and figured out what I was doing.

I heard other people doing their farewells. As the noise level continued to soften, I could tell the party was breaking up. When it got truly quiet and no one had gone in the library, I began to wonder if the kleptomaniac had taken the night off or if Jerry R had been wrong about the suspect list and it was someone who simply hadn't come to this party. It wasn't really necessary, but I did another check of the library and all was well.

When I went back into the massive living room, Mason and Jerry R were standing in a corner talking. I heard Lisa R saying good night to someone and then she came back into the room from the entrance hall. She saw me and smiled.

"I was going to grab a glass of wine. Can I get something for you?"

"Thanks, but no thanks," I said before dropping my voice. "I don't drink when I'm working." She went off to the drink room and I glanced around the interior. A moment later, she came back into the room and let out a satisfied sigh as she settled on the couch.

"Now to enjoy the afterglow of another party. I love entertaining but it's always a relief when another one is over." I glanced back at Mason and Jerry R. They had made such a point about discretion that it seemed best to say nothing about what happened, or more accurately, didn't happen.

I heard some conversation coming from the entrance hall and then Bennett came into the room and spoke to the hosts. "You'll be glad to know that I made sure Harrison had a good time. Poor kid was lost in the sea of adults."

"Thank you for looking after him," Lisa R said. "It's too bad that his father didn't spend time with him."

"It's not Kirkland's thing," Bennett said. "And not the first time I've had to stand in for him. It's all of our jobs to keep him looking good." Lisa R nodded to him as one of the catering people came in to ask her something. Bennett walked over to me. There was something unassuming and sweet about his manner.

"Sorry, I didn't live up to my promise to return. I guess it's too late now," he said. "You look like you're ready to leave." His glance went to Mason and Jerry R, who were looking at something on a phone. "I guess you have to wait for your cousin," he said.

"I was waiting for him, but I don't really have to," I said, and explained I was staying in the guest house.

"You are VIP guests," he said with a smile. "It's certainly convenient." He looked at Mason again. "It seems like your cousin has left you on your own. How about I walk you home? We could look at the stars." His lips curved into a grin. "It goes along with the whole rom-com trope."

There was an awkward moment as I considered if it was okay for me to leave without getting Mason's consent. But then everybody on the suspect list was gone.

Bennett seemed like a fun sort of person and why not let him walk me back. It wasn't as if Mason owned all my time. I made an excuse that I had to check where I had been sitting to see if my crochet hook was there.

"I'll be waiting here," Bennett said. I heard him saying his good-byes as I made a final check on the glass case in the library, just in case. The scissors and the rest were still there and the glass case appeared untouched.

When I returned, I tried to keep up the guise of being a party guest and thanked my hosts. Jerry R glanced at Bennett and then went back to me. "We'll talk in the morning before you leave," he said. I looked back and caught Mason's eye and announced I was going. Mason's gaze moved to Bennett. I wasn't sure if it was my imagination, but it seemed that he gave my escort a hard stare.

It was frustrating that I hadn't been able to find the kleptomaniac, but I was also glad to leave. I had been on alert the whole evening and I was relieved to be able to stand down.

"I thought you were just a party guest," Bennett said as we walked outside. "But that sounded like business with Jerry R." There was a question in Bennett's voice.

"No," I said in a light manner. "Jerry R is going to tell me all about how they make the olive oil from all those trees."

"I hadn't thought about that," Bennett said. "I wonder if they put all the olives in a big wooden tank and then stomp on them like in that old *I Love Lucy* episode." I could see his smile in the darkness.

"Lucy stomped on the grapes. It would have been a whole other story with olives."

"You're right. It would be messy and slippery," Bennett said. "And probably slapstick fun." We both laughed at the image as we walked outside.

When we had cleared the house and were past all the trees we looked up at the open sky. It was sprinkled with more stars than I could have imagined. Coolness was coming up from the ground and there was a sense of peace. "Which way?" Bennett asked when we got to the end of the open space behind the house.

I led the way through a fragrant garden off to the side. From there, we met up with the road. I heard him let out a sigh. "Peace at last. It's good to get out of there. It might have been all party for you, but it was work for me and I had to be on the whole time."

"I know what you mean," I said, thinking how I felt the same.

"Really?" he said. "Why? Was Fields giving you a hard time?"

"Oh, no, that's not it," I said, realizing I had made a mistake. "Mason is fine. I'm just not really a party person."

He nodded with understanding. "So that's why you were hiding out behind that potted plant doing your yarn thing."

"I didn't realize that you saw me. I thought you spent all your time in the game room with Harrison."

"I slipped out to check in with Kirkland," he said. Neither of us seemed in a rush and we were enjoying the night air and the inky sky spread with stars. "Kirkland is never off his career. You would think he would be concerned about his bachelor party or getting married again, but all he wanted to talk about is a story he's been investigating. And that he wanted to make sure the film crew got a lot of shots of the celebrity guests." He shook his head as if he'd had an upsetting thought. "It's easier dealing with serial killers being interviewed in jail. They don't worry about lighting and being caught at their best angle."

Bennett let out a groan. "I don't know if you talked to Tom Kelter, but becoming an action star has totally changed him. When he was doing comedy, he was easygoing and kind of self-deprecating, but now it's as if he believes he really is that character he plays. You know, he looks like a regular guy, but he's really some kind of superhero with a black belt in everything." Bennett blew out his breath. "If his ego gets any bigger it will explode."

I didn't mention my encounter with Tom's wife, but instead asked about Meg Rush. "It's very unusual between Kirkland and her. They met when she was working for his business manager. Kirkland might seem all together when he's reporting on a story, but deal with something like writing a check, hah," Bennett said and shook his head in disbelief. "Their divorce was amicable, and she still handles his finances. Kirkland trusts her implicitly. Who knows if that will change when he and Zoe are married." He let out a laugh. "And who cares. We should be talking about other things." We had reached the guest house. There was an outside light illuminating the door, but the inside was all dark.

"It looks pretty dark in there. I could come in and make sure there aren't any bogeymen hiding in the closet."

"Thanks, but I'm pretty good at chasing them off on my own," I said with a laugh. It didn't seem right to invite him in.

"I guess then I'll see you tomorrow and the day after and so on. There's a whole array of events before the wedding."

"I'm just here for tonight," I said.

"Oh, no, are you pulling a Cinderella?" he teased. "It seems a waste to just say goodbye forever after our cute meet and almost evening together. Maybe we could pick things up back in LA." He held out his phone and asked for my information. I couldn't think of a way to say no, and I actually liked him. It would be a lot easier when I wasn't working, so I put in my number.

"Until then," he said and gave me a quick kiss.

Once I was inside, all the lightness of our encounter evaporated and I was back to thinking about my job. I couldn't help it if the kleptomaniac didn't perform, but I still felt let down.

I was sitting in the main room when the door opened and Mason came in carrying a shopping bag. He set it on the table.

"I figured you probably didn't eat," he said. He started taking out containers of food. "There were lots of leftovers." As I began to smell the food, my hunger came back with a vengeance.

As he unloaded the bag, he told me what the containers held. He stopped when he got to a round one and flipped off the lid. "This is some olive oil from their trees. It's hand-pressed." The thick greenish oil had actual pieces of olive floating in it. "You have to taste it." He pulled out a piece of bread and dipped it in the oil before handing it to me.

I commented on how delicious it was and helped myself to another piece of bread dipped in the oil while he finished putting all the containers on the table. He took out some plates and silverware.

"Go ahead and help yourself. We can talk afterward."

"Why not talk now," I said as I spooned an array of salads on a plate. There was no reason to put off discussing what happened.

"Have it your way," he said. "You want to tell me what you've got? Who was it?"

"What do you mean?" I asked.

"Who is the kleptomaniac?" Mason said.

"I don't know," I said. "They must have taken the night off. When I left, everything was still in the glass case."

Mason shook his head. "Well, it isn't now." And he described the empty spot.

"The stork scissors are missing?" I said in a panicked voice. "That can't be true."

Chapter 8

Needless to say, I didn't eat much and tossed and turned all night going over and over how I could have missed the thief. The worst part was in the morning when Mason and I went to the big house. I was supposed to give the big reveal.

"Well," Jerry R said expectantly. An untouched cup of coffee sat on the small table next to me and I absolutely felt on the hot seat.

The word hung in the air as I felt Mason looking at me. I knew if I didn't say something soon, he would speak for me and I would look even worse. I was a big girl and had to deal with it myself.

"When I left last night, the scissors and the rest of the things were all still in place. And it appeared that all of the people on the suspect list were gone," I said.

"Then you don't know who took the stuff," Jerry R said, sounding disappointed.

"I bet it was Heddy," Lisa R said, but then her husband gave her a cease-and-desist scowl.

"If you give me another chance, I'm sure I will catch them in the act," I said, but he shook his head resolutely.

"There is too much going on now with Kirkland and Zoe's wedding. Lisa R can put out more sparkly stuff in the glass case for the weekend to keep the person from moving on to somewhere else in the house." He shook his head in a dismissive manner.

I had a hard time not hanging my head. I was Molly Pink, Bad Detective. I berated myself for failing. Even though I didn't know what else I could have done. There was nobody there when I left.

"I'm sorry I let you down," I said to Mason when we were back outside.

"It happens," he said with a shrug. "I'm sure you did your best."

"But I don't understand how it could have happened. You were there after I left. Did you see anyone?"

"I didn't see anybody, but Jerry R and I went into his office,"

Mason said. "Lisa R went to check on the caterers and make up the care package."

"Maybe it was someone not on the list, like someone working for the caterer," I said, but Mason shook his head.

"Jerry R considered workers when he made the list of suspects. The people on the list are the only ones who were there for all the parties where something disappeared." He touched my arm in a reassuring manner. "Let it go. I'll get you back with the Hookers. I'm sure Adele will pull some kind of nonsense and you'll forget all about the disappearing scissors."

"I'm sure you're right about Adele. In fact, I know you're right," I said, thinking over what I had seen during my visit to the Hookers' house before turning my attention back to him. Mason appeared to be very understanding, but I wondered how he really felt.

We walked back to the guest house and Mason got my bag and put it in the SUV. I was staring straight ahead as we went up the long driveway to the road. Instead of leaving with a triumphant feeling, it all felt so unfinished. I didn't even look back as we passed under the arched entrance to the ranch and got onto the road.

"And you're sure I can't have another chance," I said. "I heard there are gatherings going on this whole weekend."

"You heard Jerry R. He just wants to let it go for now. His focus is on Kirkland's wedding and all that goes with it. It is much more than just a wedding. It's all about making it into something the media will pick up. Jerry R said he might make another try to find the culprit in the future."

Mason didn't say it, but I felt sure it would be without me. "I'm so sorry I let you down," I said again.

"Most likely the thief realized what you were doing and figured out how to go around you. It's okay. Nobody wins all the time."

"Yes, but a good detective never gets made," I said, using the lingo that meant my cover had been blown. He didn't say anything and I wondered if that meant he agreed. I didn't want to ask him directly, but

I worried that he would never hire me again. My shoulders drooped as I thought about saying goodbye to my double life. It had been fun and exciting for as long as it lasted.

I was so wrapped up in being upset that I hadn't paid attention to where we were. I finally checked out our surroundings when Mason pulled the car into a driveway. Instead of the Hookers' house, we were in downtown Pixie in the parking lot of a coffee shop.

Mason noticed my surprise. "You don't think I would drop you off without giving you breakfast? I always take care of the people who work for me and you must be very hungry since you didn't eat last night." He pulled into a parking spot. "You really shouldn't have pushed me to talk before you ate." He was right. As soon as I had heard that the scissors were gone, my stomach clenched and I could not face the plate of food. I was trying not to think that as understanding as Mason was acting, this was probably my farewell breakfast.

Then Mason said something that totally caught me off guard. "Do you think you might have lost your focus because you were all flirty with that guy?"

"Flirty," I said with a laugh. "I don't think so. He approached me and I thought being social with someone was a good cover."

"And you needed cover on the way back to the guest house?" I was surprised at the sharpness in Mason's voice.

"What was I going to say when he offered to escort me back there?"

"How about, no thank you," Mason said. He seemed to catch himself after that. "Never mind. It's over with."

"Maybe not," I said. "He suggested we get together back in LA." I wasn't sure why I added that. Okay, I did know. I was irked at Mason's whole speech that he had moved on from us and I wanted to make it look like I had too.

Mason seemed to think it over for a moment before he turned to me. "You'll be off the clock then," he said. "Whatever you do is none of my business." He opened the car door. "Let's eat."

The coffee shop smelled of bacon and coffee. It had an authentic classic feeling with red booths and Formica tables. I was beginning to accept my fate that my detective career was over and the tension was going away as I could feel my hunger return.

This was the first time I had been to a sit-down restaurant with Mason since our breakup. He had always done the ordering and then we had shared the food. I was about to pick up the menu, expecting to choose my own breakfast, but when the waitress came by with the coffee pot, he ordered an omelet, silver dollar pancakes, orange juice and two extra plates.

When she was gone, he closed his eyes and smiled, realizing what he had done. "Sorry," he said. "It was habit. If you want, I'll flag her down and we can order separately."

"It's fine," I said. "I always liked the way you made all of our meals into mini buffets."

I was done with the case and the cast of characters, so there was no reason to talk about any of it anymore, and there didn't seem to be anything to say other than comments about the food as we both dove in. And then out of the blue, Mason asked about my family.

"Peter never says much," Mason said. "How are they all getting along?"

"You must have seen the She La Las in my living room when you picked me up."

"I did see some action through the window," he said with a laugh.

I mentioned the upcoming PBS special and he was impressed. "Is your father still acting as their road manager?" I nodded. "It's nice to see how they operate as a couple after all this time."

I didn't really want to talk about my family with Mason and told him about the bookstore remodel and my concern about kids juggling glue guns and most of all having to deal with Adele if there was a knitters' group. "You know Adele. It'll be like the Sharks and the Jets," I said. "She would try to get the She La Las to choreograph the encounter." I began to describe what I thought it would look like and told him to imagine the music from *West Side Story*. "Adele would be in the lead, of course, with the rest of us dancing behind her. Everyone would be waving their hooks. Those knitting invaders would be complacent and superior. They'd just be doing some small moves while they stayed in place and worked their needles." I started laughing at my description.

"And then there'd be the big moment as the crocheters danced through the knitters and knocked their needles to hell. The big finish would be the jugglers tossing around glue guns."

Mason had joined me in laughing by the time I finished. "Thanks, I needed a good laugh to start the day. There's one thing missing from all of Jerry R's gatherings—fun. Even the game room is intense." Mason stopped himself. "Don't tell anyone I said that."

We had finished all the food. "Time to get you back to Adele and company," Mason said. "Unless you want dessert. The carrot cake looks pretty good."

I shook my head and told him about Dinah stuffing my bed with pillows. "I better get back there before anyone checks." I excused myself to use the restroom while he dealt with the check.

I was on my way back to the table feeling good that at least Mason and I were ending on a light note. I glanced toward the entrance as a man wearing a suit came in. It got my attention because the outfit was completely out of place with the rest of the customers, who were dressed in jeans or shorts.

I could only see his back as he talked to the cashier and she pointed to a table. I waited for him to turn, sure that it was just a resemblance. It couldn't really be him. And then I saw the side of his face and my breath caught. What was Barry Greenberg doing up here? I knew the answer by the clothes and the dark shadow on his chin. He was a homicide detective and must have been working on a case, probably seeing the morning from the other side. I was too familiar with how he worked. Once he picked up a murder, he was off on the hunt and nothing got in the way. Day, night, sleep, relationships—all got lost. But apparently not hunger. He passed Mason and I was sure they saw each other, though neither showed it. There was definite hostility between them. It wasn't just about me, but a natural animosity between lawyers and detectives.

I froze for a moment wondering what to do. The only thing I knew for sure was that I didn't want him to see me. There were a multitude of reasons, but mostly it was because we were definitely done forever and yet I couldn't manage the indifference that Mason seemed to have mastered.

I waited until Mason looked toward the hallway I was in and I pointed at the exit sign. I was already outside in the parking lot when Mason came out.

I didn't know what to say, so I said nothing and just got into Mason's SUV. I didn't want to even think about what a disaster it was after the two weeks in Hawaii. The trip had been like the happy ending in a romance novel, but the trouble was that the story went on after that, and as soon as real life had come into it, everything fell apart.

It was a relief when Mason's phone rang and he got out of the car to take the call. I took the time to collect myself and was feeling back to normal when Mason returned.

"Is something wrong?" I asked since he seemed agitated and in a rush as he started the car.

"There's no time to drop you off. You'll have to come with me," he said, putting something into the GPS.

I waited for him to say more, but he drove out of downtown Pixie in silence. The voice kept giving directions and we were out in a rural area again. There was nothing to do but go along for the ride.

Police cars and the paramedics' rig were already there when he pulled into the driveway of a rustic piece of property. "Stay here," he said. "And don't say anything to anybody." All the lightness of our breakfast was gone and he was in serious mode when he got out of the SUV.

I watched him go to the front door. It was opened by a police officer in a midnight blue uniform. The house was vintage Spanish-style with stucco walls and a tiled roof. The walls were a dusty color and the tiles on the roof darker than the usual orangish color I was used to seeing. A covered porch ran along the front and there was an old-looking rocking chair and lots of potted plants. When I glanced toward the street, it definitely felt like we were out in the wilds. There were no sidewalks or houses in the vicinity. My gaze stopped on the loaf-shaped mailbox by the curb. It was painted with a scene of trees and mountains and then I saw the name in black letters: *Mariano*.

Despite Mason's order, I was out of the car in a flash, heading for the side of the house to investigate. There was no fence and I looked past some gnarled oak trees to an orderly grove of trees in the distance. There were rugged hills beyond. I knew that the Hookers' house property touched it somewhere and scanned the area wondering where the border was. Before I could take a step forward, I was stopped by a uniformed cop running yellow tape to block access.

"What's going on?" I said in a friendly voice. "I'm a neighbor and I heard all the sirens." I hoped he wouldn't think about what I said too closely. Out in the country like this, would the first responders even need to use their sirens on empty roads?

"There's been an incident," the cop said.

"Was it Heddy?" I asked. "Like I said, I'm a neighbor and know her. Is she okay?"

The officer seemed to hesitate and finally just said, "It's not her."

"Then who is it?" I asked.

He glanced over his shoulder and then turned back to me. "I can't divulge that," he said.

"Can you tell me how badly whoever is hurt?" I asked.

The cop shrugged. "All I know is that the paramedics are still back there with him, I mean the person." When I tried to get more details, he waved for me to leave. I accepted that was all I was going to get and turned to go back to Mason's SUV. Just as I got to the front of the house, a black Explorer pulled up. I scrunched my eyes, looking through the windshield to identify the driver. As soon as I recognized Barry Greenberg, I looked for a place to hide.

I pushed myself between a twiggy bush and the stucco house as I heard the car door open.

After a moment, I heard Barry talking to the officer who had shooed me away. It was hard to make out all of what they were saying. There seemed to be some negotiating and then Barry went back to his car. It was harder to get out of my hiding place than it had been to get into it. The twigs caught on my sweater and in my hair as I pulled myself free. I crouched down and rushed back to Mason's SUV.

I stayed out of sight in the car until Mason finally returned. He pulled a twig out of my hair and looked at me with a question in his eye.

"Sorry. I know you said to stay in the car. But you know me. I couldn't just sit here and not know what was going on."

"Tell me what you figured out," he said.

"The house belongs to Heddy Mariano and something bad happened to someone in the back somewhere. Heddy is probably telling everyone her space people are responsible. Jerry R asked you to come here and act as her lawyer to keep her from talking." I was glad to show off I had at least some investigative skills after the flop at catching the scissors thief.

"Very good and you're exactly right," he said.

"And there's something else," I said. "Barry Greenberg was nosing around here." Mason asked if Barry had seen me.

"No, and I intend to keep it that way." The last bit was really an explanation for me ducking out of the coffee shop and to make it seem clear that anything between Barry and me was over. I pointed at the bush where I had hidden and Mason chuckled. His phone rang again and he went off to take it. I picked some more twigs out of my hair while I waited for his return.

He got back into the car and heaved a sigh as he sat back against the seat.

"So what happens now?" I asked.

Mason pushed the ignition. "The easy answer is I drop you off with the Hookers and we say goodbye. Or, I have a proposition. That was a call from Jerry R. He's worried the cops are going to pin what happened on Heddy. It's worse if it turns out there's a death. Jerry R wants me to find some other suspects to push on the cops before they arrest or charge her. It would be even better if there was evidence that really tied somebody else to it." He took a heavy breath. "That's all I can say unless you're working with me." He faced me. "I know you are supposed to be finished and free to spend the rest of the time with your friends. But would you consider another job? Will you work on this case with me?"

Would I? Absolutely. I was so relieved that my double life wasn't over that for a moment I forgot how serious this all was. "Yes," I said, leaning over and giving him a spontaneous hug. I pulled away as soon as I realized I had overstepped the employee-employer relationship and rushed to repair the damage. "I hope that doesn't count as some kind of sexual harassment," I said, and he chuckled.

"I won't report you," he joked. "But back to the matter at hand. It will be good to have your help. Now I can tell you the rest. For now, they are letting her be. Before I got there and could stop her, she had already told them that her space visitors were there late last night and she was sure they were responsible for what happened. I took over speaking for her after that. They aren't going to arrest her until they do some more investigating, which gives us a little time. I made sure she didn't give them permission to search the place, and now they're waiting for a warrant."

"What do you want me to do?" I asked.

"As you can imagine, there's a lot of confusion at Jerry R's. Their house is the center of all the weekend plans. I was supposed to go horseback riding with Jerry R today, but now I don't know. I'll drop you off with the Hookers until I know what's going on. Have your crochet day and I'll be in touch."

"Okay," I said. "I'm sort of in charge of this getaway so I really do need to spend time with the group. I'm not sure it will be helpful, but according to Elise, part of Heddy's property abuts the land the Hookers' house is on." When I explained that from what I'd seen, the area where the properties touched was all wild, he nodded and told me not to worry about it.

"Don't go climbing over the fence or anything. I don't want to have to bail you out of jail here." I was relieved to see he was smiling when he said it.

He started the car and followed the GPS's convoluted directions to get to the Hookers' house. I promised to stay out of trouble, and he looked past the house to the uncultivated wilderness. "If you hadn't told me, I never would have guessed the properties are adjoining. One thing is for certain, they aren't orderly rectangular-shaped plots."

"Elise said there's a creek and some kind of pond back there on Heddy's land."

He waited while I took my suitcase out and stowed it in the bushes to bring in later. "I can't blow Dinah's story that I arrived late last night and slept in. She left the patio door unlocked so I could sneak in."

"Right, and your bed is stuffed with pillows," he said, seeming to enjoy the image. "I forgot about all the stuff you get into. Never a dull moment." He repeated that he would be in touch and drove away. It was only then that I realized he had never given me the identity of the victim.

Chapter 9

The plan didn't quite work. The patio door was unlocked and I made it into the bedroom, but when I made my grand entrance and started doing a yawning routine as if I had just awakened, Adele shook her head. Before she could say anything, Dinah interceded.

"They know," my friend said. "I told them that you ran into Mason and he asked you to do a favor for him and be his plus-one at a party. And it was a house party so you stayed the night."

"Dear, you could have just told us," CeeCee said. "And even if you're back with Mason, none of us would pass judgment."

"Are you back with him?" Elise said. "You must be some negotiator if you got him to forgive and forget what you did." Elise saw everything in terms of real estate and making deals.

"I'm not back with him," I said. "It was just one friend doing a favor for another." I embellished on it a bit and said that the woman he was supposed to have as his date backed out at the last minute and it was awkward for him to show up alone. I didn't explain why it would be awkward and thankfully, they didn't ask. I was actually glad that it was out in the open since it seemed as if I might have to duck out again.

"Dear, it's good that you're finally here since there doesn't seem to be much of a plan for anything. Adele said you were the one who made the arrangements," CeeCee said. "I was trying to suggest we do a group project. I see that there's yarn, but it would have been helpful if there was a pattern." I looked at the stack of plastic bins against the wall. With all the chaos at the bookstore, I had packed a bunch of yarn without paying too much attention. I lifted the lid on one and saw there were packages of cotton yarn. Each one had some colors that worked together and a skein of off-white. The bin underneath it had some lightweight acrylic yarn in basic colors. A tote bag full of yarn sat on the coffee table and seemed to be all reds and pinks. Adele's hearts were on the table next to it.

"Adele is pushing us to just work on the hearts for her," Elise said. "We can all knock off some of them for her, but it would be nice to make something we could keep."

"I never said that the hearts were the only thing we could work on," Adele said. "I just thought you would all want to help me, considering my circumstances." She sniffled a few times. "My heart is broken. There hasn't been even a text from Eric. I don't think he even cares that I'm gone." She looked around at the group. "You all have supportive husbands, like Rhoda, Elise and Dinah. Or a crazy family like Molly, or a fabulous career like CeeCee." Adele pouted. "All I have is crochet."

We were all feeling sympathetic and on the verge of a group hug, until Adele continued. "Our group project should be making one of these to show solidarity." She held up the tie to her body. It added an over-the-top touch to her already crochet-heavy outfit. Her wavy brown hair was held in place by a headband with a big flower. Her white shirt was unadorned, but the jeans made up for it. They were embellished with tiny granny squares, a school of goldfish that appeared to be swimming around one of her knees, and a crescent moon with a couple of stars sewn below it.

"Solidarity to what?" Rhoda said. "We didn't tell you to make that tie for Eric."

Adele struck a pose. "Well, we're all crochet sisters and we should stick together." And then she went into the whole diatribe about Mother Humphries ruining everything and turning Eric against her passion. "I'm wearing this in protest." Her voice became more melodramatic as her gaze moved across the group. "It's not just against me, but a diss against all crocheters." She held up her hook like it was a symbol for all who took part in the craft. She glanced at the others, expecting some kind of backing, but they all just shrugged it off since they were used to all her fussing. She started on again about how her marriage was over and that she couldn't stay with someone who wouldn't support her artistic endeavors.

"Why don't you put it on the back burner for now, dear," CeeCee said. "This trip is supposed to be for all of us. We all have our reasons to have wanted to get away. In case anybody is interested, I needed a rest after the rigors of my game show and a distraction while I wait to hear from my agent on something big." She left it hanging and seemed to be expecting the group to ask for details, but instead Rhoda went into her reason for needing to get away.

"I love Hal, but there is just too much togetherness. Now that he sold the business, he is just there all the time," Rhoda said. She looked at Dinah. "You're practically a newlywed, so it's probably still all champagne and roses."

Dinah chuckled at the comment. "Maybe when you get married when you're young and stupid. It is a whole other situation when you are used to doing things your way. It's as silly as Commander can't stand to have a roll of paper towels unless they're in a holder." She smiled at the group. "And I just needed some time with girl talk." She glanced at me. "Sorry, Molly. I mean women's talk."

All eyes were on Elise. "It's not fair. Logan has been in real estate much longer than I have. He got an award for being salesperson of the year and keeps gloating about it. I couldn't stand it anymore."

"Your turn, Molly," Rhoda said.

"It's my job since the bookstore is sponsoring our weekend. And, well, you all know what it's like at my house."

"And don't forget it was a chance to do that favor for Mason," Rhoda said. I smiled to myself as I thought *if they only knew*.

Adele, upset that she had lost the spotlight, let out one of her melodramatic sighs and flopped back into an easy chair while CeeCee attempted to take care of business. She glanced at Adele and continued. "I have an idea for a variation on the tie," the actress said. "We could make a scarf using the same size granny squares, but make more of them." She took one of the packages of cotton yarn out of the bin. "We could mix up the colors for the first few rows of the granny square and do the last row in the off-white." She mentioned a TV program that featured a female version of Columbo who had worn something similar in the show.

"I know the program you mean. I loved that scarf," Dinah said. "I could wear it as a replacement for the long skinny scarves I used to wear."

Elise was looking at something on her phone and wasn't paying attention, so CeeCee just counted her in. I said it was fine with me, glad that the yarn I had packed for the group would work for it. Rhoda said her daughter loved that TV show and she would give the scarf to her. Adele made a lot of harrumph sounds, but once she realized it was based on her original plan, she went along with it.

"Wait until you hear this," Elise said, still looking at her phone.

Before she could speak, there was a loud knock at the door, startling the group. It was punctuated by a bellowing voice announcing it was the police. Adele was out of her chair and on her way to the door. "Eric is so dramatic. I knew once he realized I was gone, he would come after me."

She had a stormy expression when she returned. There was no barrel-chested Eric but two uniformed Ojai Valley PD officers and someone else. Barry Greenberg stepped from behind them. I barely heard what Adele was saying about their desire to talk to us regarding something that happened nearby. This time I couldn't slip away unnoticed. His presence wasn't lost on the others either. They looked at me for my reaction. I had learned a lot during my on-and-off relationship with Barry and was pretty sure I was keeping my expression neutral. But he was the master of the cop look, and there was no way to evaluate his real reaction to seeing me there. He didn't even appear surprised.

"There was an incident on the property behind here," one of the officers said. "We're talking to everybody in the area to find out if they saw or heard anything." He glanced toward the back patio and the trees beyond. "It happened back there. Beyond all that."

Adele seemed more interested in trying to show the tie to them.

She saw that Barry was wearing a suit and tried to put it around his neck. He put his hand up to stop her. "We're here on official business." It was hard to tell with the flat expression, but there was just a glint in his eye that made me think he was fighting back a laugh.

"That's what I was going to tell you," Elise said to the group before addressing the police. "I'm in real estate and I knew that Heddy Mariano's property is behind us." She tapped the screen of the phone. "It says there's a police investigation going on back there."

One of the uniformed officers who seemed to be in charge put up his hand to silence her. "We want to talk to each of you separately," he said. While he and the other cop worked out the logistics of that, Barry nodded in my direction.

"I'll start with her." He was totally nonchalant as he waved for me to follow him and was acting like I was just another witness. I felt Dinah's eyes on my back. She more than anyone knew about the roller-coaster ride my relationship with Barry had been. She also knew that no matter that it was over between us for good this time, there was some leftover emotion.

He looked around at the main room for someplace private. "How about we talk out here?" I said, leading the way to the back patio and pointing to the chairs around a table. I focused on the strings of little lights crisscrossed above us as I tried to keep my cool. No way was I going to show how shaken up I felt.

Once he sat down, he took out his notebook and pen. "Let's start with what you're doing here," Barry said.

"Are you asking as a cop or out of personal curiosity?" I said.

He let down some of his detective demeanor and smiled as he shook his head in frustration. "Really? You're still playing that game? Answering a question with a question? How about this for an answer. Both."

I'd had a reaction when I saw him in the coffee shop and again at Heddy's, but it was mild compared to being this up-close and personal. The suit and shirt looked spotless and his tie was still pulled tight. He kept his dark hair close-cropped so it never looked mussed. But there were circles under his eyes. The five-o'clock shadow was gone from his chin and I guessed he had shaved in his car. The rest of the world blurred out when he was on a case. I fought back against the buzz of heat I felt being so close to him. That didn't matter in the whole scheme of things. It didn't blot out days and nights of not hearing from him, then leaving messages that weren't answered, which made me worry that something had happened to him.

I hid my reaction under what I hoped was a flat expression. "I'm not saying anything until you explain what you're doing here," I said.

He laughed this time. "Molly, this is official business and you know I don't have to explain anything. But instead of doing more of this back-and-forth, I'm going to cut to the chase. I came up here looking to talk to someone connected to a homicide in LA. Now it looks like there might be a connection to what happened here and I'm working with the local PD." He flipped open the pad. "And you were going to tell me why you're here."

I glanced toward the house. The officers had spread the Hookers apart and had started interviewing them individually. I felt sorry for the poor guy who was in the dining area with Adele. She was back to showing off the tie and trying to get the officer to try it on.

"It doesn't seem like such a hard question," Barry said.

Of course, he was right. It seemed evident I was there with the Hookers. I would leave it at that and make no mention of being there to work for Mason. It wasn't a lie. It was simply not the whole story. "The bookstore is closed for repairs and Mrs. Shedd arranged for the Hookers to have a getaway trip up here." I threw in a little color about Adele and the tie. "She's all upset that Eric's mother badmouthed it and he refused to wear it."

Barry looked down at his own tie, which was a conservative burgundy and cream-colored strip. "I can't say I blame him."

"You wanted to talk about what happened back there. Did someone die?" I asked.

Barry seemed irked that I had been the one to bring him back to the point of the visit. "Yes, but don't ask me who because I won't tell you. It won't be public until the next of kin has been notified."

I had a sinking feeling. If someone was dead, everything against Heddy became more serious. I did a good job of hiding my thoughts and Barry continued. "I was going to ask if you heard or saw anything last night. Bright lights or loud noises, something like that. Did you see anybody in that back area?"

I could honestly say that I hadn't and hoped that would end it before he asked anything else, like if I knew Heddy Mariano. I would be caught in a bind then. I didn't exactly know her, but she was a guest at the party and a possible kleptomaniac. Well, more than possible. She had been at the top of my list. My mind wandered for a moment to what might be going on between Jerry R and Heddy. He was her manager, but since she wasn't working, did she even need a manager? The way that Lisa R had been quick to point out that she thought Heddy was the scissors stealer made it seem that she was hostile to the singer. Could there be something personal going on between Jerry R and Heddy? I pushed it out of my mind and went back to dealing with the present and how to deal with Barry. I let go of my flat expression and smiled at Barry. "You look tired. How about a cup of coffee," I said.

He blew out his breath and nodded. "But don't think a cup of coffee is going to make me grill you any less."

I went inside and used the single-cup coffee maker. I didn't need to ask how he took it to know he drank it black. I found some cookies and brought it all out to him. He took a sip of the brew and ate one of the cookies. "I needed some caffeine and sugar. Thanks."

My gesture seemed to have softened his manner and I wanted to keep it that way. Let him think it was just a coincidence that the incident, as it was being called, had happened where the Hookers were having their vacation and I had no other connection. I asked him about his son Jeffrey, who I had always had a soft spot for.

"He went back to spend the summer with his mother. It's just as well. Carol and I broke up."

"Oh," I said, surprised. "You seemed like a good match."

He let out a mirthless laugh and rocked his head. "An ER nurse and a homicide cop. Too much adrenaline."

I was already connecting the dots. That meant he was all alone. I could only imagine how that affected his lifestyle. Living on fast food with no one to ground him and keep him in touch with people who weren't cops or killers. He seemed to read my thoughts. He looked at the surroundings as if seeing them for the first time. "I can see why you all came up here. I bet you can see a lot of stars at night." He turned back to me. "How's being a grandma going?"

"She doesn't call me that," I said a little too quickly. "I'm LaLa, the fun person who lets her have dessert before dinner." His smile broadened at my reaction to the old-sounding version of the title.

"And all your animals?" he asked.

"If you mean Cosmo," I said, referring to the black mutt who Barry and his son had adopted, but who ended up staying with me, "he's fine."

"Thanks for giving him such a good home." He started to push away from the table. "I think we're done here."

As we walked back inside, he turned back. "Good luck with your weekend," he said, then he looked me in the eye. "I saw Mason Fields a little while ago. Did you know he was in town?"

I suddenly felt cornered. I answered the only way I could that wouldn't be a lie. "Oh, really," I said and shrugged.

Chapter 10

"I'm glad that's over with," Rhoda said, carrying a cup of coffee as she joined the rest of the group in the main room. "Who would have thought we would end up in the middle of a police investigation. The cop I talked to just said there was an incident but wouldn't give me any details." She looked around at the group. "What about the rest of you?"

"I thought when my officer recognized me from the game show he'd give me some inside information, but he just wanted to know how to become a contestant," CeeCee said. She looked down at the gray joggers she was wearing and then patted her blondish hair, which had a bed-head look. "I wish I'd known they were coming so I could have spruced myself up."

"My philosophy is always be attired so I can show a property at a moment's notice," Elise said. She had definitely dressed accordingly and wore gray slacks and a white shirt. Even her ballet flats were dressier than the sneakers and slippers the rest of us were wearing. "I do wonder what happened back there. It could alter the value for this place and the place behind us." Elise's total focus on whatever she was into at the moment fascinated me. It was like she had on blinders to the rest of the world.

Dinah picked up the thread of our interrogation. "I tried some tricks I learned from Molly," she said. "Like act like you know more than you do, but it didn't work. The cop I talked to was absolutely by the book."

"It was different for me," Adele said. "I'm a police wife and speak their language. I knew to call the one who questioned me by name and made sure that he knew he wasn't talking to some clueless civilian. And he told me right away that Heddy Mariano was fine and that it seemed like any danger had passed. He was very interested in the tie when he heard I had made it for one of his police brothers. He even tried it on. I asked him if he would wear it if his wife had made it. He said he would for sure and he couldn't understand Eric's problem with it." She looked at her phone on the table. "Do you think I should call Eric and tell him that?" As usual it had become the Adele show. We were all shaking our heads, but she continued anyway, asking for the group's opinion of what she should do.

"Why are you even asking us? You're not going to listen to what we say anyway," Rhoda said, cutting right to the point. "But here's what I think anyway. You should leave it alone for now. I mean really leave it alone. As in stop talking about the silly tie. Let's get back to what we came for. This was supposed to be a getaway from stresses for all of us." She turned to me. "You haven't said anything. How did it go with the detective? You haven't seen him in a while. Were there sparks flying between you two?"

"No sparks," I said, which was more or less true. "He mostly kept it businesslike and he wouldn't tell me much." I wondered if I should mention what he did say, letting on that there had been a death. They already seemed agitated and I didn't want to make it worse. This was supposed to be a relaxing trip away from the worries of the world. I ended it with a shrug and looked at my watch. "Hey, it's lunchtime. Let's talk food."

"Good idea since we barely had breakfast," Rhoda said. "Now that you're here, you see how we're in the middle of nowhere."

"I need to get myself presentable if we're going to try one of the cafés in town," CeeCee said.

"We have the groceries you all picked up last night. Molly and I could whip something up with them," Dinah said. That suggestion got the most traction and we both got up and headed to the kitchen. Meanwhile, Adele tried to get them all to turn out some hearts while they waited.

"I hope you don't mind that I volunteered you," Dinah said as we stopped in the compact kitchen. "I thought we could get some privacy to talk. I want to hear all about everything."

"First we better come up with something to make for lunch." I opened the refrigerator and checked the cabinets to see what we had to work with. "Seeing the food there is, let's make a charcuterie board and they can make sandwiches or eat the stuff plain." Dinah agreed and we started working on it.

"Okay, now spill," my friend said. "What's the real story about seeing Barry?" I had found a wood board that was perfect to use. And she took out some different cheeses and cold cuts. The point of a charcuterie board was presentation. People did all kinds of cute things like making faces out of cheese, and rolled-up salami slices for hair, with olives for eyes. We were not up to making something that fancy and started arranging things nicely but without the fun touches.

"I was uncomfortable to say the least. I wanted to be distant, but it was hard. There are still a lot of memories." I detoured and told her about seeing Barry earlier when Mason was bringing me back. "And then again when we stopped at Heddy Mariano's." Dinah was wide-eyed when she heard where I had been.

"Then you know a lot more than you let on," she said, making cucumber spears to go with a little container of hummus.

I nodded. "There were police and paramedics. Mason was doing his lawyer thing with her and I tried to find out what happened. All I got was that the paramedics were working on an injured person somewhere on the property. Barry told me he came up here to talk to somebody connected to a homicide in LA and now he's helping the local police."

"Does that mean Heddy Mariano is involved with the LA homicide?" Dinah asked.

"I don't know. He wasn't generous with the information, and he actually dropped the cop stuff and got a little personal. He told me that he and Carol broke up," I said.

"Wow, that is being personal. Maybe he wanted to let you know he was available," Dinah said.

"It doesn't matter. I'm not getting caught up in that again. Maybe it is better to be single right now," I said. I was still getting used to single meaning unattached as opposed to the old meaning of not married. "Marlowe is practically living at my place. Peter is there because his daughter is and he's using the converted garage for his office. My mother and the girls are getting ready for the PBS special and over all the time. Samuel texted me last night that he has top billing at a music night at the Tarzana Cultural Center and needs to practice when the She La Las aren't. Then there are all the animals, and that doesn't include my job and my friends," I said.

I knew it might sound like I was protesting too much, but she was a good enough friend not to bring it up. "It sounds like you have enough to adjust to without having to deal with a partner," she said, nodding in agreement. "It's like I told the others this morning. It's not easy weaving together our different lifestyles." She got a triumphant smile. "But maybe Commander's coming around. I got a text from him this morning agreeing to go to Cabrillo Beach at midnight to catch the grunion run."

"That's an achievement," I said, knowing a big issue was the difference in the hours they kept and that he tended to go to bed much earlier than her. I knew all about the late-night event she was referring to, having gone to the beach in the past to see it for myself. The grunion that would be doing the running were small silver fish that came out of the water to lay their eggs in wet sand. It was all timed to the tides and phases of the moon. Lots of people showed up on the dark beach. Some were there to catch the fish, which apparently were quite tasty, but most came out just to see the spectacle.

"He is such a good guy," Dinah said. "It's hard with our different ways of doing things, but I love his character. I love him." Then she seemed embarrassed. "Listen to me," she said, shaking her head. "I sound like a gushy greeting card." She transitioned into talking about a note she had gotten from one of her students that was written almost entirely in letters standing in for words. "They weren't even abbreviations. I thought *sut* was some new word, but it means see you tomorrow." She shook her head and laughed as she put a small bowl of green olives next to a cascading row of cheese slices. "It's always good to go off for a while. I needed a break before I face summer school. I have to build up my reserve to deal with them." She shook her head in frustration. "Just when I get used to their slang and text talk, it all changes. I feel like I'm deciphering a code when I read their papers. And trying to get them to understand grammar rules?" She rocked her head again. "I was trying to teach them about commas and gave them two sentences. Let's eat, Jerome. And Let's eat Jerome. They didn't get it, even when I explained that in the first sentence Jerome was one of the people having the meal and in the second one, Jerome was the meal." Dinah ordered herself to take a deep breath and relax. "At least I still have the rest of the weekend to decompress."

I stuck a wedge of brie cheese next to a tiny bowl of spicy apricot preserves. Dinah found a loaf of bread and stared arranging the slices in a basket. "I can't believe I forgot to ask you. How did it go with your job for Mason?"

In all the excitement, I had forgotten about it, but now it came back and I felt bad all over again. "Not good," I said, making a face. "To put it bluntly, a pair of fancy scissors disappeared and I missed out on who did it."

Dinah gave me a sympathetic pat on the shoulder. "How did Mason take it?"

"He was very nice about it. He even took me out to breakfast and we had a few laughs. But I wasn't so sure he would be hiring me again." I gestured toward the French doors leading to the back area. "And then all of this happened." I dropped my voice before explaining the task Mason had been given to find some other suspects. "He asked me to help him, and that was before Barry let on that the victim had died."

"He told you that?" Dinah said, incredulous.

"He wouldn't tell me who it was. They have to notify next of kin before making it public. That's why I didn't say anything to the others."

"Mason will really need your help now. What do you think he will want you to do?" my friend asked.

I shrugged, explaining I had no idea what it would entail. "But for the rest of the weekend I'll be doing double duty. Dealing with the Hookers and whatever comes up with Mason." I let out a sigh. "I know I should be upset that someone died, but I'm so relieved that Mason wants me to work for him."

We had stopped what we were doing, but then Dinah looked at the unfinished serving board and said we had better finish up. "How nice that this place came stocked with sauces and condiments," she said, putting together a selection of packets of different mustards, along with mayonnaise, in a basket, while I put together another basket with the bread and rolls.

Dinah's asking me about my job reminded me of Bennett and I wanted to share. "I sort of met someone," I said.

"When, where and who is he?" Dinah said, surprised. After I gave her a brief rundown on the lanky field producer, she looked at me and laughed. "All that talk about being single and it sounds more like it's raining men."

Chapter 11

The charcuterie board got a lot of compliments as we put it on the dining room table along with the selection of bread. Rhoda came in just as we were figuring out if it was better to pass the board around or leave it in one place and treat it like a buffet. She was looking at her phone and shaking her head.

"I just got a text from Hal. He said there was a breaking news alert that Kirkland Rush died. You all know who he is," she said, looking over the group as they nodded. "The report said it happened in Pixie on the eve of his wedding and that he had been found in a rural area. There weren't any more details beyond that it was being investigated as foul play." She swiveled her head toward the French doors at the back of the main room. "That has to be what the police were here about." Everyone followed her gaze and shuddered.

"I'm sure you're right," Elise said. They all started talking about the news person. I barely heard all their prattling as the news sank in. It was one thing to hear that a nameless someone had died, and then it changed when a name was added. But it was totally different when the victim turned out to be someone I had been checking out as a possible kleptomaniac the night before. It felt too strange to think back to seeing him with Zoe in the library and realize that now he was dead.

Rhoda let out a heavy sigh. "Hal wasn't happy with me going away and this has just given him a reason to tell me I should come home now. And he doesn't even know how close we are to what happened."

"The officer told me that the danger was past," Adele said. "As a police wife, I know what that means."

"It means they think it was something personal rather than a killer on the loose," I said, getting to the point before Adele somehow managed to bring the granny square tie into it. Adele seemed annoyed that I had finished what she was going to say.

My mind was whirling as they all started throwing out questions and comments. What was Kirkland doing there? Didn't it seem obvious that Heddy Mariano must have done it? As they went on, Dinah looked at me with a question in her eye. I nodded in answer.

"Molly might know a little more about the whole thing," my friend said, and then all eyes were on me.

"Kirkland Rush was a guest at the party I went to. So was Heddy Mariano and Kirkland's fiancée, Zoe. It wasn't on the eve of his wedding, more like a pre-pre-event. The wedding is this weekend."

"You mean *was*. You can't have a wedding without the groom," Rhoda said. "What if he went off with Heddy for a last fling and his wife-to-be found out? Now I remember hearing he was marrying one of those weather girls." Rhoda shrugged. "It's hard to tell them apart. It doesn't even matter what their hair color is, or even their skin color. They all look the same."

A discussion erupted about how all the weather women wore super-fitted sheath dresses and heels that looked like murder weapons. "You're right," Elise said. "She could have followed him and used her shoe."

"That seems a little far-fetched," CeeCee said. "But I suppose it could have happened."

"That is, if she could move around enough in that tight dress. Can you imagine what she has to have on under it. I bet she wears a spandex body suit to hold everything in," Rhoda said. "They can't have even the slightest bulge over the belts a lot of them seem to wear." She looked down at the dark blue pull-on pants with a white tunic top she was wearing. "Not for me."

"Not for any of us," Elise said. "But more importantly, who gave the party?" As soon as I mentioned Jerry R's name, CeeCee let out a sound.

"That's who the host was?" CeeCee said, surprised and impressed. "Do you know who he is?" It turned out to be a rhetorical question and she continued. "I don't really need a manager, but if I did, I would pick Jerry R." She turned to the others. "His real last name is Rayner, but everyone calls him Jerry R. He's the best because he really cares about his clients, like they're his family. I had heard he moved up here. Everybody likes his wife, too. She's a kindhearted soul who has a cat rescue."

Elise announced that she had pulled up an aerial view of the Rayner ranch on her laptop. "What a spread," she said. "It's got everything—a huge house with some outbuildings and then a barn, corrals, and a grove of olive trees." She wanted to know what it was like on the inside. I told them all about how it seemed designed for entertaining, including the game room. I added that they had a reputation of putting on a party for every holiday and hosting events like Kirkland's wedding.

"Who else was there?" Rhoda asked. I mentioned the people I thought they would recognize, like Tom Kelter and Rory Bijorn and Verona Gilroy. "There were some other local people, like a couple who moved here from Silicon Valley, and Kirkland's ex-wife."

"Tom Kelter turned into a hunk," Rhoda said, and they all laughed at her choice of words. She shrugged it off and went to comment on Rory Bijorn. "She seems like the moody type." I was going to tell them about my encounter with her but stopped myself, realizing I would have to give up my undercover job in the process.

"I like Verona Gilroy," Elise said. "She's so perky and cute."

"That's her persona. But maybe she's not so perky and cute in private," CeeCee said.

"Am I the only one who thinks it's weird that Kirkland's ex was there?" Dinah said. "What was she doing there?" I explained that Kirkland's ten-year-old son was supposed to be the best man and she had brought him. I didn't go into the fact that she seemed to be handling Kirkland's financial business.

"She could have done it," Rhoda said. "She could have lured him to Heddy's and then—" She looked at me. "I wonder how he died."

I realized I didn't have a clue and shook my head as Rhoda continued. "But maybe it's someone else entirely. He was known for getting himself into the middle of the stories he reported on. He probably stepped on a lot of toes."

"I bet the cops have already pinned it on Heddy," Elise said.

"She is the most obvious," Rhoda said. "It happened in her backyard."

"Actually, she's claiming that she has space creatures visiting her property and that's who killed Kirkland," I said. I worried about bringing it up, since we were so close, but they all seemed to shrug it off as ridiculous.

CeeCee shook her head with concern. "Poor dear has probably lost it and is seeing things. You know, she had a breakdown in the middle of a show. I don't think she has performed since. I suppose it would be easy to make her the prime suspect. That space visitor story makes her seem even more crazed. But what if it wasn't her," CeeCee said. She looked at me. "Can't you do something? You're really good at ferreting out the solution to crimes and have done it so many times before."

Mentally, I was breathing a sigh of relief. CeeCee's concern had just given me the excuse I needed to be able to go with Mason. "I'm sure you're right about the cops settling on her. I would hate to see her wrongly accused. Maybe I can nose around a little." I stole a look at Dinah and she gave me a nod of approval. "Mason and I are just friends now. I'll see if he can get me back in the middle of things."

Adele had been strangely quiet and then she let out an upset moan. "Who cares about that? The real problem is why didn't Eric call me to tell me what happened." There were eye rolls all around.

When we finally got around to eating, the charcuterie board was a big success.

I decided to be proactive, and as soon as lunch was over I called Mason to let him know that I had cleared the way to be able to work with him without it being a problem with the Hookers. I got his voicemail and left a message.

Dinah had already begun clearing the table, and I grabbed what she couldn't carry. We went into the kitchen while Adele herded the rest of them into the main room, insisting it was crochet time. When the dishwasher was loaded and everything put away, we slipped outside and retrieved my suitcase and took it into the room we were sharing. "You really did it," I said, laughing as I saw my bed loaded with pillows under the covers to make it look like someone was there.

After that, Dinah went to join the others. I felt like I was in a whirlwind and needed a little time alone to process everything. I knew crochet was good at helping when I felt stressed, but I couldn't deal with the company that went with it just then.

I slipped back to the kitchen and made myself a cup of coffee. No one even noticed when I took it outside and sat down at the table. It was the same spot I had shared with Barry. I was still getting over the shock of seeing him at the coffee shop. And just when I thought I had avoided meeting him, he had shown up here. And now there was a murder. Peaceful weekend, hah!

A bird flew by and landed in one of the trees at the point where the yard became wild. The California oak trees had dark green leaves that were much smaller than the hand-shaped leaves of the other kinds of oak trees. The ground was covered with a tangle of undergrowth that seemed low enough to maneuver through. There was nothing that said I couldn't explore the property the group had for the weekend. Even so, I checked to make sure no one was looking. I didn't want company or to explain where I was going. I left the cup and began to make my way back into the wildness.

Just like Heddy's back acreage, this part of our place seemed too big and too wild to be called a yard. When I glanced back to get my bearings, all I saw were more trees and undergrowth with no sign of the Hookers' house. I kept going what seemed like forward and then up ahead saw a low chain-link fence mostly hidden by bushes. I moved in closer and looked into the next property. In the distance it sloped upward and there were a lot of big rocks. A row of bushes and trees grew along the bottom of the hill there and made me think there was water. As my gaze moved closer, I saw the sun glinting off of what appeared to be a free-form pond surrounded by large rocks and foliage. Then I sucked in my breath when I saw one of the white tents the cops use to cover a body near the water. I didn't want to imagine what was under it. There was an evidence marker on the ground next to a large rock covered in a dull-looking red. My stomach did a flip-flop as I realized it was dried blood. I considered going over the fence to have a better look, but there was someone there. I slipped behind a bush, and as the bushes on the other side of the fence rustled, something silvery-looking appeared for a moment and then disappeared in the overgrowth of ground cover and trees.

I waited a moment to see if it was going to reappear and when it didn't, I left my hiding spot. When I turned away from the fence, there were just trees and ground cover and I had no sense of what direction I had come from. My natural thought was that the house was somehow behind me, but as I walked, all I saw were more trees and brush. Now I wished I had left a trail of breadcrumbs or something to find my way back. I stepped over some dried grass and my foot slipped on something.

It wasn't until I thought I heard the ping that I realized I had my phone in my pocket. A piece of red yarn fell to the ground as I took it out. Just as I was going to read the text, a voice said, "There you are."

I looked up and a man in a cowboy hat approached me. It took a moment to realize it was Mason. "What are you doing back here?" he asked, looking at the rustic area. Then he cocked his head. "I know what you were doing. You didn't go onto Heddy's property, did you?"

"No. I wouldn't do that, and besides, there was someone back there. Probably a CSI person dressed in one of the suits they wear when they go into a crime scene. I always thought they were white, but this one was silvery-looking."

"Last I heard they were still waiting to get the warrant. And you're right, the suits are made of Tyvek and are white."

"Maybe it was one of Heddy's alien visitors making a daytime appearance," I said, joking.

"Shush, don't even say that," Mason said. "I wish she would stop saying that. It isn't helping her case." He glanced in the distance. "Did you see anything else?"

I mentioned the tent and the evidence marker next to the blood-covered rock. Then the surprise of seeing him registered. "What are you doing here?"

"Looking for you. Dinah said she heard you go outside. I saw the cup on the table and figured you had gone exploring. I tried sending you a text and followed the ping. I was prepared to send more, but then there you were."

"Impressive," I said.

"You don't know this about me, but I was an Eagle Scout and I know my way around in the wilderness." He was dressed in jeans and an olive-green collarless shirt. The cowboy hat was a total surprise. He saw me looking at it and took it off and smiled. "It's bad manners to wear your hat around a lady."

"It's a whole new look for you," I said. I looked down at his feet. "Cowboy boots too."

"You have to dress the part," he said with a shrug. "I ended up going riding with Jerry R. He needed to get away from it all and clear his head. As you can imagine, everything has hit the fan. There's so much to deal with. Kirkland's ex-wife isn't really responsible for decisions about obituaries and arrangements. And his fiancée, well, she's in no condition to deal with anything. It's all falling on Jerry R and Lisa R. They're having to adjust all the plans. He moved Heddy to the ranch for now and she isn't taking it well."

"Do you think it's more than a business relationship?" I asked.

"I don't think so, but I don't know for sure. I do know that Jerry R thinks of his clients as being like family. I think that's why he was hosting Kirkland's wedding." Mason paused and glanced back in the direction we had come from. "If the tent was there, it probably means the medical examiner hasn't arranged to pick up the body yet." He explained they used a funeral company to transport the body. "I got your message. I gather you worked something out with the Hookers," he said.

I nodded. "It was tricky, but I handled it."

"Great. Then can you come with me now?" he said.

"Yes. That is, if we can find our way back," I said, seeing nothing but trees.

"Remember, I said I was good in the wilderness." He took out his phone and opened the compass. He glanced at me with a smile. "Do you need me to hold your hand?"

Chapter 12

Thanks to Eagle Scout Mason, we made it back to the Hookers' house with no problem. And no, I didn't need him to hold my hand. On the way, he apologized for not telling me who the victim was from the very beginning. "It was a slip-up but there was so much coming at me at once," he said by way of explanation.

"Do you want to come in and say hello?" I asked when we were at the glass door.

"Sure, why not," he said. "I'm a brave soul."

Everyone was in the main room and they did a double take when we walked in. Once he took off the hat, they all relaxed. All I had to do was make a vague excuse about leaving and they all gave me knowing looks, thinking that I had maneuvered my way back into the middle of things instead of being called back to action by Mason. Only Dinah knew the truth. Adele was looking at Mason with keen interest and I knew any second she was going to whip out the tie and put it on him. I said a fast goodbye and we were out the door.

"I hope you appreciate that I saved you from the assault of the tie," I said as Mason steered the SUV.

"Oh, no, what is Adele up to now?" he asked with a smile.

I told him about the granny square tie and how she had forced it on the cop who had questioned her. "Every man she sees is fair game," I said.

"I didn't consider that the cops would come here, but it makes sense since you are so close," he said. "There's a lot to process." I didn't want to bring up that Barry was the one who questioned me and just assured him that we had all said we didn't know anything.

"Does Jerry R know I'm helping you?" I asked.

Mason hesitated. "I think I told him. I'm sure he'll be happy to have your assistance. It's an all-hands-on-deck situation right now."

"It's just that after what happened, I wasn't sure how he would feel about my skills. But it could be another chance for me to find the kleptomaniac," I said.

"Jerry R has put that on the back burner for now, but sure, if you want to," Mason said.

"I do," I said emphatically. "I don't like leaving loose ends. You hired me to do something and I didn't come through."

"Oh," Mason said, turning to face me while he was stopped at a red light. "I didn't realize that it meant that much to you."

I decided to tell him the truth. "When I failed, I worried you wouldn't have me work for you again—all things considered." The last part was vague, but I was sure he knew I was referring to the way things had ended with us. "I really appreciate how you set aside any negative feelings you had about me. It probably sounds silly, but I love having a secret life." I turned to him. "Who would think this plain woman in khaki pants was actually working as a private private investigator?"

Mason had his eyes back on the road. "Are you fishing for compliments?" he said in a light tone. "You're not plain-looking, far from it." There was an awkward moment of silence and I tried to figure out how to respond to his comment. He seemed to realize things were going in the wrong direction and quickly changed the subject. "So, what did you say to your crochet buds? They were all giving me weird looks."

I laughed as I started to explain. "I twisted things around so they were actually telling me I should find a way to get involved."

"And how did you do that?" he said, sounding genuinely interested.

"Mostly, I got them sympathetic to Heddy. They know all about the sleuthing I've done before. I didn't even have to say anything about finding out what really happened. They suggested it."

"I'm impressed," he said. He chuckled as I took a mock bow. "We should talk about tonight. There's going to be another party—well, maybe it's better to call it a gathering. It's more like a vigil or wake. You can just mingle and see what you hear."

I looked down at what I was wearing. The leggings and denim shirt were fine for hanging out with the Hookers but hardly something for a gathering at Jerry R's, particularly when it was for something so somber. Other than Adele, who always dressed to get attention, and Elise, who was always dressed to sell, we had all brought clothes meant for sitting around and crocheting in.

"I only brought one outfit that counted as casual elegant," I said. "And it's back in my suitcase. We better go back for it. I'm sure no one would notice that I was wearing the same thing again since it was so bland-looking."

"I have a better idea," he said, making a U-turn with the SUV. "We'll just get you something new. It's a business expense." I was surprised by his offer, but it seemed better than resurrecting the outfit from the night before that I had thrown in the suitcase without regard for whether it turned into a mass of wrinkles.

"You're the boss," I said. He drove into the downtown area of Ojai with all the cream-colored stucco buildings and little shops. We left the SUV in a lot next to Libby Park. I glanced at the playground in the front and got a better look this time. There was a special area for younger kids. Mason noticed how intently I was looking at the park.

"What's so interesting?"

"I'm afraid it doesn't go with being an investigator. I was thinking how nice the place would be for Marlowe." I looked at him. "I take my grandmother duties very seriously, particularly when it comes to anything that might be fun."

"Just what I would expect from you. You're like the kind of grandmother every kid would wish for," he said. I was going to offer to show him pictures, but it seemed too much.

We stopped and checked out the area. Just down the street there were some shops with racks of things out front. The other side of the street had the colonnade and shops that seemed a little more formal. We crossed the street and checked out the row of stores.

"I vote we go there after we find you something to wear," Mason said, pointing out an ice cream parlor that promised it was all homemade. He must have realized that it sounded too much like fun and said we could discuss strategy while we ate.

"This place seems promising," I said, indicating a small department store.

When we neared it, Mason stopped. "I can wait out here and you can get me when you need my credit card," he said. "Or I could come in. Your choice."

"I wouldn't mind your help in picking something out," I said. "You probably have a better idea what would be appropriate."

"I'm not so sure about that, but maybe if we put our heads together we can come up with something." He held the door for me and then followed me into the store.

We found the area set aside for women's clothes. We had already agreed that I didn't have to wear something dark or too formal, but also agreed that it seemed wrong to wear something too festive.

Mason sat outside the dressing room and I came out to show him the things I had picked. It reminded me of old times when he somehow had made everything fun. We both agreed on a long tank-style dress with a colorful duster. To be sure I had everything covered, he suggested I get a couple of pairs of jeans and some shirts to go with them, along with incidentals, even though I said I had that covered in my stuff I'd left with the Hookers.

"And now for that ice cream," Mason said. He insisted on getting us cappuccinos too. We took the ice cream and coffee drinks to a table in a parklike area behind the line of shops.

"What a view," he said. "This place does feel like a faraway paradise." We both looked at the mountains in the distance, softened by a haze of moisture that blew in all the way from the ocean. It seemed like he caught himself then and sat up a little straighter before he brought up the evening ahead. "What we're looking for are other suspects with some evidence that points to them. Nobody will expect that you're investigating. All you have to do is get people to talk to you about Kirkland."

"I can do that," I said. "I'll just be your cousin again." I was glad that we were getting back to the business at hand. The shopping and ice cream had seemed too much like old times and I had to remind myself that we were in a different place.

"I was preoccupied when you mentioned the police talking to the Hookers. Was it just the local cops?"

"Barry Greenberg was with them. He's the one who talked to me." When I looked at Mason, his mouth was twisted into displeasure.

"What did you tell him?" Mason's voice had changed into something more formal.

"As little as possible," I said. "I didn't lie, but I didn't mention being at the party last night."

"Good. Did you find out why he is up here?"

I repeated what Barry had told me. That he had come up to talk to someone connected to a case he was working on and that there might be a connection to what had happened here. "I guess he's helping out the local police."

"Good work," Mason said, giving me a pat on the arm. "I'm betting it was Kirkland who he wanted to talk to." Mason drank the last of his cappuccino. "It would get the focus off of Heddy if we could tie Kirkland's death to some murder in LA."

"I know the plan is to find an alternative, but do you think that Heddy killed Kirkland?" I asked.

"It doesn't matter what I think. In my business, that's immaterial and all I'm supposed to concern myself with is getting my client off," he said. "You know that I am still trying to balance things off by doing pro bono work for people who have gotten convicted of crimes they didn't commit. So far, I've gotten new trials for all my clients." Mason's tone softened. "It makes me feel good that I've made a difference."

I wanted to say that it was one of the things I had loved about him, but it was off-the-charts personal. He must have sensed something because he grabbed the empty ice cream cups and said we ought to go.

Chapter 13

Mason and I were silent on the way back to the Rayner ranch and I was alone with my thoughts. Mostly, I thought about how unexpected this weekend was turning out. I had been so sure I was done with the Rayner ranch and here I was on my way back there.

Mason drove directly back to the guest house and parked in front of it. I grabbed the packages and we both went inside. Out of habit, I rushed to shut the door behind us. "I'm so used to a herd of animals," I said by way of explanation.

"Me, too—well, a herd of one. Spike makes up for it in personality," he said, referring to his toy fox terrier. Mason's relationship with his dog had been another soft spot for me. Mason took Spike to the office most of the time. I was surprised that he didn't bring the dog to court with him.

"I should probably get ready," I said, picking up the bags with the things we had bought.

"Ditto for me. I feel like a dust magnet after the horseback riding." He had dropped the cowboy hat on the table and was kicking off the fancy boots. He glanced at his watch. "It's always a surprise how late it is at this time of year when it stays light so long," Mason said. "People will start arriving soon."

I went into my former room and closed the door. It felt like an eternity instead of just hours since I had left there in the morning. The feeling was completely different than when I had gone in there the day before. Then I was just thinking about one night and it felt so temporary that I hadn't settled in. The world had turned and everything was uncertain. It was clear that I was there for the evening, but then what? I hung up the dress and put the extra clothes we had gotten in the closet. But I left everything else in the bag in the dressing area.

What I wanted most was a shower. I looked over the assortment of toiletries and smiled appreciatively as I read the back of the lavender-scented shower gel. It went along with the New Agey vibe of the area and promised to cleanse my aura. It sounded good to me and I turned on the shower. The water came from a showerhead almost at the ceiling and it felt like standing in warm rain. It felt sensuous as it cascaded over my body. I started to wonder if Mason was having a similar experience but shut down the thought. I was back on the clock and he was just my boss.

He was already in the main room when I came out and gave me an appraising look. "We made a good choice. It's the perfect outfit for an undercover detective," he said with a warm smile. "No one would guess your real mission."

"Are you teasing me after I told you how much I like having this mysterious double life?" I said, suddenly feeling silly about the whole thing.

"I'm sorry if that came out wrong. I wasn't teasing you. After what you said about how much you liked the whole woman of mystery thing, I was trying to show my support."

"I accept it and thank you," I said. He had changed out of the riding outfit into a pair of dark slacks and a cream-colored untucked dress shirt. "I guess the Hawaiian shirts are over forever," I said. "I thought they suited you." The words had slipped out before I could stop myself. I tried to cover myself by saying what he was wearing was probably more appropriate and it was none of my business what he wore anyway.

He let out a little chuckle. "Only fair since I helped with your outfit." He looked down at the shirt. "It was Tiffany's idea. It's something new having someone suggest what I wear." His expression darkened as he seemed to think of something troubling. "Maybe not so new."

"Forget I said anything. I overstepped. I just always thought the Hawaiian shirts gave off a fun vibe. But what you're wearing is more suited to tonight anyway."

He opened the door and I followed him out. It was showtime, again.

The mood was different at the big house this time. The din of conversation was softer and the whole feeling was more subdued. Jerry R and Lisa R were standing in the entrance hall, greeting their guests and having them sign the guest book. We got nods to bypass the guest book and go on in.

"There's plenty of food," Lisa R said. "It was too late to cancel anything, and it will probably be a smaller group than last night."

Mason and I split up as soon as we moved on from the entrance hall. I wanted to check over who was there against my list of possible kleptomaniacs. I knew that Mason had said to forget about it, but if I could catch the person, why not. Mason was a master at social gatherings and immediately joined a group of people who were hanging near the drink room.

I made a beeline for the library to check out the glass case. The empty spot where the scissors had been was filled with a red pen. I wasn't sure if they would strike again with everything going on about Kirkland's death, but then it might even be more likely to happen if it had to do with stress relief.

"You're here," Bennett said in happy surprise as he came up behind me. "What happened?"

"It seemed wrong to desert my cousin," I said. "I thought he might need moral support."

Bennett looked over his shoulder into the main room. Mason was surrounded by a knot of people. "He seems to be doing okay and it looks like he abandoned you again." He smiled at me. "I'm happy to pick up the slack and keep you company." He let out a weary sigh. "It's hardly the expected event."

"It must be hard on you," I said. "I'm sorry for your loss—business and personal."

"Thank you, but it was almost completely a working relationship. And he was always threatening to have me replaced." He dropped his voice to a whisper. "I'm sorry to have to say this, but he wasn't a very nice person, totally self-absorbed. All that passion and supposed caring about people and justice was an act." We had a view of the entrance hall from where we were standing. He shook his head as Meg Rush and her son came in. "The whole reason he wanted Harrison in the wedding party was so he would look like a good father. But I'm pretty sure he didn't know when the kid's birthday was."

Meg seemed stunned, but Harrison appeared the same as he had the night before—like a kid stuck at an adult party. Jerry R was giving them extra attention and escorted them into the living room.

"Did you have any idea that Kirkland was going to Heddy's?" I asked Bennett.

"Yes. Me, along with anybody else who knew Kirkland, could have figured he was going to go there. Anything for a story. We all heard Heddy going on about some sort of alien invasion. Knowing Kirkland, he would have figured that whatever was going on, he would come out ahead. Getting something on a space invasion would be spectacular. This area does have a reputation for being rather mystical. But the more likely story, that Heddy has lost it and is hallucinating, would still get a lot of attention. Sad but true, the public eats up stories about the messed-up lives of celebrities. Even though she's been out of the public eye for a while, people are still fascinated by her. She's been a star since she was a kid and has turned into a nature girl singing to avocado trees."

"You seem to know all about it," I said.

"It's what I do. Kirkland might have started it by going there and getting some info, but then I would have been the one to pull it all together." Bennett paused for a beat before he continued. "He tried to get me to go with him, but I refused. He could get away with stuff like going places where he shouldn't because he was the famous journalist. And then he would leave me to be the fall guy."

"That had to be tough," I said.

"It goes with the job. I'm pretty good at keeping myself out of trouble though." Bennett seemed open to talking and maybe trying to impress me. I realized he might have useful information. I felt a little guilty about taking advantage of his friendliness, but I was just doing my job.

"There must have been other stories that Kirkland was cultivating. Did you get pulled into those? Maybe there was something in LA," I said. I was thinking about whatever Barry was working on. Mason had said it would help if Kirkland's death could be made to appear connected to that.

"For the moment, he was focused on the wedding and getting the most out of it." His expression softened. "I'm glad you came back." Bennett didn't seem to have a clue what I was doing and had gone back to his flirty manner.

"I had to come back since I forgot to leave a glass slipper," I joked, going along with his claim that I had pulled a Cinderella by my sudden departure. I felt myself smiling all the way to my eyes as I continued. "Well, it probably would not have been a glass slipper anyway. These days I think Cinderella would have left something more comfortable like a glass ballet flat or sneaker." I was surprised at how easy it was for me to be flirty with him. I would have liked to have thought it was a sign at how good I was at being a secret investigator, but the truth was, it was a genuine reaction to him. I thought of Dinah's comment about it raining men and chuckled to myself. Then I pulled myself together and got back to business.

"I think we're breaking the rules by having fun. Aren't we supposed to be talking about Kirkland in hushed whispers? Maybe talking about all the stories that wouldn't come to fruition now that he was gone?"

"Anything big will go the distance," he said. "The BNN people have already been in touch."

"Even that story you were telling me about. The one in LA," I said. Bennett seemed confused for a moment, for good reason. He hadn't really told me about any LA story. I was using a trick that I had learned from Barry. Cops would bend the truth when questioning someone. And yes, I felt bad about doing it.

"You mean the disgruntled accountant who had some information about a financial firm he had recently been fired from. He claimed to know something about some sleazy investments they were making with their clients' money. A lot of their clients were celebrities. I told Kirkland that nobody cares about celebrities' business managers."

I filed that information away to deal with later and turned back to something more personal to make up for my twisting the truth. "I suppose his death messes up your work," I said.

He smiled. "It feels a little callous to say this but I have already gotten a step up. I was given complete control of putting together all the pieces for the media. The film crew who was coming to cover the wedding will be doing it for the memorial service. I learned a long time ago that in this business you have to be ready to deal with all kinds of changes, and no matter what you have to stay hydrated and fed." He gestured in the direction of the dining room, where the buffet had been laid out.

I shook my head. "I'm really not hungry," I said. The truth was that I didn't want any distraction from mingling and seeing what I could find out. I was going to tell him to go on himself when we were joined by Kirkland's fiancée, Zoe. I imagined that she was used to keeping up appearances under pressure. She was dressed in another weather girl outfit, this time a tight yellow dress that had crisscrossing zippers, which made me think it would be a good dress for a stripper. The shoes had heels so thin they looked as if they could snap at any moment. Her long blond hair cascaded over her shoulders and her makeup was perfect. She dabbed at her eyes, but it seemed very theatrical and I wondered if they were real tears or just an illusion.

She focused on Bennett. "What happens now? Are you going to film something about me?"

"I talked to Jerry R about how we're going to adjust things. We'll get something at the memorial," he said. "This must be a very difficult time for you. I'm sure that Jerry R and Lisa R will help you figure out what's next."

She hugged him. "I'm sure you're right." I quickly added my condolences and she thanked me and dabbed at her eyes again. "I'm starving," she said. "But if I eat more than a grape this dress will come apart." She said something about a glass of wine might work and went off to get it.

He watched her go and shook his head. "What's the term for a fiancée whose husband-to-be dies? Maybe something like bereft bride?" He realized I didn't know what he was talking about. "I'll need to know how to refer to her in the piece I do for BNN and clips for the rest of the media. It's really strange but it's just the kind of story Kirkland would have liked. A wedding that becomes a funeral. A mysterious death possibly, by a space alien invasion, a former pop star who grows avocados, all in a town called Pixie."

He looked at me. "Are you sure you don't want to get food? Remember what I said about staying hydrated and fed." I urged him to go without me. He shrugged and started to do the Arnold Schwarzenegger impression, but then realized it might seem improper under the circumstances and whispered the rest of it before he walked away.

I froze for a moment as I thought about the things in the glass case. I had not been paying any attention to who was going in and out of the library. I made a quick check and everything appeared untouched. It was fine for now, but there was no way I could watch the library and do the mingling my current job required.

I hated to admit it, but unless I got a lucky break, I was going to have to leave the kleptomaniac search on the far back burner. I had stopped in the area outside the library where I had done my sleuthing the night before. I was determined to go back and get into more conversations or do some eavesdropping, but I heard voices getting louder, meaning someone was headed my way. I slipped behind the potted tree next to the wicker settee just as Jerry R and Lisa R brought Heddy into the area between the living room and library. They each had one of her arms. The singer seemed agitated and was trying to pull away from them. She was wearing a similar outfit to the one she wore the day before, but without the bag of avocados.

"We only want what's best for you," Lisa R said.

"And it's not good for you to be here. You should really lay low for tonight's gathering," Jerry R said.

"Why should I have to hide out?" the singer said in a defiant voice. "I had nothing to do with what happened." She pulled her arm free. "I found him this morning when I went for my meditation soak. There he was lying in the water, all red like a cooked lobster. It was the aliens. They were trying to cook him in the mineral bath. It's like that classic *Twilight Zone* episode I just saw where everybody thinks the aliens came to help Earth people. They even have a book called *To Serve Man.* Except it turns out to be a cookbook."

Jerry R put his arm around her in a protective manner and urged her to quiet her voice. "I thought we agreed that you ought to stay away from scary shows." He glanced toward the living room, hoping her voice didn't carry above the conversations.

"It's not my imagination about the aliens," she said. "Why won't anyone believe me? I only watched that *Twilight Zone* because I was trying to do research on alien visitors."

"You do realize that was fiction," Jerry R said.

"Or maybe not," she said indignantly. "You didn't see the news guy in the water. Who knows what those aliens planned to do with him."

For a small woman she had a big voice, probably from learning how to project her singing voice. I heard she had started in a choir and had managed to make herself heard over the rest of the group. From there she had been on a kids' show called *Ben and Sissy*, about a brother-and-sister singing duo. When they got a little older, Ben fell by the wayside and the show became *Sissy Sings.*

Lisa R looked at her husband and there was a wordless communication as he stepped away and let his wife take over. She changed the subject by asking Heddy about her avocado trees.

Instantly, she stopped going on about Kirkland being cooked by the aliens and became obsessive about the trees and how they must be upset because she hadn't sung to them as usual. Lisa R's face lit up with an idea. "I know you miss your trees, but I bet our olive trees would love to hear you sing." Heddy brightened at the thought and Lisa R escorted her to the same door that Rory Bijorn had gone out when she thought I was a crazed fan.

I knew my task was to find other likely suspects, but it was going to be hard. When it came to the basics of means, motive and opportunity, Heddy had means and opportunity for sure. There were plenty of rocks laying around and he had shown up on her property. As for motive, she could have thought he was one of the aliens and gone after him.

I went into the living room just as Ash and Bayleigh Selinger joined the gathering. They seemed ill at ease as they glanced at the crowd. I figured it was probably how most of the people felt. Were they supposed to have fun or walk around with serious expressions?

They hadn't altered their dress style from the previous night. He had a wheat-colored outfit on with a similar colored filmy fabric scarf loosely wound around his neck. She wore a gauzy dress in shades of purple. It seemed like all-occasion clothing. I saw them focus in on Tom Kelter and Rory Bijorn, but as the Silicon Valley coupled moved toward them, the actor couple moved away and disappeared into the warren of side rooms.

Verona Gilroy walked into the living room. She was wearing a black dress and heels. She checked out the rest of the crowd, who all seemed more casually dressed, and kicked off the shoes before heading to the drink room. She came back a few moments later with a very generous glass of red wine. Without her photogenic smile, there was just a ghost of the perky girl-next-door appearance that one of the Hookers had mentioned. She stood drinking and seemed at a loss for what to do. I went over thinking I could start a conversation with her. Her face lit up in what I could best describe as a grateful smile as I approached and she latched on to me. "I'm overdressed," she said, looking down at her dress. "I thought, you know, someone died and all." Her shoulders slumped and her smile faded. "I always wear black."

"It must make it easy to get dressed," I said in a light tone. "No worry about matching anything."

"And it's forgiving if you have a little too much wine and get sloppy," Verona said, smiling as the wine sloshed around in her glass. "And don't forget it's great if you want to blend into the background."

She had almost finished the wine. "Do you know what this get-together is about? Are we supposed to sit around and share stories about Kirkland?" she said. "I'm guessing they are all supposed to be complimentary. That thing about don't speak ill of the dead. Then I better not say anything about the cameo he did in *Justine and Jeremy*." I recognized the name of an iconic rom-com she had been in. She let out a tipsy chuckle. "Oh, well, I'm going to say it anyway. He was a rude egomaniac who was on the set for a day but made a bunch of ridiculous demands, like he had to have a trailer larger than mine. I was the star, for heaven's sake." She looked at the wineglass as if she was considering a refill. "And then there was that horrible interview he did when he was on the red carpet at the Oscars. I had just moved up here with my husband and my kids, and Kirkland started asking if we were part of the swinger scene." She leaned into me. "He was just making stuff up. I kept saying it was nonsense and then he twisted my words and implied I was protesting too much." She seemed exasperated thinking about it. "We were hopelessly dull. That was why we moved up here. My kids were just becoming teenagers and I wanted them to have a more normal life. It really is a small-town sort of place where the sidewalks roll up at night. If it weren't for all of Jerry R's parties, I would have probably left a long time ago." The wine was affecting her, and she seemed more relaxed. "It's all different now. The kids are off at college and my husband is now an ex. I probably should think about moving. At least to someplace actually in town." She drank the last little bit of wine.

"What else can I say about Kirkland. The guy was all about his next big story. It was a few nights before his wedding, and he wanted to know who handled my business. I thought he might be looking for a referral. When I gave him the company name, he asked if I would mind showing him one of my statements for a story he was working on. Of course, I told him no. Then he said I might be sorry." She started to move away. "The best thing about these parties is the wine and that game room." She saw Ash and Bayleigh coming toward us. "I'm out of here before they corner me. All they want to talk about is their wellness resort and they are so boring. Besides, I need a refill."

As soon as she slipped away, I noticed the couple changed direction and headed to the room where the buffet was set up.

Mason had changed locations and was with a new group. Bennett hadn't returned and I guessed he had gone to the game room. I was thinking of checking it out but stopped when I saw a group of men with Jerry R in the entrance hall. There was something different about them and I eased my way closer so that I could hear what was going on.

A gray-haired man in a sport jacket seemed to be in deep conversation about something with Jerry R. "I was willing to do it your way. We're all in plain clothes and everybody has instructions to be casual and friendly," the man said.

Jerry R offered an office for them to use, but the man who I was now sure was a cop said it would be better to use the seating clusters in the gallery that ran along the living room. "We want everybody to feel at ease."

Jerry R didn't seem happy with the situation. "This is like a vigil for Kirkland. It seems inappropriate to be questioning them about his death."

"I'm sorry but we have to talk to the people who were here last night. We all want the same thing—to find out who is responsible for what happened to Kirkland Rush."

"Do you have any more information about cause of death?" Jerry R asked.

"We're really not supposed to give out any of the information until it's official," the older man said. "But you've always been a friend to the Ojai Valley PD, so off the record, it's not clear if it was the blow to his head or if it was the effect of the hot springs." As I heard what the cop in charge said, I thought of Heddy's mention of the *Twilight Zone* story and shuddered at the thought of Kirkland in essence being cooked.

Jerry R thanked him for sharing the information and it seemed he was agreeing to let them go ahead with the interviews, as they called them. One of the people stepped away from the others and began to look over the party guests in the large room.

I had a sinking feeling when I saw who it was and tried to duck away, but it was too late. He couldn't cover his reaction with his cool cop stare. Barry Greenberg's eyes were blazing as our gazes met. "I'll take her," he said, pointing at me.

Chapter 14

Barry Greenberg was next to me in a couple of steps and had taken my arm in a manner he probably learned in cop school. There wasn't enough pressure in his hold to hurt, but enough so that I had no choice but to go where he was taking me.

He looked refreshed, and I thought he must have managed a shower and a change of clothes. It was amazing how together he appeared. But years of being a homicide detective had taught him to get by on little or no sleep and a haphazard diet with too much coffee and a lot of junk food. Despite all of that, he had managed to stay in shape. He could still run down a suspect if he had to, or as I was discovering, keep a hold on me until he found a place to sit. He looked over the main room and at the long adjacent space that ran along it. What I guessed was a former porch had clusters of small conversation arrangements with a couple of chairs and a small table. The outer wall was all windows. He led me to a pair of chairs in the corner.

He let go and gestured for me to sit. I doubted it had been a concern of his, but he had chosen a spot that had a view all the way back to the hillside where the olive trees grew. There were lots of shadows now as it became evening, but I could make out the rows of trees and I wondered if Heddy was back there singing to them. It seemed like a better place to be than where I was as I realized my earlier omissions were going to haunt me. I squirmed in the chair, waiting for him to begin. I was trying to think about how to handle it. Should I speak first and explain why I was there or try to do a word dance, telling him as little as possible?

I could feel his eyes on me as he sat down on the chair across from me. He took out his notebook and flipped back to something. I knew he was reading over his notes from our earlier tête-à-tête. I couldn't take the tension of the silence anymore and had to say something. "It's a great view. Those are olive trees," I said. "They make their own olive oil. I tasted some from a hand pressing. It was really delicious and had bits of olives in it." I gestured back toward the living room and beyond. "There's a lot of food. I'm sure they wouldn't mind if you made yourself a plate."

Barry looked up from the notebook. "Are you done with the party hints?" He seemed to have gotten control of his eyes and the blazing had turned into piercing.

"I'm done," I said. "Go ahead and ask away. But remember what the cop with the gray hair said. You're supposed to have a casual friendly manner."

My comment broke through his cop shield and he laughed. "Right. So I won't be shining any lights in your eyes. But that doesn't mean I'm not going to get the whole story from you this time." He kept his gaze on me and I knew he was referring to the partial story I had given him before. "Let's start with what you're doing here."

I avoided looking at him and instead checked out the living room and beyond. Mason was walking with Heddy and one of the other cops. "I guess she got back from singing to the olive trees. She sings to her avocado trees regularly," I said.

"I'll make note of it," Barry said, looking in the same direction I was. Mason was trying to be cool, but there was a reaction when he saw who I was with. It wasn't lost on my inquisitor.

"Does he have anything to do with why you're here? You told me that you were here for a weekend with your yarn group but I don't see any of them here. I thought you weren't back with him," Barry said, looking at me intently.

I didn't want to answer, so I tried to divert him. "So you think what happened to Kirkland is related to your LA homicide?"

He rocked his head skyward with frustration. "Can't we get past where you answer my questions with one of your own." He blew out his breath in exasperation.

"I learned it from watching you," I said.

"I shouldn't have been such a good teacher," he said. "How about you unlearn it and just tell me the whole story this time so we can get this over with."

"I answered your questions truthfully," I said. "You asked me if I had seen or heard anything from the property behind the place the Hookers were staying. I told you the truth when I said I hadn't."

Barry's eyes narrowed. "Yes, but what did you leave out?" He turned in the direction of another group of chairs. Mason was standing next to Heddy while an officer talked to her. "It has to do with him, doesn't it? What's going on?"

"Okay, I didn't see or hear anything because I wasn't exactly there last night."

"So then where were you?" he asked. It was a direct question and I never lie with those.

"I was here." I gestured toward the window. "There's a guest house back there."

"I suppose you have someone who could verify where you were."

I rolled my eyes this time. "You know I'm not a suspect, so I don't need someone to vouch for where I was," I said.

"It's been a long day. Could you just be straight?" He sounded worn out and it had been a long day for me too.

"Okay, I was there with Mason. But not with him, with him."

There was a glint in Barry's eyes now. "Then what exactly were you doing with him?"

I was going to say it had nothing to do with anything that concerned him, but I decided it was easier to just tell him the truth. "I'm working for him," I said.

Barry couldn't contain the surprise in his face. "Working as what? His escort?"

"No," I said indignantly. "I'm like a private private detective," I said with a certain amount of pride. Then came the questions about whether I had a license and what was I doing exactly.

"I don't need a license. I'm working under the PI his firm uses. Just very quietly."

"So then what are you investigating here?" he said. I told him about the missing keys and now the scissors and he laughed. "So then nothing exactly dangerous."

"There you are," Bennett said, stepping between Barry and me. He seemed to have no idea what was going on and used his Arnold Schwarzenegger voice. "I told you I would be back." He held out a plate. "I know you said you didn't feel like eating, but I brought chocolate cake. And not just any cake either. This is the famous chocolate cake made with olive oil that comes from back there." He looked to the rows of trees in the distance. His gaze flicked to Barry. "I don't think I know you." He held out his hand. "Bennett Edwards. And you are?"

Barry lifted his suit jacket and showed off his badge. "Detective Barry Greenberg," he said.

"What's going on here?" Bennett asked, seeing the notebook on the table.

Barry looked at me. "We're done here. You can go." He waited until I stood, and nodded at Bennett, pointing at the chair. "We're just having some friendly interviews about last night. Now, who did you say you were and what's your connection to Kirkland Rush?" Barry saw me still standing there. "I said you can go."

Bennett seemed unruffled by it all and handed me the plate. "Don't forget your cake. And remember, I'm walking you home again. Can't wait to see all those stars."

I felt Barry's eyes on my back as I took the plate and nodded at Bennett.

• • •

I actually took a bite of the cake. I was drained after the encounter with Barry and needed the sugar to deal with the rest of the party. It was amazingly moist and delicious without even needing icing. Even so I set the plate down. If I had been keyed up before, it was nothing compared with now. I was sure that Bennett could hold his own with Barry.

I thought over what Bennett had told me and wondered if he would tell Barry the same. He knew where Kirkland was going, but it seemed like almost common knowledge that Heddy's aliens story was like catnip to the journalist. Bennett had made a point that he had not gone with Kirkland. But what if that was taking control of the narrative by answering the question before it was asked? He had gotten an instant career boost with Kirkland out of the way. I felt a shiver. Bennett could definitely be considered a suspect. Mason wanted someone to distract the police from Heddy, but I didn't want Bennett to be the distraction. Besides, I was sure he didn't do it. There had to be someone else I could come up with.

I wandered back to the library to check on my other mission. The room was empty and I was expecting to see the glass case appear untouched. But when I got close enough to view the contents, the spot where the red pen had been was empty. The klepto had struck again and I had missed it again.

I forced myself to stop thinking about the missing trinkets and focus on the current goal. I needed to mingle and went to the room with the food. I couldn't just stand there, so I began to load up a plate. Meg Rush was holding a plate and eyeing the array of dishes. Harrison was standing next to her. He seemed bored and distracted until she said he could leave. She shook her head as she watched her son go.

"I guess I should be glad there is the game room." She seemed to be speaking to the air, but it was a chance to interject myself into the conversation. An ex-wife at her ex's wedding could be full of murderous emotions and a good candidate to be a suspect. I opened by offering her my condolences.

"Thank you. But as Kirkland's ex, I'm not sure I'm the right one you should be offering them to," Meg said. "I'd say my son, but he barely knew Kirkland." She let out a distressed sound. "I knew this was going to be a hard weekend, but it's gone from bad to worse." She was rail thin with wiry dark hair. I guessed her faux-wrapped dress had a designer name attached to it. It had a grayish look from a distance, but when I got closer I saw that it was speckled with black and cream.

She noticed me looking at her dress. "I had no idea how to dress. I mean, we are on a ranch. This is an old standby that seems to work for any occasion." She put a large blob of mashed potatoes on her plate, which surprised me. I took her to be one of those women who barely ate in public. As if they were above the need for food and it was somehow virtuous not to eat. She saw me examining her plate.

"Don't judge me. I'm dealing with a lot and I need some carbs." She let out a heavy sigh and added some sweet potatoes. She looked at me again. "I don't recognize you. Are you a guest or the help?"

I didn't bother mentioning that I'd been with Bennett the night before when he had taken her and her son to the game room. I suppose that her not noticing me was good in a way. It meant I had succeeded at blending in with the crowd. And, well, I was sort of part of the help.

"Molly Pink," I said. "I'm here with Mason Fields. I'm his cousin."

She definitely knew who Mason was and regarded me with a little more interest. "Does he know any more about what happened to Kirkland? I can't get a straight answer whether it was murder or an accident. I heard Heddy talking about her alien visitors, and knowing Kirkland, he went there to see what was going on. He never had any sense of boundaries and he probably snuck in. If she caught him there and killed him thinking he was an intruder, wouldn't it be self-defense?" She moved down the buffet, and now that she felt under scrutiny, she stuck to grilled vegetables and a tiny slice of turkey. I followed her into the living room when she had finished loading her plate.

She seemed glad when I took the chair next to her. "I could do with some company. This whole experience has been hell. Being the ex-wife at Kirkland's wedding was bad enough. But now this."

Zoe crossed right in front of us with Lisa R. The weather person could only take tiny steps in the tight dress, and she seemed agitated.

"I already talked to the police. Why did they need to talk to me again? I told them everything I knew," Zoe said, taking no notice of us. Lisa R seemed to be trying to calm her by walking her around the room.

"If you think she's upset now, wait until it sinks in that if this had happened a few days later, she would have gotten a lot more." Meg's lips curved into a small smile. "But now she gets nada." She watched Lisa R and Zoe turn back when they neared the space the cops were using. "I don't think she really understands that I handle all of Kirkland's business. His image was the courageous journalist going where the news was happening." She turned to me and shook her head. "He didn't want anyone to know that he didn't even know how to balance a checkbook. She probably doesn't know how to do it either," Meg said as she scraped the last of the mashed potatoes from her plate. "You know her real name is Bertha."

Meg had barely said it when the pair stopped next to us. The hostess smiled and suggested Zoe join us. Zoe made an annoyed sound when she recognized Meg. "I'm almost his widow and I should be the one making the decisions about—" She hesitated and put up her hands. "Well, everything, whatever that is."

Did I really want to be in the middle of this? I had enough to tell Mason already. I was just supposed to come up with some possible suspects and it seemed like both of them fit the bill. It was pretty obvious that Meg had control of Kirkland's money. Maybe he wasn't really the dufus about it that she was claiming. The wedding could change things. What if there was missing money? As for Zoe/Bertha, her relationship with Kirkland just seemed strange.

"I'm sure you two have a lot to talk about and need your privacy," I said, getting up.

As I looked around the living room for somewhere to go, I saw Lisa R leaning against a chair in the corner. She looked all in and I felt for her. "Can I get you a drink or something?" I asked when I joined her. "This has to be a lot for you to deal with." I looked back toward the pair I had just left.

Lisa R gave me a grateful smile. "It was already overwhelming with the wedding and all the events around it. Jerry is a sweetheart the way he wants to take care of everyone, but . . ." Her voice trailed off.

"But you're the one who gets stuck with putting it all together," I said. She looked like she wanted to hug me.

"Jerry R loves to be the host, but the logistics always fall on me. Now we have to change the wedding to a memorial service for Kirkland. It's too late to cancel anything so we, or I, have to figure out what to do with all the rose petals. I suppose we can change the playlist for the dance band." Her eyes closed momentarily as she mentioned the stack of waxed bags to pack the pieces of wedding cake in. "And then there's the cake itself. We went to so much trouble to get a bride and groom that looked like them for the top of the cake. The wedding planner we hired said we could separate the figures and have Kirkland recline across the top of the cake and she could create a coffin out of Hershey bars. Then she had a meltdown and quit." Lisa R seemed overcome by it all. "Who even decides what happens to Kirkland when they release the body?" She looked at the two squabbling women.

I started to apologize for not succeeding at the task Mason had brought me for, but she brushed it off. "I don't have any more of the stork scissors to sacrifice, but I have a drawer full of stuff to keep filling up the empty spots until we can figure something out. In the meantime, the klepto can build up their collection."

"Maybe I can offer some suggestions for the changed event," I said. I told her about my other life working as an event coordinator at the bookstore. "I know a little about dealing with catastrophes." I had her laughing when I finished with stories about the burned food at a cookbook event that set off the smoke alarm and brought the fire department, and the time a guy who wrote a fix-it book started a flood at the bookstore when he demonstrated a plumbing repair. I described some of Adele's antics as the queen of crochet.

Lisa R followed through with a hug this time. "Thank you. I needed a laugh. Anything you can come up with would be appreciated."

I promised to text her anything I thought of, and she let out a sigh of relief before she rejoined her guests. If I couldn't help with the disappearing trinkets, maybe I could make it up by helping with all that Lisa R had to contend with. I went back to the settee near the library to think about everything and put some initial thoughts I had in my phone.

Because it was more of a reception than a party, it broke up early. When I went back into the living room, people were already leaving. Jerry R and Lisa were standing by the entrance hall saying good night to their guests.

Mason was off somewhere, probably with Heddy, and there didn't seem to be any reason for me to stay. Meg Rush caught up with me as I headed for the door. I was surprised when she squeezed my arm in appreciation.

"Thank you. It was so nice to have someone to talk to who didn't make me feel like the odd man out." She waved a goodbye to the hosts. "See you tomorrow," she said as she went out the door. Harrison was lost in a handheld video game and stumbled as he followed behind her.

"What's tomorrow?" I asked, looking at the Rayners. I wondered if it was going to affect me.

"It was supposed to be a rehearsal for Kirkland and Zoe and just a party for everyone else," Jerry R said. "We're keeping it as a gathering for all our regulars. It helps to deal with the shock of what happened by being together."

I wasn't sure if that included me and wished them a good evening.

I took a moment when I got outside. I had an awful lot going on at the same time and it was a relief to just focus on the sky and all those stars. I hadn't gotten any more instructions from Mason and it seemed like the best idea was to go back to the guest house and wait.

"There you are," Bennett said, coming up to me. "Were you going to leave without me? The rom-com gods would frown at that," he said with a grin.

"I thought you might be tied up with something," I said. I knew that he was there as part of his job, and it would come before any flirty walks to the guest house.

"I do have a long night ahead of me putting together the piece about Kirkland, but it can wait until after I see that you get home safely."

"Aren't you the gallant one," I said with a laugh.

We stopped outside when we reached the guest house. He looked at the dark windows. "I trust that you didn't find any bogeymen last night," he joked and I nodded. "There could be some tonight though. I would be glad to do a check."

"Sure. Why not. I could offer you a cup of tea or something," I said. I liked his manner and it seemed like the hospitable thing to do.

"Tea and company. Just what I need to keep me going." He followed me inside and I turned on the lights. After a mock search, he announced it was bogeyman-free. "Nice digs," he said, looking around. "It's sure nicer than a room with a view of the parking lot." I invited him to sit and went to make the tea using the single-cup maker. I came back with two cups of Darjeeling tea. I wasn't sure where to sit. He was on the small couch and it seemed a little too close to sit next to him. I chose the chair across from it.

He seemed like somebody who was comfortable wherever he was. He took a sip of the tea and held on to the mug. "You haven't said much about yourself. You must do something outside of being Mason Fields's cousin who stands in when he's stood up." He seemed amused with his clever wordplay.

"I do have another life," I said. Honestly, by now I couldn't remember who I had told what about myself. I brought up working at the bookstore since it didn't mess with the idea that Mason and I were cousins. I even mentioned the getaway weekend with the yarn group and the coincidence that it was next to Heddy's. "I wonder if I would have seen anything if I had stayed there," I said. I left it at that, not wanting to say anything that might sound like I was investigating. I transitioned into mentioning that I was a widow and talking about my family.

He laughed when I told him about the She La Las practicing at my house and all the animals. "Going to work at the bookstore is peaceful compared to all that," I said.

"It sounds full of life and more exciting than my condo in North Hollywood. Though I'm on the move a lot," he said. "Things always come up at the last minute. Hurricanes don't make appointments." He went on how it was up to him to gather his crew and go where the story was. "There's always a short deadline—like what I'll be working on when I go back to my room."

"It sounds stressful," I said.

"I'm blessed with huge tolerance for stress. I have an overlying feeling that everything will work out." He grinned at me. "And you know, it always does, one way or the other."

"I like your optimism," I said.

The door opened and Mason came in. He was carrying a shopping bag and set it on the table. "Peace at last," he said, and then he saw Bennett and did a double take.

"No worries. I was just leaving," Bennett said, picking up on the awkwardness of the situation. I got up and walked him outside.

"That was nice," he said. "So, will you be going back to stay with your crochet buddies or staying here?" His smile widened. "I need to know where to bring the glass slipper or whatever shoe style you decide on in case you do another Cinderella."

I was noncommittal about my plans and he continued. "I hope the cops won't be there again. That detective who talked to me really pushed it. He wanted to know all kinds of personal stuff, like about my divorce." He turned to me. "It was years ago and I'm completely available."

"Good to know," I said. "What did you tell him about last night?"

Now that he had brought it up, I was curious about what he had said.

"My rule with cops is always the same. Tell them as little as possible." He let out a sigh. "I hate to say it, but I better go. My night of work awaits. Until we meet again," he said and swept me into his arms. This time it was a real kiss.

Chapter 15

Mason was waiting when I came in. He had emptied the shopping bag of food containers on the table. "I figured that you didn't eat again."

"Thank you. You're right, and now I'm famished." I sat down and started to open the containers.

"I didn't eat either," he said. "There was too much going on to think about food." I glanced up expectantly, thinking he was going to offer details, but he just indicated the open containers and told me to help myself.

I had been more interested in talking to Meg Rush when I had been in the room with the buffet to pay much attention to the offerings beyond the potatoes she put on her plate. My mouth started to water when I saw the selection of dishes. It was totally not the usual food offered at parties given by people in the entertainment business. I thought of all the events I had been to when Charlie was alive. The food had been all about presentation and tiny bites. This was all comfort food and carb heaven. I took some of the macaroni and cheese, barbecued brisket, corn pudding and a biscuit. I balanced it off with some grilled vegetables and spinach salad.

"There's dessert, too," Mason said, showing me a container that had slices of the chocolate olive cake. We talked about drinks, and he said the refrigerator was stocked with sparkling water. I got bottles for both of us.

I figured we would eat first and then talk since we were both so hungry, but I'd barely gotten a taste of the macaroni and cheese when Mason asked me about Bennett.

"What's going on, is he your boyfriend now?" Mason said. "I hope he isn't distracting you from your job." I looked to see if he was joking, but he seemed serious.

"I wouldn't call him a boyfriend," I said. "Just a friend—for now, anyway. Don't worry, he didn't interfere with me working the crowd," I said. "I was off duty by the time we walked back here."

Mason shrugged. "Sorry if I'm sounding like your son. I know he is upset with the idea of you dating, except—" He stopped himself and I knew what he was about to say. Peter was upset with me dating, if you could call it that, except if it meant Mason. My whole family loved Mason. He fit right in with them. We were from similar worlds, and I was still getting flack from them for messing it up.

He saw that I had stopped eating. "Let's just eat for now and you can tell me if you found out anything useful while we have dessert."

"It sounds like a good plan," I said before taking a bite of the biscuit. It was heavenly and I picked one out of the container and put it on his plate. "You have to have one of these."

We ate in silence, both lost in the flavors and textures of the food. I gave up before my plate was cleared and joked about overestimating how much I could eat. "I did the same," he said, pushing his plate toward the middle of the table. "Besides, I saved room for dessert. I would love a cappuccino, but I guess we'll have to rough it with what's available." He got up and made us coffee with the single-cup maker.

I got a plate and put several slices of the cake on it and set it between us. He came back to the table with the improvised coffee drinks. "Why don't you start with your conversation with Barry," Mason said, handing me a mug.

I took a couple of sips of the coffee and began. "Mostly it seemed he wanted to know what I was doing there since I had led him to believe that I was strictly with the Hookers for the weekend. I didn't lie in the morning, just left out stuff. I probably should tell you that I admitted that I was working for you." Mason's face clouded and I put up my hand. "Not about this. I made it sound like my only assignment was ferreting out the scissors thief. I think he blew it off as fluff. And that was about it."

"Try to keep it that way," Mason said. "What about after that? Did you pick anything up?"

"I'll just tell you what I found out and you can decide if it's useful," I said. "Verona Gilroy seems to like her wine and is considering moving somewhere. She is definitely not a fan of Kirkland's. None of the encounters she had with him were good. Meg Rush is still handling Kirkland's finances. She claimed that he didn't know how to balance a checkbook."

Mason laughed. "It's probably true." He broke a corner off the chocolate cake and tasted it. He pushed the plate closer to me. "You have to taste this." I took a small piece. It was moist and chocolatey without being oversweet.

"Is there anything else?" he said.

"She and Kirkland's fiancée, Zoe, seem hostile to each other. Meg did tell me that Zoe's real name is Bertha," I said with a shrug. "There is something off about her. I guess I would have expected her to be more broken up about Kirkland. But then I saw them together the first night and well, he seemed indifferent to her. She came to the vigil dressed in her weather girl clothes and seemed most concerned about being featured in the pieces being made up for the media."

"I wonder who knew he was going to Heddy's?" Mason said.

"From the people I talked to, it seems like everyone who knew him thought he would be entranced by her alien story." I took another sip of the coffee. "Is any of that helpful?"

"It's all good," he said. He gestured toward the cake and offered me more, but I put up my hands in capitulation. He sat back in the chair and let out a sigh. "Yeah, I'm there with you."

I mentioned hearing Jerry R talking to the cops and wondered at their relationship.

"He definitely has a friendly relationship with the local PD. He's a big contributor to any events or fund drives."

"Just a guess, but is he going to feed what I find out to his cop friends to steer them away from Heddy?" I asked. Before Mason could respond, I had another thought. "But how would Jerry R feel about us putting the spotlight on any of the other people in his circle?" I said.

"I'm sure Jerry R has considered that," Mason said.

I thought about the whole situation and shrugged. "I know it's not supposed to be your concern, but I wonder what really happened."

I could tell Mason had something on his mind, and I gave him space, hoping he would speak. "I wonder too," he said finally. Then it was like he caught himself. "Forget I said that." He let out his breath. "This is not about playing Sherlock Holmes and connecting the dots. All I want from you are the dots." He was trying to sound serious.

"You're the boss," I said with a shrug.

"It would be a lot easier if it really was some space aliens," he said. This time when our gazes met, he was smiling and his eyes were warm. He seemed about to say something more, but the door opened, interrupting the moment.

Lisa R came in with someone. "Here he is," she said to the person with her. Before I could take it all in, I heard a yippy high-pitched bark.

"Spike," Mason said in a happy tone as he got up and retrieved the squirming little dog from the woman's arms. The toy fox terrier wiggled and licked Mason's hand and then his face in an excited greeting.

"I was able to get out of my commitment early," the woman said. "I knew you missed the dog, and of course me. I know you said you were caught up with Kirkland Rush's death, but you have to have some free time," she added with a cool smile. Lisa R made her exit, and the new arrival continued talking to Mason while ignoring me. She looked at the food on the table and started shaking her head in disapproval. "I thought we agreed nothing after six o'clock." She picked up one of the containers with more head-shaking. "Macaroni and cheese? It's like the devil's concoction of dairy, fat and carbs."

This was obviously Tiffany. While she went on, I assessed her appearance. She was around my age, which meant fifty-something. She gave off an air of confidence that I had never mastered, and seemed to have taken over by just walking into the room.

I couldn't see her features other than she had dark brown hair that hung loose to her shoulders. The stark designer outfit of wide-leg black capri-length pants and a loose-fitting ecru top with a long black sweater over it seemed to go along with her persona. She brushed some dog hairs off of her sweater as if she was glad to have handed him off. Finally, she glanced in my direction. No surprise, she had sharp features and the puffed-up lips that were the style. I thought they made it look like she had been punched in the mouth.

"You must be the one working for Mason." She gave me a critical appraisal before turning back to him. "You're right, no one would think she was an investigator." Spike squirmed to get out of Mason's arms and came over to me, putting his little paws on my leg. It was his way of asking to be picked up. His stubby tail was wagging, and he gave a few yips as I took him in my arms. He gave me the same excited kisses he had given Mason.

I started talking to the dog without thinking. I had so many animals that it came naturally to me and I never thought about how it appeared to others. "It's so good to see your cute little self," I said, looking into his eyes. I gave him a kiss on the top of his head and cuddled him. "You remind me how I miss my menagerie." He licked my face and I laughed, cuddling him some more.

"Tiffany, this is Molly Pink," Mason said. She acknowledged me with a nod and turned back to Mason, doing her best to make it clear she saw me as unimportant.

"Where should I put this?" Tiffany said, indicating the suitcase that Lisa had left by the door. It was taupe and had the markings that I recognized as Louis Vuitton. I tried not to show what I thought of the absurdly expensive luggage. I caught a glimpse of her purse and it was a Chanel classic-style bag, which also had a crazy price tag. Not that it ever happened, but if anybody had asked "who" I was wearing when Charlie was alive and we went to red carpet events, they would probably have cut away when I said Nordstrom's Rack.

"You mean you want to stay here?" Mason said. "It's late but I'm sure I could get something at the Ojai Inn. You could use all the amenities while I'm tied up here."

"Here's fine," she said. "From what you said, what you call working is under the cover of social events. You told me that you introduced Mary here as your cousin, so your girlfriend arriving shouldn't be a problem."

"It's Molly," Mason said, throwing me an apologetic look. "Sure, you can stay here, but the inn is more in keeping with your style."

"If you can rough it, so can I." She glanced around the room. Mason shot me a helpless shrug.

I put the dog down and pushed away from the table. "We were just finishing up talking about the developments in the case we're working on." I turned to Mason. "I could call Dinah for a ride."

"No, I should provide your transportation," Mason said, handing me the keys to the SUV and telling me how to use the GPS. "You can bring it back when you come for tomorrow night's festivities."

"Then you want me to be there?" I said.

Tiffany was already clearing the table and seemed to have contempt as she put the containers back in the shopping bag.

"Absolutely," he said. He went to touch my arm but caught himself and retracted it. "Who knows what you might find out."

I didn't even consider the things I had left in the room I had stayed in and went out into the night.

As I drove through the dark roads, I thought over Tiffany and how she had shown up unannounced and immediately planted herself in the middle of things. I wondered if she was as oblivious to me as she had acted. I was sure Mason hadn't told her about our past.

She reminded me of Mason's ex. She even looked a little like her. But then they said that people had a type they kept going back to. That made me start thinking about my type. An outside observer would say that Mason fit the bill. He came from the same world as my late husband and fit right into my family. He was glad to help my two sons with their careers. He even seemed to think a lot of the kookie stuff I got involved with was fun.

After seeing Tiffany, I understood that I had been the outlier for him. The one that didn't fit in with the pattern of women in his life. Unlike Tiffany and his ex, I didn't need to feel in charge of things. It never occurred to me to try to control the people or situations around me. I was more of a roll-with-the-punches type.

Barry had been the outlier for me. I was sure that was a big part of his appeal. He was elusive and lived in a world so different than mine. He wandered the streets at night on the tail of killers when I was snuggled in bed. He dealt with the dark side and saw things on a regular basis that I could barely stand to think about. But when we had spent time together, I somehow thought of myself as the light in all that darkness. Until I couldn't. I couldn't take how unpredictable his life was and that when he was off on a case, he forgot all about me and everything else. My family didn't even try to hide their hostility to him. Peter was the worst.

I wondered how Bennett might fit in. He had a laid-back easy sort of charm, but his work meant that he floated around a lot. The way my life was now, that might be fine. I decided that he didn't seem to be either an outlier or my type and wondered what that meant.

The disembodied voice of the navigation system did a perfect job of leading me through the dark roads, but I was still relieved to pull the SUV into the driveway of the weekend house. I took a moment to collect myself before I went inside.

The group was sitting around the main room. Rhoda was intent on crocheting while Adele and CeeCee were arguing over whether they should all make the exact same scarf.

"I say we should all make the scarf any way we want," CeeCee said. She held up a granny square that had orange for the first round and then a delft blue yarn for two rounds, with a last round done in the off-white cotton yarn. She picked up another square that had three rounds of purple yarn with the last one done in the off-white. She held it next to the first one.

Adele shook her head and held up a square she had made with

three colors. "All the squares should be the same. Just like the tie that inspired the idea."

"Says who?" Rhoda exclaimed. She had started ripping out her work. "I'm with CeeCee. I'm going to redo the squares I've made and then make them with all different arrangements of the colors in the middle part. I like keeping the last round in the off-white."

Elise was looking at something on her laptop and Dinah was on the back patio, and by the way she was talking to her phone, I guessed she was video chatting with her husband.

With all that was going on, it took a moment before anyone noticed I was there. And then there was an onslaught of questions, mostly about the dress and duster since I had been wearing something else entirely when I left. I glossed over it and made it seem that I had been the one to purchase the pieces with no mention of Mason.

Dinah came in just as Elise showed her computer screen to the rest of them. "That's where Molly went." There were a bunch of oohs and aahs at the size of the house and the land around it. "I wonder if the Rayners want to sell their place in Malibu since they seem to be spending all their time up here."

"It must have been a short event. You're back early. Did you find the killer?" Rhoda said.

"Mason's girlfriend showed up," I said.

"Oh, no," Rhoda said. "I get it, three's a crowd."

"Come and sit," CeeCee said. "Tell us all about her. It's better than having Adele play the crochet police and tell us how we have to make the squares."

My cell phone rang, startling me and the rest of them. "We're trying to have sort of an electronic cleanse," CeeCee said. "We all agreed to keep our phones on silent."

"And do any calls or video chatting outside," Dinah said. She walked across the room and found a seat.

I apologized and went out to the back patio while the ringing persisted. I assumed it was from somebody at my house who couldn't find the paper towels or something. I had already gotten a lot of texts asking about things like that and ignored them. I clicked on the green button without looking at who was calling.

I had barely gotten out a hello and asked what the emergency was when I was interrupted.

"Greenberg here. I need to talk to you."

"Barry?" I said, surprised. "You sound pretty formal. What's up?"

He let out a tired groan. "Sorry, it's habit," he said. "But it is official business. I'm calling as Detective Greenberg. I have a few questions."

"Okay," I said. "What do you want to know?" I attempted to sound like it was no big deal and I would gladly answer whatever. But really my guard was up and I was determined to tell him as little as possible.

"Nope, talking on the phone won't work," he said. "It needs to be in person." He didn't elaborate, but I knew what he meant. In person there were body language clues that didn't show up on the phone. It was a lot easier to be evasive when he was not sitting in front of me. He was probably still upset that I had managed to leave a lot out when he had questioned me the first time.

"Where are you?" he asked. "I went to that guest house and there was a woman there who thought your name was Mary." There was dead air after that and I assumed he expected me to explain who she was. Instead, I just told him I was back with the Hookers.

"Oh," he said with a groan. "I can't deal with Adele. She'll try to get me to talk to her husband again about that tie. Just because he's a cop too doesn't mean I can play marriage counselor."

"Not your forte anyway," I said. The words were out before I could stop them. Barry had been divorced twice, things hadn't worked out with us, and now his latest relationship had tanked. There was just a moment of silence on his end.

"Right," he said in his professional voice. "We could talk in my car, if that's acceptable."

I just wanted to get it over with and agreed. It felt later than it was, but it had still been a long day. And the truth was, talking to Barry was difficult. There was the whole personal thing and the cop part. "Okay," I said and agreed to meet him outside.

I went to tell the group that I was leaving. I explained that the police had shown up at the party and Barry had questioned me again. I hesitated about what else to say. This was when having a double life got confusing and wasn't fun. It was getting hard to keep track of who knew what. Only Dinah knew I was working for Mason and the rest of them thought I had just joined the investigation on my own, like what I had done in the past when I had played amateur sleuth and solved some murders.

I had decided the best way to deal was to tell them as little as possible. "Barry probably wants to ask me about some of the other people who were there," I said.

"Or he could just want to spend time with you," Rhoda said.

I shook my head. "He knows that's a dead issue."

Chapter 16

I went outside the house to wait for Barry's arrival. I wanted to be done with the questioning as quickly as possible. Jump in his car, tell him as little as possible, and get out. I had hurriedly changed out of my party clothes and put on one of the outfits I had expected to wear during the Hookers' getaway. It had cooled off from the warmth of the day and I added a hoodie to the leggings and T-shirt. I wanted to take a long shower when I got back and wished I had grabbed some of that shower gel that promised to cleanse my aura. And then a hopefully long sleep in the bed that was supposed to be mine.

I had left the Hookers still fussing about the squares for the scarves and upset that I was having all the excitement while they were stuck in the middle of nowhere. Dinah had stepped in for me and tried to keep the peace by offering hot chocolate with marshmallows, which was part of the stash left by the hosts.

As I waited in the darkness, the quiet was a bit unnerving. I almost wished for the freeway whoosh sound that seemed to be in the background everywhere no matter how far away from the highway you were. There were no streetlights, or lights from neighboring houses. All I could make out were the silhouettes of tall old trees.

I saw the reflection of headlights coming around the curving street and tensed up about the coming encounter. I was bathed in the headlights as the unmarked SUV stopped at the edge of the driveway. He leaned over and pushed open the passenger door for me to get in.

He had just cut the motor and was looking for his notebook when the door to the house opened and the light from inside illuminated Adele, who appeared to be about to step outside.

"Nope," Barry said, starting the motor and backing the Ford Explorer out of the driveway. I thought he would just park down the street, but he kept going, driving back in the direction he had come from.

I stifled a laugh at his reaction. "I can't believe you are that freaked out by Adele," I said.

He glanced over at me. "I don't have your knack for dealing with her," he said, sounding defensive.

"She does seem a little more supercharged than usual and it's even worse with all of them stuck in that house," I said. "Everyone's nerves seem a little frayed. Can we just get to whatever you want to ask me about?"

"Not yet," Barry said. "Wait until we stop somewhere and I have my notes." I couldn't tell where we were by looking out the window. All I could see in the darkness was that there were a lot of trees and open fields. When we got into town, he pulled into the parking lot of the coffee shop where I'd first seen him. The place was dark and closed up for the night. He cut the motor and turned on an interior light before starting to thumb through his notebook.

It suddenly felt like too close quarters. He had changed out of the suit and was wearing jeans and a collarless shirt. With the light on, I could tell that he'd shaved and I picked up the scent of body wash. It might sound strange, but I could feel his energy and it made me uncomfortable. "Can we take this somewhere else? It feels too weird being grilled in here."

He looked over at me. "Let me see if I can come up with an alternative." He glanced at the darkened street through the windshield. "Nothing's open," he said. "And the motel where I'm staying doesn't have a lobby." He blew out his breath and took a moment to think. "I have an idea if you don't mind sitting outside." He glanced back at me as he started the engine. "I wasn't planning to grill you," he said in a worn voice. "I save my grilling for someone I think is a suspect. I'm just looking for some information you might know."

He drove on into downtown Ojai. It was a lot different than when Mason and I had gone there earlier in the day. All the stores were dark and the streets were empty. He pulled into an empty parking lot next to a line of small shops I recognized. The headlights illuminated two benches near a stairway to some offices that were above them.

"Is that acceptable?" he asked and I nodded. We got out of the Explorer and each took a bench. As I checked out our surroundings, I could just see Libby Park. I strained my eyes to look at the playground and thought about Marlowe and how much I missed the little girl. I wondered how old she would be when I explained that her fun grandmother was actually a professional PI. But for now I just wanted to get this over with.

"Okay, ask away," I said, and he chuckled.

"And you will just answer?" he said, sounding hopeful.

"It depends on the questions," I said with a shrug. He looked at his notebook and, realizing it was too dark to read, shut it. "I'll wing it," he said. "You want to tell me who Tiffany is?"

"That's an easy one," I said. "She's Mason's lady friend. She handles travel arrangements for musicians." I was going to leave it at that, but I suddenly had a thought. "Or maybe she's something more. Maybe she has something to do with what you came up here to investigate."

"I'll make note of that," he said.

"Is that it?" I said, starting to get up. He shook his head and gestured for me to sit.

"I couldn't read my handwriting on the notes I took about Bennett Edwards and I thought you might be able to confirm some information about him." Barry looked at me. "The way he brought you the cake and talked about walking you home, it's obvious that you know him." He let it sit there for a moment. "What exactly is the nature of your relationship?"

"What's that got to do with anything?" I said.

Barry grunted in frustration. "Couldn't we just keep going with you answering my questions easily? Like you did about Mason's girlfriend?"

"She's kind of old to be called a girlfriend," I said.

"What I call her is not the issue here—" He paused a beat. "But you do sound a little hostile."

"Only because of how she treated me," I said, wishing I had said nothing. "I barely know Bennett. It was really all about the cake. It's a big deal because it's made with olive oil from the Rayners' olive trees. It's too bad that you missed it." I was going to go on about how great it was but he put up his hand to stop me.

"I had a piece and yes, it was great."

"Then you did get a chance to have some food," I said, surprised. "When was that? I thought you and your cop bros did your interviewing and then left."

I expected him to object to my asking him about it, but instead he picked up the thread. "We went off to Rayner's office to compare notes. Then after everyone had left, he invited the group of us to eat and drink and enjoy the game room. He seems to have a very friendly relationship with the Ojai Valley PD." He looked at me for a reaction, but I had none and Barry continued. "Rayner hung around in the game room acting like he was playing host. I heard him talking to one of the guys about Kirkland Rush's death being an accident. Rayner laid out a scenario where the newscaster was looking for a story and trespassed on Heddy Mariano's property. In the darkness, he could have somehow fallen, hit his head and stumbled into the hot water pond."

He turned and looked at me intently. "Do you know anything about that? Maybe Mason said something about a plan or strategy?" I thought back to my earlier conversation with Mason when I had wondered how Jerry R would feel about getting Heddy out of the suspect spotlight, only to put his other guests in it. Mason had been noncommittal, but now I thought I knew why. Jerry R probably did have a strategy. Get the cops to accept the incident as an accident. It was only supposition though and I was going to keep it to myself.

"Why would they tell me anything? I told you that I was here to catch a scissors thief."

Barry looked me in the eye. "You want me to believe that's all that's going on? That you haven't heard anything about Kirkland's death? Like maybe where his phone is?"

143

"Do you think that Mason would hire me to help with a murder?" I said with a laugh. I was actually pleased with my response, even if it was kind of a diss at myself. I had answered without it being a lie and I hoped he would let it go.

Barry shook his head and made a grumbling sound. "I know what you're doing," he said. "Just like you know my tricks, I know yours." He put up his hands in frustration. "Never mind about that. Let's get back to Bennett Edwards. You were telling me how well you know him."

"Not much at all," I said. "I met him at the party. That's all." I pulled my hoodie around me. The evening had turned chilly and being on the hot seat made me feel cold.

"You know him well enough that he was walking you home," Barry said, reminding me that he had heard Bennett mention the plan.

"Oh, that. He was just being a gentleman."

It was hard to tell in the dark, but I was pretty sure that Barry rolled his eyes. "And did he suggest that he come in to help you turn on the lights or make sure the place was safe?"

"He might have joked about that." I tried to shrug it off, but Barry kept on.

"Did he suggest you get together when you are back in LA?"

"What if he did?" I said, trying to brush it off.

"Whatever your connection to him, you should know that I saw right through his claiming not to know anything." Barry gave me another of his direct stares. "And as far as I'm concerned, he is a person of interest."

I didn't mean to flinch, but I did. Being a person of interest was like being engaged to being engaged. It meant that Bennett was one step away from being a suspect.

"I don't think so. He's too nice to be a killer."

Barry laughed and shook his head. "Being nice doesn't mean anything. What do you know about him? He could have a string of secret families." Barry seemed to have realized what he had said sounded a little crazy. "Okay, scrap that last thought. But just remember he's a field producer, which means going off with a crew wherever a story takes him. And the assignments come whenever something like a disaster happens. Sort of like with a homicide detective. A guy like that might not make it through a meal without having to leave."

"Thank you for the advice," I said. "Are we done now?"

Barry nodded as he stood up. I peeled off the hoodie and we drove back in silence. After not talking to him for months, it was the third time in a day. I tried to will away any feelings seeing him had stirred up. But I knew they would always be there. And I didn't want to admit it, but he had made a point about Bennett.

He stopped the SUV in the driveway and seemed to have something on his mind. "What is it now?" I said, reaching for the door handle.

"I was thinking that when this is all done and we're back in Tarzana, we could get dinner sometime. Just two friends having a meal."

What?

Chapter 17

"You waited up for me," I said, surprised to see Dinah sitting in the main room when I came in. She was still dressed and was crocheting something with red yarn.

"I figured you would have something interesting to tell me." She looked around at the empty space. The rest of the group had left their projects where they had been sitting, ready to be picked up and worked on the next day. "I'm sure it will be more interesting than what went on here." She had a dismayed expression and let out her breath. "We've never stayed together like this. It's one thing hanging out in the bookstore, but being together twenty-four-seven is a whole other story. Of course, Adele was the worst. No wonder she doesn't get along with Eric's mother."

"So the hot chocolate offer didn't help," I said and Dinah threw back her head.

"You have no idea. The minute she realized it came from a pouch, Rhoda complained it was full of artificial everything. With Elise it was about too much sugar."

"Was that it?" I asked, brushing away some yarn scraps before sinking into the couch.

"I wish," my friend said with a laugh. "What would a night be without Adele making a fuss."

"What did she do this time?" I ask.

"She's obsessed with making money after Elise showed her some condos online. She dominated the conversation when we were crocheting, trying to come up with ideas. They all went to bed to get away from her." Dinah laughed. "I wasn't enough of an audience for her, so she did her distressed diva move and went off in a huff. She's just lucky that we have agreed to view her as that difficult relative you have to include. Thank heaven she has a room to herself. Can you imagine what it would be like sharing one with her?" Dinah said, shaking her head at the concept.

"I knew things were a little tense, but I hoped that everyone would mellow out." I stopped to reconsider what I said. "Well, I guess I figured Adele would be a holdout in the mellow-out department." I looked at my friend. "I'm sorry you were left to deal with them," I said.

"I'm probably as bad as the rest of them. Teachers do have a rep for being bossy. But with my students, I have the hammer," she said with a laugh. "They may fuss and try to argue that they should be allowed to make up their own words, but I'm the one who gives out the grades." She did a few stitches and held up what she was making and I recognized the shape of a heart. "I gave in to Adele to keep the peace." Dinah pointed to several finished hearts on the side table. "I'm only making the quick ones though." Adele had left the stuffed one on the coffee table as a hint of what she really wanted everyone to make.

Dinah leaned back against the couch. "It's also turning out that all their fussing is pretty boring. Adele keeps going on about her marriage problems and that tie. Elise can't stop talking about real estate. I never realized how she gets so totally focused on one thing. Rhoda—well, she's a good soul, but a little dull. And CeeCee's thing now is she wants to get a spa treatment." Dinah took a deep breath. "Tell me about your evening. It has to have been more interesting than that."

I had been so wrapped up in what I was doing and who I was seeing that I hadn't thought about Dinah being bored. I felt bad for leaving it all on her and suggested we try to make it into one of our girls' nights like we had in her she-cave. I was wired from my outing with Barry on top of everything else and was only too glad to tell all. We made tea and got a box of cookies.

"I don't want to have to whisper," Dinah said as we went back into the main room. "Let's go outside."

The days were warm, but it always cooled off at night. Even more so out here, where there was no concrete to absorb the sun's heat. I realized I had left my hoodie in Barry's cop car. I wasn't going to contact him and chalked it up to a loss. I grabbed a sweater instead.

The overhead string of lights gave off a warm glow that made it seem festive and separate from the darkness beyond. We got situated and Dinah turned to me. "Tell me everything."

"I don't know where to begin," I said. "It's all in a jumble in my head."

"Then start with Barry. What did he want? What was it like seeing him again?"

"It was actually the third time today of interacting with him," I said. Dinah's eyes widened and she laughed.

"Third time? When was the second time?"

"The local cops showed up to discreetly question everybody at the wake or vigil, or whatever it was supposed to be. Barry was one of them. He wasn't happy when he realized I had left a lot out when he questioned me in the morning. He made up for it by doing a good job of pinning me against the wall, and I ended up admitting that I was working for Mason."

Dinah's eyes lit up. "What did he say when he heard you were a professional now?"

"I downplayed it and made it sound like my only job was the hunt for the elusive kleptomaniac. And then Bennett showed up with a piece of cake and he said something about walking me home after the vigil." I stopped for a moment. "I don't know why they pretended it was a vigil. Nobody was talking much about Kirkland. Except for his almost-widow. And she seemed mostly concerned about herself."

"Did Bennett walk you home?" she asked.

I nodded and explained inviting him in. "And Mason walked in on us." Dinah's eyes widened again and I rushed to correct what she was thinking. "We were just talking. Mason had brought leftovers because we had both been too busy to eat."

I got sidetracked when Dinah asked about the food and I described the delicious barbecue. "It was definitely not for the diet-conscious." I lost track of the thread about Barry and Bennett when I mentioned Tiffany's arrival.

Dinah seemed to have come back to life. She didn't seem to be bothered that I was hopscotching all over the events of the evening and wanted to know all the details about Tiffany.

"To cut to the chase—she's the in-charge sort who is trying to run Mason's life, as in telling him what to wear, what to eat and when to eat it. Mason said she wants to get married, but he doesn't. I bet she already has the ring picked out," I said with a laugh.

Dinah leaned forward. "Enough about her. What happened on that third time with Barry?"

"He wanted to make sure I understood that Bennett was a suspect and then he suggested he and I get dinner sometime." She reminded me that Barry had said I was the love of his life and I shook my head. "No, his job is."

"What did you say to the dinner offer?"

"I didn't know how to answer so I said nothing."

Dinah laughed again. "Like I said, it is raining men for you. Romance, mystery—you have it all going on. I'm jealous." She let out a sigh "At least we can talk about the mystery. What did you find out about Kirkland's death? Do you think Heddy Mariano did it?"

I put up my hands and shrugged. "She keeps going on about space aliens on her property and that they did it." I brought up the *Twilight Zone* story. "She thinks they were trying to turn Kirkland into soup in the hot springs," I said. Dinah nodded, remembering the episode of the old TV show and the twist at the end.

"Jerry R is keeping her at the ranch for now. I don't know if it's a hallucination or her attempt at pushing the blame away from herself."

Dinah's mouth went into a mock pout. "I miss being part of it all." She looked back toward the trees and the rest of the property. "I wish I had been with you when you got a look back there."

Dinah had been my sidekick in the past and I felt like I owed her some adventure. "I'd say we could go have a look, but I got lost before and it was daylight then."

Dinah was too enthused about doing something on the edge to give up that easily. "We can work it out." She went inside and returned a few moments later. "Where there's crochet, there's a way." She smiled and held up a large skein of yarn. It was an odd greenish color. She held it under the table, and in the darkness it gave off an eerie glow.

"It's a yarn way of leaving breadcrumbs," she said with an enthusiastic smile as she went up to a nearby tree and tied the yarn onto a branch. Then the two of us moved on into the woodsy area following the beam from a flashlight I had found.

As we moved further into wild area, she hooked the yarn onto another tree and then another. We got to the end of the yarn just as the low fence came into view. Dinah seemed disappointed that it all appeared peaceful. I was about to point out that the tent was gone, when a bright light appeared on the other side of the fence. It seemed to hover and then abruptly started to move toward us.

"Enough adventure. Let's get out of here. I don't want to end up as dinner," Dinah said, running back into the darkness. I followed along behind her, taking a quick look back over my shoulder. The light seemed even bigger but had stopped coming after us as soon as we moved away from the fence. It was so bright it was hard to tell for sure, but it seemed like there was a silver figure below it with big buglike black eyes.

We tripped as we tried to follow the trail of the yarn. I took another look back and all I saw was darkness.

We were breathless when we got back to the house. "Should we call someone?" Dinah said.

"And say what? That we saw Heddy's aliens, but they're gone?" I said as we got back in the house and made sure to lock the French door we'd gone out of.

We fell asleep with the light on.

Chapter 18

I was really confused about where I was when I awoke in the morning, particularly since I was still wearing my clothes and I had dreamt that Heddy was singing to a spaceship. Mason was in the dream, too. He was too busy with Tiffany to notice that a creepy silver figure with big eyes and a soup ladle was coming after me.

It was a relief to see Dinah asleep across the room. I felt like I had to tell somebody what we had seen. Mason probably was too busy with Tiffany, but I sent him a text describing our adventure anyway.

I had barely hit send, when my phone rang. Dinah was still asleep, so I went into the main room to take the call.

"That's a joke, right?" Mason said when I finally answered the phone.

Some of the others were in the kitchen and Adele had just come into the main room. I'd never seen her nightwear before. She was wearing a red T-shirt-style nightgown that said *Hot Honey* on the front. Her slippers were crocheted booties. I ducked outside with my phone in my hand before she saw me. It felt chilly and the dew had made the tile floor of the patio slippery. I heard Mason's disembodied voice coming through my phone. "Are you there, or did the aliens come back to snatch you," he said, chuckling.

"I'm here, sorry, but I didn't want to talk in front of the others. They'll freak out if they hear," I said. "And it's not a joke." I repeated what I had seen.

"Are you sure you weren't dreaming?" He had lost the chuckle.

"No, I definitely wasn't dreaming." I could see the yarn hanging from the tree where we had first tied it. I heard Tiffany in the background and Mason explaining he was talking to me and that he had made coffee. There was a discussion over whether it was caffeinated. As soon as he said yes, she said she would make decaf for both of them.

"Here's a hint that it might have been a dream. How did you manage not to get lost in the darkness?" he asked. He certainly wasn't expecting the answer I gave him about the glow-in-the- dark yarn.

"I'm looking at it right now on the tree that we attached it to," I said.

"Why did you go back there?" he asked. I didn't want to tell him that it was because Dinah felt left out of everything, so I said I was curious about the hot springs pond.

"It seems like a lot of trouble to see some hot water. If you want to try a mineral springs soak, there are places where they pipe the water that comes up from underground into pools. There are towels and lounge chairs to relax on afterward," he said. "And no worries that you're trespassing."

"Got it," I said.

"And to put your mind at rest, it was probably someone connected to the medical examiner who wanted to check out the temperature of the water and the situation there at the time when Kirkland died. The light could have been a headlamp and the rest your imagination filled in." He was chuckling to himself. "I suppose you were playing that Sherlock Holmes game," he said. He knew all about the deducting we did to see if we could figure things out.

"Not exactly," I said, and decided to tell him the real story. "Dinah felt left out, and it turns out the Hookers are getting on each other's nerves. I just wanted to let her feel a part of things."

"You and Dinah are fearless. Now I feel bad that I missed out on your adventure." He had been talking freely and I guessed that Tiffany was off on the hunt for decaf coffee.

"Let's get back to last night and where we left off and what's going on tonight." He'd barely finished the sentence when I heard Tiffany, who had obviously returned with the decaf coffee, telling him that he needed to get dressed and something about going horseback riding again.

"It's better if we talk in person anyway," he said. "What about at the farmers' market."

"Farmers' market?" I said.

"You have to go and take the—" He stopped himself and I realized he didn't want to say *hookers* in front of Tiffany. He finally just called them my associates. "Everybody in town goes to it. There is a lot more than stalls selling vegetables. It's like a bazaar with everything from clothing to cooked food. They probably even have a booth selling yarn."

I glanced back at the group in the house and I could tell by Adele's hand-on-her-hip stance and the way the others were looking at her that things were getting dicey. An outing would be good.

I agreed and we set up an approximate time. Just before he hung up, he added something else. "Did Bennett show up at your place? Tiffany said a man came here looking for you last night when I was in the shower."

"I'll tell you about it when I see you," I said, and we ended the call.

I went inside and told them about the farmers' market. They all thought it was a great idea. Even Adele.

"What's going on?" Dinah said, yawning as she finally came out of the bedroom. While they were all telling her about the plan for a trip to the farmers' market and claiming it was their idea, I took her into the kitchen to get some coffee.

We had a quick discussion about the previous night's escapade. I assured her it wasn't a dream and that I had told Mason about it. I offered her his explanation. We agreed not to say anything to our housemates.

"Thank you for taking me on an adventure," Dinah said. "Now I feel like I can get through the rest of the weekend without losing my mind."

Dinah played transportation captain and set up who would drive with who. I was out of the discussion since I was taking Mason's SUV and planned to hand him back the keys.

I let them all go off ahead. They set aside their electronic cleanse and had their phones' sound back on so we could communicate about meeting up later.

Once I got into town, it was easy to find the farmers' market. A row of colorful banners flapped in the breeze and live music was coming from somewhere. The mass of white tents and canopies was set up in an open field. Food trucks were parked nearby and there were plenty of umbrella-shaded tables spread around the grass. It all seemed very festive and I could see why it was a magnet for the residents. The sense of community seemed important in Pixie.

I had gone to a weekly farmers' market near Tarzana, but it was not nearly as elaborate as this. I was early for my meeting time with Mason and went to explore the temporary shops in the meantime. Thinking ahead to it, I hoped it was going to be sans Tiffany.

I took a moment to take in the setup and saw that the rows of booths had an organized arrangement. The first rows were devoted to local produce. There was lots of color from the crates of orange pixie mandarins, along with other produce like baskets of deep purple eggplants and displays of bright red tomatoes. Everything was artfully arranged and had a sign indicating the farm where it came from.

The next aisle was filled with delicious scents. I passed baskets of freshly baked breads, trays of homemade tamales, and pots of spicy curries. Ears of corn were roasting on a grill. A booth had bowls of salads made with pixie mandarins. There was even a sushi chef making up vegan sushi rolls. People were taking plates of food and walking out onto the grass to the umbrella tables.

The next row of booths seemed to be all racks of clothes, handmade jewelry, and such. Mason had been right. There was a booth selling hand-spun yarn, but I veered away from it when I saw Rhoda stopped in front of it. I needed to be on my own until I connected with Mason.

I stalled, waiting for her to move on by looking at a booth filled with incense, dream catchers, candles and other New Agey stuff. A man in a long red velvet robe came forward and offered his assistance. There was something otherworldly about him that went with the vibe up there. I smiled back at him and said I was just looking. By then

Rhoda was gone and I moved on.

Mason had left it that we would find each other. It would have been easier if he just texted me, but I assumed he had a reason for doing it this way. It wasn't a stretch to figure out it had something to do with Tiffany. I went back to the beginning for another walk through since it was close to the appointed time. On this go-round, I paid more attention to the individual booths. I was surprised that I had missed one on the first go-round. A banner said *Rayner Ranch* and offered olive oil tasting. When the crowd moved, I saw Jerry R and Mason standing by a display with bottles of olive oil and a tasting setup. Lisa R was hanging in front of the next booth, which promised organic catnip plants. Tiffany was positioned near Mason. They were both dressed for horseback riding but without the hats. His clothes had a patina of dust. Hers appeared so fresh that I had a feeling she had just dressed for the event, but not taken part. I watched her body language. She was definitely not staying in the background, but seemed intent on taking an active part in the conversation between Mason and Jerry R.

I wanted to let Mason know that I was there and stopped next to Lisa R, waiting for him to glance my way. Lisa R offered me a friendly smile. Ever since I had offered to help with some suggestions for turning the wedding into a memorial for Kirkland, she seemed to view me as support and didn't care that I hadn't found the trinket taker. We talked over some suggestions that I had texted her. She looked at Jerry R and shook her head with a weary smile. "He's such a micromanager about everything. We have whole crews of people to deal with making the olive oil and running the booth, but he has to make an appearance here and rearrange the display."

Her comment made me think of what Barry had said about Jerry R trying to influence the local police into thinking that Kirkland's death could have been an accident. It was a clever plan that would get the heat off of everybody. I guessed that was more important to the manager than getting justice for his client.

I assumed that Tiffany had seen me by then because she moved closer to Mason. Dinah might think I was having a rainstorm of men, but it was all so complicated. I kept to my place as his employee and waited until he looked up and then gave him a wave.

He said something to Jerry R and Tiffany. I think he expected her to stay put, but she followed along with him. When he reached me, she made sure to stand close enough to make it clear they were a couple.

Mason greeted me and turned to Tiffany. "We have some logistics to discuss. Why don't you look over the rest of the booths. Molly and I won't be long."

"I can just wait," she said, not making a move. Mason pulled her aside and said something and she finally walked away, still giving us a few looks back.

"Sorry. She's a little possessive," he said. I heard Spike give a yip and Mason showed off the cloth cross-body bag he was wearing that held the little dog.

"It seems that way." I knew I should leave it at that, but I couldn't help myself. "Does she remind you of anybody?" I asked, and he shrugged. Then he seemed to understand.

"You're right. How did I miss it? She even looks a little like my ex. I guess it's true that we all have a type." He looked at me. "I have to say that you never reminded me of Jaimee—or anybody else." He started walking up the aisle as if he had someplace specific in mind.

He stopped when we got to a tent that had the heavenly scent of freshly ground coffee. I followed Mason into it. "It's locally grown and was roasted yesterday," he said. There were bags of coffee for sale and also a menu of coffee drinks. I sucked in my breath when I saw the prices. Mason talked to the man running the booth about the coffee and how exciting it was to try locally grown beans. Mason ordered cups of coffee for both of us. The man explained that it was a medium roast that was high in caffeine.

"Just the way I like it," Mason said.

We found an empty table that was shaded by the trees growing along the edge of the open field. Before we talked about anything, he suggested we savor the coffee.

"At the price, we definitely should," I said.

We touched cups in a toast and each took a sip while he gave me the lowdown on California-grown coffee. It was a big deal because it was the farthest from the equator that coffee was being grown. The beans were actually seeds of the coffee cherry that grew on shrubs or small trees.

"Heddy told me all about her coffee trees. She has them planted between her avocado trees. They have similar needs. She is very excited about having her first harvest." Mason looked at his cup of brew. "I had no idea it took so long for the plants to produce. She has a whole setup arranged to handle the beans and get them roasted."

"I'm certainly going to savor this," I said, looking at the brown liquid. The flavor was nutty and delicious. We went back to drinking in silence so as to concentrate on the flavor. But then he put down his cup. "We better drink and talk." He started with Dinah's and my trip into the wild the night before. "Did you take any pictures?" he said.

I laughed at the thought. "All I could think of was getting out of there," I said.

"As I told you, I'm sure there is a non-alien explanation, but please keep what you saw to yourself," he said.

"Only Dinah knows and she won't tell the others." I left it at that and moved on to the tease I had left him with when he had thought it was Bennett who had asked Tiffany about my whereabouts.

"It was Barry who was looking for me," I said. "But he was acting as Detective Barry Greenberg and after information." I brought up what Barry had said about Jerry R having a strategy.

"It's not a surprise that he figured it out. It's not the most original idea," Mason said. "What did you tell him?"

"I just shrugged it off as if I didn't know anything about it. It was the same when he asked about Kirkland's phone."

"Yeah, the cops didn't find it," Mason said. "Did Barry have anything else to say?"

"Not really. He just seemed intent on telling me Bennett Edwards was a person of interest," I said.

"He is right about that. All the flirting stuff could be a cover. Be careful that you don't give him any information, as in that you're working for me." Mason took a sip of the coffee as if it was fine wine. "But back to Greenberg. How many times has he questioned you?"

"There was the time in the morning when the cops came to talk to all of us. Then at the party or vigil, and finally last night when I was back with the Hookers."

Mason wanted details of the late-night meetup and seemed upset when I mentioned Barry wanted to talk in his cop car. "It seems excessive. Three times in one day and you're hardly a suspect." Mason paused. "Or was it personal?"

I shook my head. "He really did seem to want information."

Mason looked back toward the people milling around. "Let's finish this up before Tiffany finds us and sees the coffee," he said with a smile. "She is a fanatic about caffeine. Was there anything else about last night?" he asked.

I took a moment to remember who else I had talked to at the party. I considered mentioning that I had noticed the red pen had disappeared from the glass case, but it seemed unimportant at the moment. "I think I told you everything," I said.

"Good. Then we're done," he said.

I took out the SUV's keys and put them on the table. "I guess this is it."

Mason didn't make a move for the keys. "No, you're still on the clock," he said. "Who knows what you might pick up tonight. It's a pre-memorial for Kirkland. Same time, same place." We both saw Tiffany approaching. He crushed his empty coffee cup. "Could you get rid of the evidence," he said, pushing the smashed cup across the table. "Enjoy the afternoon with your crochet buds and then it's back to work." He touched my shoulder as he got up to leave. And then he was gone. I drank the last drop of the coffee and tossed our cups. It was time to find the rest of the Hookers and see how it was going with them.

Adele was standing in front of the booth selling yarn. She had a group around her and was showing off her white shirt, which was like a crochet sampler. It was embellished with tiny granny squares and flowers.

Dinah came up to me as I was watching. "Leave it to Adele to gather a crowd. I heard her talking. She was pitching the wonders of crochet and her ability to give lessons."

Dinah suggested we get some ice cream. There was a food truck with soft serve and we both got large cups of it and sat at one of the tables shaded by a yellow umbrella. I told her about my meeting with Mason and repeated that we shouldn't tell anybody what we saw the night before. She laughed when I told her he had asked if we took pictures.

"It was the last thing on my mind," Dinah said. "I'm glad too, because if I had tried to, I would have just dropped my phone and lost it in the process." She asked me if I was done with my undercover assignment.

"He wants me to go to the event they have going on tonight." I looked back at all the booths and said I needed to get something to wear. "I can't show up in a repeat outfit since it's the same crowd."

Elise pulled out a chair and sat. "I've had enough. I'm staying here until we go back to the house." Rhoda joined us a moment later with the same sentiment. CeeCee was all aflutter when she showed up at the table.

"I had no idea that anyone would recognize me up here. But two people wanted to take selfies and another told me she loved the game show." CeeCee began patting her hair and face. "I wasn't expecting the attention. I must look awful. I really need a facial."

"Here we go again," Rhoda said. "I'm sure you will get your spa time. In the meantime, you look fine."

I left them waiting for Adele while I went back to shop for

something to wear.

I found a gauzy dress in shades of green and blue that seemed perfect and was about to walk away. The exotic smell of incense caught my attention and I stopped in front of the booth run by the man in the red robe. I was thinking about asking if they had the bath gel that promised to cleanse your aura when Tiffany seemed to have come out of nowhere and stepped in front of me.

"What is it?" I said, startled by her sudden presence.

She seemed a little breathless, as if she was in a hurry. "I think you ought to know what's really going on. I heard Mason talking to Jerry R about you. Mason was apologizing for your failure and said he was going to fire you. He only told you to come tonight out of pity." Tiffany's face seemed full of concern. "Mason even said it was a mistake to hire you. If I were you, I would save myself the embarrassment and just not come. Who wants to go somewhere where they are not really wanted?"

She didn't wait for me to respond and took off. I stood there in shock at what she had said. Did Mason really feel that way?

"That wasn't very nice," a man's voice said. "Here's something that might help." When I looked up, the man in the long red robe had come out of his booth. He held out a little drawstring bag made of purple velvet. I took it and started to open it, but he stopped me. "The magic will only work once. When there's something or someone your heart calls out to, open it and follow the instructions."

It was such a nice gesture. I thanked him profusely and tried to pay him, but he wouldn't take it. "I like to play fairy godfather," he said with a smile.

Chapter 19

I was stunned by what Tiffany had said and took my time going back to the Hookers' house. I was still in a fog when I went in. The din of voices coming from the main room snapped me back to reality. It was way too loud to be just the Hookers. I rushed ahead, wondering what had happened now.

Adele was standing with a group of people, while Rhoda, Elise and CeeCee were grumbling to Dinah.

"Do something, Molly," Rhoda said. "Adele has gone too far this time. This is supposed to be our weekend and she brought back a bunch of strangers for a crochet class." Rhoda sputtered before she added, "That she's charging for."

Everyone had turned in my direction, and as I looked over the people with Adele, I realized they weren't strangers to me. The drab clothes had fooled me at first, but I recognized them all. CeeCee announced she was going to her room and left it to everyone else to work it out.

"You were at the party at Jerry R's," Rory Bijorn said, sounding surprised. "You're my super fan who followed me for the autograph." She looked down at her cargo pants and graphic T-shirt and felt her hair, which was pulled back into a plain pony. "I'm sorry, but if you're hoping for a selfie with me, I can't do it dressed like this."

"That's right," Bayleigh Selinger said. "You were the one who showed Ash how to crochet."

Adele was displeased that she had lost the spotlight. "Don't bother with her. I am the master teacher here."

"I remember you from the Rayners' too," Verona Gilroy said.

"What are you doing here?" Ash Selinger asked, seeming perplexed.

They were all looking at me now, and I thought over how to explain. There was nothing saying I couldn't be Mason's cousin and be with the Hookers. "I came up with my friends for a weekend away, and since I was up here anyway, I did my cousin a favor. He hates going to parties alone. And then after Kirkland died, it seemed rude not to pay my respects."

Adele focused in on me. "Who's your cousin?"

"She was there with Mason Fields," Verona Gilroy said.

"That's ridiculous. He's not her cousin," Adele said before I could stop her. All eyes were on me again as I tried to save myself.

"Okay, we just said we were cousins. I was going to be up here already and it was a favor."

"So, then, what exactly are you to each other?" Rory asked.

"Friends," I said.

Adele always had to have the last word. "And weren't you doing something else?" She turned to the group and I tried to cut her off, but there was no stopping Adele. "Molly likes to think she's an amateur sleuth. As soon as somebody died, she had to get involved."

"No sleuth, amateur or otherwise, is needed. Everybody knows that it was Heddy Mariano. She's totally lost it. I don't know why she hasn't been arrested. It makes me kind of nervous to see her at Jerry R's. What if she decided to take us all out?" Bayleigh said.

"I didn't think about it, but you're right," Verona added. "Did you see the look in her eyes? I hope Jerry R has made sure she doesn't have a weapon."

"But I wonder if he knows that she always carries a knife?" Rory said. "I went to her avocado farm once and she offered me one right off the tree. She had a knife in a sheath tucked under her shirt. You should have seen how easily she whacked the fruit off the branch. I will say it was delicious, though. Maybe there is something to her singing to the trees. She sliced it up and we ate right there in the grove."

Adele was tapping her foot and had a peeved expression. I ignored her and asked them how this lesson had come about.

"It was because of you, actually," Rory said. "I saw you crocheting at the party. I'm looking to take up a hobby. I thought of pottery, but this seems a lot less messy. When I saw your friend at the farmers' market and she was offering a lesson, I thought why not."

"I've been looking for something to do that might help calm me without any side effects and that is portable," Verona said. "I was in right away when Adele offered us a group lesson." Verona's black capri pants and black top reminded me that she had made a point that wearing black all the time made dressing easy. She seemed to have the same nervous energy she'd had at the parties. I had the feeling she needed something bigger than working with a hook to release it.

"So, Molly, it looks like they're all here because of you," Adele said in a self-satisfied tone. It was a stretch to somehow blame me for her impromptu lesson, but I did see her point. More importantly, I wanted to smooth everything over. I didn't want anyone to go back to Jerry R's and complain about me since, according to Tiffany, I already had a bad rep. And the Hookers had a right to expect the space to be theirs. I felt like I was straddling two worlds.

"What about this?" I said. "Adele, why don't you take your students out on the back patio? It's a beautiful day and there's shade." I turned to my fellow Hookers. "Then you can go on with no bother."

There was still some grumbling from the Hookers that Adele had turned our getaway weekend into a commercial venture for herself at their expense. But they finally went to settle in and Adele led her students outside. Dinah stayed with the inside group and I followed the patio people.

I didn't trust Adele not to stir up something else, so I stayed out there as she set up for the class. They looked around the back area, commenting on how wild the surrounding land was. "You were talking about Heddy Mariano," Adele said, taking a self-important stance. "Her place is back there. The police came here to question us to see if we saw anything." As she was talking, I was glad she had no idea that I had done the recent exploring. I didn't want to talk about what I saw.

"I'm a police wife, so I talk their language," Adele said. She started handing out hooks and balls of yarn and it seemed that the discussion about the location of Heddy's land had ended. I let out a breath and started to relax. It was too soon because when she was done handing out the supplies, she took out the tie and dropped it around Ash Selinger's neck.

"This is my latest design," Adele said. "I'm very proud of it." She looked at Ash. "You would be glad to wear such an original handmade creation, wouldn't you?"

"Maybe," Ash said with a smile. "But not with this." It did look ridiculous with his outfit of a white T-shirt and a pair of khaki shorts with a torn pocket. It was a far cry from the linen outfits he had worn to the parties and it seemed as if he had reached in their closet and picked out the first thing he touched.

"I think it works with anything," Adele said. Ash turned to his wife and asked her opinion.

To my surprise, she was positive. "It might just be the quirky accessory we need."

"You are right," Ash said. "We could have the front desk staff wear them, like a signature thing." He told Adele about their wellness retreat and asked if she had them for sale.

"I could do a custom job for you. We could come up with your own color scheme." Adele flashed a look of triumph at me.

Verona was still checking out the surroundings. "What's that?" she said, pointing at some yarn hanging off a tree. It was daytime so instead of glowing in the dark, it was the odd shade of green.

"It's nothing," I said, trying to dismiss it. "It's some yarn that got wet and we hung it up to dry." Adele gave me a strange look.

"I sure wouldn't want to go wandering back there," Bayleigh said. "What if Heddy isn't hallucinating?" I didn't know if anybody heard her comment because Ash was tapping his hook on the table.

"Could we get to the lesson," he said, pursing his lips in impatience. Adele happily took back the spotlight and had them start with making a slip knot. She did a demonstration of how to make chain stitches, and then had them begin on their own. I sat there for a while to make sure there were no more bumps in the road. Once I felt confident it would stay peaceful, I went inside. I needed to talk to Dinah.

All the fuss about the crochet lesson had diverted me from thinking about what Tiffany had said, or more importantly, what I was going to do about it. If ever I needed to talk to my best friend, it was now. Dinah looked up when I came in. She had read my expression and knew there was something wrong and suggested we go into our room, where we could have privacy.

"What is it?" Dinah said as soon as I shut the door.

"Tiffany gave me some friendly advice," I said sarcastically and then told her the rest of it.

Dinah took a moment to absorb it before she spoke. "It sounds to me like she's jealous and trying to make you disappear."

"Yes, but it doesn't mean that what she said isn't true. I told Mason how much I liked having this secret life and he, being the nice guy he is, could have figured he would give me this last evening of it. And then later, I'll get a text saying something like thanks for the help, but he's going in a different direction for investigating."

"What are you going to do?" she asked.

"I don't know," I said with a shrug. "It seems like my options are that I could not go and, as she said, avoid the embarrassment. And just accept that my time of being a private private investigator is done. I did flop at finding the kleptomaniac. I would finish out the weekend here with the Hookers and go back to my normal life."

"Or?" Dinah said.

"I could show up and tell Mason I was hanging up my deerstalker hat. You know, quit instead of waiting to be fired." I thought it over for a moment. "Facing him would be uncomfortable, but it would feel better than running away." I took a deep breath, thinking over Tiffany's little talk. "And I don't like the idea of letting her chase me off."

"I think you have your answer," Dinah said.

"I have to get his car back to him anyway."

Chapter 20

I was a mess of emotions. I felt sad at the thought of giving up my secret profession, but also better about taking control and quitting before I could be fired. Mostly though, I wanted to get the moment with Mason over with. I also wanted to look my best for it. I had hoped to be able to concentrate on just getting ready to go, but I still had to deal with the Hookers.

Adele's lesson was over and our group was hanging out in the main room crocheting and squabbling about the plans for dinner and the evening after when Dinah and I joined them.

"Molly, I think we should go into town for dinner," Elise said. "But CeeCee wants to get takeout and bring it back here. She doesn't want to be seen in public until she gets a facial." She turned to the actress. "Did you see how Rory Bijorn looked? Nobody cares up here."

"Maybe not for someone like her, but I'm old school. People have expectations of how I'm supposed to look."

Rhoda started to bring up Adele's lesson and how she had overstepped, but Dinah stepped in and shushed her. True blue friend that she was, Dinah took over for me and told them all that she had just read that cooking a meal together inspired a joyous feeling.

"So, that's what we're going to do," she said. "I noticed some staples in the pantry. There's pasta and jars of sauce. We have stuff for salad in the refrigerator. And we will eat it alfresco." She pointed to the back patio. Surprisingly, they all went for it. I excused myself, saying that I needed to get ready for my evening at the Rayners' without giving any details that it was my swan song.

Dinah left them in the kitchen fussing over who was going to do what and followed me back into our room to keep me company as I got ready to go.

She gave me a pep talk and was full of compliments when she saw me in the dress I had gotten at the farmers' market.

"What's that?" she asked as I put the purple velvet drawstring bag on the dresser. I was feeling too tense to talk about it and said it was something for a future wish.

When I was ready to go, Dinah walked me out to Mason's black Mercedes SUV. She gave me a supportive hug before reminding me to call her when I needed to be picked up. I used the GPS to find my way back and then parked a distance away. I wanted to wait until the event at Jerry R's was in full swing. That way I could have my moment with Mason without it being noticed.

My stomach was doing flip-flops by the time I finally drove into the Rayner Ranch driveway. I left the SUV parked with the other cars, not wanting to go near the guest house. I still had some clothes and things there, but I didn't really care what happened with them.

I took a couple of deep breaths and tried to will myself to relax before I walked into the house with a feeling of finality.

I was glad there was no one in the entrance hall handling greetings. I hoped to get in and out with as little notice as possible. I would just find Mason, say my piece and leave. I deflated when I realized it wasn't going to go as quickly as I'd hoped. The guests were all gathered in the main room watching something on a screen. I stood at the back of the room. After a few minutes of hearing about the life and times of Kirkland Rush, I realized it was the piece on him that Bennett had talked about putting together. But this wasn't a five-minute piece for the entertainment news shows, this was longer, and probably meant to be a special on BNN. Mason was sitting with Tiffany and it seemed inappropriate to approach him until it was over. And I wanted to talk to him alone anyway. I was too keyed up to sit or even pay much attention to the video. Though what little I did manage to absorb seemed quite good.

The video finally ended and after a moment, everyone applauded. Bennett was dressed more professionally in slacks and a dress shirt and took humble bows as he was showered with compliments.

I watched Tiffany go off toward the bar, carrying two glasses. It seemed like the right time to make my move. I wanted to say my piece and get out of there before Tiffany came back or I got waylaid by any of Adele's crochet students.

Mason was talking to some people. I came alongside him and tapped his arm, whispering that I needed to talk to him right then. He excused himself and I led the way to an empty spot.

"What's up?" he said in a friendly voice. I swallowed and took a deep breath.

"I really appreciate the chance you gave me," I began. I willed away the quiver in my voice. "But I realize that it's too much for me with everything I have going on. I'm sorry that I failed." I stopped to regroup. "I've already told you all I've managed to find out about other suspects . . ." I took a deep breath. "So, I'm resigning, quitting. Whatever you want to call it."

His expression dimmed. "I don't understand," he said. "You told me how much you liked having a double life."

I saw Tiffany come into the living room holding two glasses of wine and looking around. I wanted to end it quickly. "I want to thank you . . ." I hoped to say more, but Tiffany was on her way toward us and I just wanted to get out of there. I pressed the keys in his hand and took off. I passed Bennett on the way out and without stopping, gave him a compliment on his work. I heard him say something like *Cinderella does it again.*

Once I was clear of the house, I stopped to regroup, glad to be lost in the darkness. I'm not usually a crier, but I felt my eyes welling up. "No," I said out loud to myself. "It is what it is. Get on with it." I texted Dinah that I was ready to be picked up. Then I let everything settle as I walked down the long driveway to the road. It had been fun while it lasted, but it wasn't as if I didn't have a lot going on. I told myself that I would be okay.

I was leaning against the white fence around the front of the ranch when a car pulled off the road onto the dirt. The headlights blinded me and it wasn't until I got closer that I saw it wasn't Dinah's car.

The passenger door swung open and I hesitated until I saw the driver. "Barry?"

He held up a sweatshirt jacket. "You left it last night and I came by to drop it off and Dinah said you needed a ride." He watched me as I got in. "She made it sound like you needed something more than transportation." He glanced back at the property. "Did something happen?"

I nodded. "But I don't want to talk about it," I said. He pulled the Explorer back onto the road. "I was going to tell Dinah that I needed some time before I went back to the house and had to deal with the Hookers."

"So then you're saying you want to go somewhere else with no explanation," he said.

"Yes," I said and leaned back against the seat.

"I'm guessing a bench by the park isn't going to cut it this time," Barry said. "I know a place if you don't mind a ride." I answered with a nod and he made a U-turn. "Why don't you tell me what's going on," he said after a moment. "You'll feel better if you talk."

I laughed at his phrasing. "Isn't that what you say to suspects you're trying to get a confession out of?" I said.

"Sort of," he said. "But I tried to temper it and make it more personal to you." We were passing little houses that hugged both sides of the road. Beyond, the mountains loomed in the darkness. "You would feel better if you let it out."

"You really are a cop through and through," I said.

"It's what I do," he said. "It's a ruse when I tell suspects that I can work things out if they will tell me what happened. But I mean it with you."

"Or has it become a challenge to get me to confess to what's going on?"

I heard Barry let out his breath. "Like I said, it's what I do. But it would make you—"

"Feel better," I said, finishing his sentence. I think he expected me to continue and give him the tell-all he was pushing for, but I said nothing. The whole episode was still rolling around in my mind. No matter what Mason said, I was sure he felt I had let him down. He was just humoring me by saying that he wanted my help finding a way to get the heat off of Heddy. I felt like I had let myself down. I should have been able to catch the kleptomaniac. If only I'd had another chance, I could have succeeded.

The road got wider and turned into a highway as we left the mountains behind. We got on the 101 and were back in Ventura. A light fog was blowing in off the ocean and there were lights on in some of the businesses we passed. I was beginning to wonder if he was going to keep driving all the way back home, but Barry got off the freeway and pulled into the parking lot of a strip mall. One shop was still open. When I saw what it was, I started to laugh.

"I know it's a stereotype," he said as he stopped in front of Earl's Donuts. "But there's a reason. Donut places are open." As we got out, he turned back to me. "I've been known to loosen up a resistant suspect with something fried and sweet."

The interior was bright and pink and smelled of oil and sugar. I shrugged it off when Barry asked me to pick something. He got a selection of donuts and a couple of cups of coffee. I thought he was going to suggest we take one of the three tables in the place, but he led the way outside back to the black Explorer.

He got back on the road and drove on until we reached Ventura Harbor. After he parked, he led the way past the closed shops and restaurants to a bench with a view of the boats. There was a mixture of pleasure crafts and odd-looking commercial fishing boats. The sidewalk that went around the water was empty except for a lone person walking a dog.

"Donut?" he offered, holding open the bag. There were napkins and the cups of coffee in a cardboard carrier sitting on the bench.

"If it's a bribe, it's not going to work," I said. The truth was I was too embarrassed at how things had turned out to talk about it.

"No strings," he said and held the bag closer. I finally extracted a buttermilk bar and took a bite. It was freshly made and had just the right amount of sweet. "Have some coffee," he said, handing me one of the cups. I took a few sips. "I thought you needed something extra and added some cream."

I had to admit that the richness did soften the bitterness of the coffee and thanked him.

"Now, don't you feel better?" he said. "Just imagine how even better you would feel if you didn't have whatever it is weighing on your mind."

"Nice try," I said. "The donut and coffee did the trick and I'm fine now. Why don't you tell me how your case is going." I said it as a way to get the spotlight off me. I didn't expect him to tell me anything more than he had before and say something vague about an LA homicide. By now I had figured that he must have wanted to talk to Kirkland. And then my mind took off. Maybe it was the stress of it all, but I had a sudden aha moment as I realized what Barry's homicide was about. I should have thought before I said anything, but, well, after the abrupt end to my investigative career, I needed to prove that I still had it. Maybe it was more like showing off my skill. "I'm guessing it was connected to a story Kirkland was working on. Something about a disgruntled accountant who had the goods on the financial firm he worked for." Barry seemed surprised and I should have stopped there. But the words just tumbled out. "I figured it out from something I heard from somebody," I said, feeling proud of myself.

Barry snapped to attention and had a piercing stare when he faced me. He had instantly changed from teasing me about what was bothering me to his cop persona. "Who is the somebody?" he asked in his interrogation voice.

"Huh?" I said as I realized what I had done. Showing off and being full of yourself is never a good thing and now I had gotten myself in a trap. I couldn't tell him it was Bennett who had told me. Barry already had Bennett pegged as a person of interest and this would only add to it. When Bennett had told me about the accountant, I had never thought about him being dead. Now I realized that the disgruntled accountant was probably the victim in the case Barry was working on.

I had to think fast to come up with something. When asked a direct question, I usually gave an honest answer. I didn't want to lie, more like smudge the answer. "I'm not sure who it was," I said. "I might have even overheard Kirkland talking about it that first night. I was hanging out trying to catch the kleptomaniac in the act and I overheard him talking. That must have been it." I quickly added that I had heard that Kirkland had warned Verona Gilroy to check with her business manager as to how her money was being invested.

"I knew that," Barry said. "Did you happen to hear anything else?"

I shook my head. "All I was interested in was finding the kleptomaniac." I was glad when Barry seemed to dismiss that as unimportant and didn't ask if I had succeeded.

"That's right. You said that was your job for Mason. Then I suppose you don't care that the medical examiner ruled on the manner and cause of Kirkland's death."

"Not really," I said.

"Why is that?" Barry said. He knew me well enough to know that I was too close to the whole thing to not be at least curious. I realized that I had gotten out of one trap and into another. There was a glint in Barry's dark eyes and he waited for me to answer. I was worn down from the whole thing with Mason and didn't know how long I could hold out before Barry squeezed the story out of me. I still had the energy to use one of Barry's tricks back on him.

"What I meant to say was that I don't care because I already know. Inconclusive on both manner and means," I said. I didn't really know anything for sure, but the idea was that if I was wrong, he would rush to correct me. I was just throwing something out there to distract him from his last question anyway.

"Oh," Barry said, seeming a little disappointed.

I tried to hide my surprise at being right. I thought over the image that Heddy had described and put it together with the rock with dried residue that I had seen. "I guess they couldn't prove that someone hit him with the blood-stained rock."

Barry nodded. "There's no proof that anyone else was even there since they never found his phone. He could have fallen and hit his head on the rock and then fell into the water." Barry shrugged. "The only thing for certain was that he didn't drown. It will probably get chalked up to an accident and that will be the end of it. Just as Jerry Rayner was hoping for." Barry's tone made it clear it all seemed too convenient to him and that he wasn't buying the medical examiner's report.

I didn't say anything and reminded myself it didn't matter. I was off the case. It was not my business to get Heddy out of the crosshairs or find out what really happened anymore. The niggling desire to know the truth was just personal.

We watched the boats for a while, but it didn't take long for the ocean breeze to become cold. Even with the hoodie over the gauzy dress, I shivered. Barry noticed and offered me a spare windbreaker he had in the car, but I suggested we head back.

As I got back in the SUV, I had a sense of being okay. The ride, the verbal dueling with Barry and the coffee and donut had smoothed out the edges and then I had done the rest myself. It was how I dealt with everything—just keep going.

"Thank you for all of this. It really helped," I said as we drove away from the harbor.

"I'm glad to have been of service," he said. "You do realize that you would feel even better if you told me what happened to start all this up."

"Really, you're back to that?" I said with a laugh. "You don't give up."

"A good detective never does. I was planning to bring out my super-duper special interrogation methods on the way home."

"You can keep them under wraps for another time," I said.

"Aren't you even curious to see if you could talk your way around them," he said as he steered the Explorer back on the street.

I shook my head and looked out the window. As we passed the beach, I saw the moon glimmering on the ocean. It was too dark to make out the Channel Islands in the distance, but I knew that Santa Cruz and Anacapa were out there.

We turned away from the water and passed through groves of citrus trees and fields of strawberries. Then he got on the freeway and headed back to the Ojai Valley.

He put on the radio and the music became an accompaniment to our ride back.

"This is your stop," Barry joked when he pulled into the driveway of the house. I didn't make a move to get out. I wasn't sure how to say good night. I wanted to let him know how much I appreciated what he had done, but I didn't want to start anything up. With all of our ups and downs, there was still a connection that seemed permanent. I would never manage to feel indifferent toward him. Upset and frustrated at the way he was maybe, but never no feeling.

Finally, I leaned over and hugged him, but pulled away as he started to hug me back. "Thank you," I said, looking back for a moment before I got out.

I hadn't realized how late it was until I saw the clock when I went inside. It was already Saturday. Even Dinah was asleep. I guessed that her plans of them cooking together had worked out. It looked as if they had spent the rest of the evening sitting around the main room crocheting. Their projects and yarn were all over the room.

As I gave the room a last once-over before turning off the lights, I noticed that one of the French doors to the back was ajar. It was probably just carelessness, but it still gave me an unsettled feeling. I closed and locked it, glancing out at the patio and beyond. I turned back to the room, examining it more carefully this time. When I focused on the coffee table something seemed off. There was a sprinkling of the easy-to-make hearts that the Hookers had been making to help Adele with her order for the party. But the larger stuffed one was off to the side. I sucked in my breath when I got a closer look. It had been stabbed numerous times by tiny plastic sword picks, like the ones I'd seen stuck in appetizers at the Rayners'. I moved closer and looked at the banner attached to it. The original uplifting message had been crossed out and a new one written in. *Back off if you don't want trouble.*

Chapter 21

No surprise, I didn't sleep well, and I slipped out of the room I was sharing with Dinah while she was still off in dreamland. Dawn came early at this time of year and the sun was already shining through the trees. Not a creature was stirring in the rest of the house as I went into the kitchen and made myself coffee.

My first thought was to text Mason and tell him about everything, from what I had learned from Barry to the voodoo-like stabbing of the crocheted heart. But then I remembered I wasn't working for him anymore. He probably already knew the information about the medical examiner's ruling anyway. I was sure that the stabbed heart was meant as a warning for me since things like that had happened before. If it was, it was a waste of their effort because I was off the case.

It had given me pause when I first saw it, but now I was ready to forget about it. I had taken some photos of it before pulling out all the plastic swords to have a record. The banner seemed hopeless to fix, so I ripped it off. The stabbing hadn't done any permanent damage to the red crocheted piece and the only hint that anything was amiss was the missing banner, which I doubted anyone would notice.

I was glad that it wasn't the Hookers who found it. More specifically, that it wasn't Adele who had been the one to see it first. I let my imagination go as I pictured her reaction. With all the talk of space visitors, she would have put on a whole melodramatic show with nonsense like how sorry Eric would be when the aliens carried her off. Then she would probably wonder if the aliens would like the tie. Thinking about all that lightened the moment.

I needed to put the whole episode with Mason behind me and let go of the fact that I had failed. My life had to go on. I looked down at my phone and saw there were a bunch of new messages and voicemails. I was at leisure now and went through all of them. There were numerous ones from my family members with questions about things like where were the circuit breakers and should they throw out some cheese that had mold on it.

There was a later message from Samuel assuring me that he had dealt with the circuit breaker situation and what to do with the cheese. Peter was the only one who knew I was working for Mason and I wondered if I had to tell him it was over or if it was better to just let it fade away. The fade-away option seemed better. I didn't want to have to tell my son that it had ended because I had failed.

I was glad that my parents were in the dark about my secret job. They were still upset I hadn't married Mason when I had the chance. They liked Mason and he fit right in with my family. I could ignore Peter's criticism, but my mother knew every button to push. A sigh of disappointment, along with a disapproving look, was enough to start the same kind of tussles we'd had when I was a teenager.

It was the universe's joke to let you think when you were an adult you could do what you wanted. There was always someone to answer to.

I made myself a second cup of coffee and thought of the day ahead of me. The idea of letting go and doing whatever felt strange after being so focused on helping Mason. Even after the stabbed heart warning, I missed being in the middle of the action.

Dinah was the first one up and came into the main room stretching and yawning. "I tried to wait up for you, but I'm afraid that Commander's early bedtime is having an effect on me. It got to be ten o'clock and my eyes just closed. I have always been such a night owl." She made herself a cup of coffee. "Tell me everything," she said.

The rest of them were bound to be up soon and I didn't feel like sharing all the details with them. I suggested we take our coffee to the back patio. The sun had warmed the air, and it felt perfect to be outside.

"Okay, spill," Dinah said as soon as we sat down. I took a breath and gave her the rundown on my brief encounter with Mason.

"How did he react?" my friend asked.

"I didn't really notice. I just wanted to get out of there. Tiffany was heading toward us and I didn't want to take a chance she would make a scene."

"I bet Mason will be sorry," Dinah said. "It's only the one time that it didn't work out. There were all those other jobs he gave you that were fine." She gave my arm a squeeze. "I hope it was okay that Barry picked you up," she said. "He offered, and well, I thought he might get your mind off of things."

I nodded with a chuckle. "He did a good job of that. He tried to use all his interrogation skills to find out why I needed to be picked up. And I used my skills to not tell him. Guess who won," I said with a smile. "He was very nice about the whole thing even if I never told him what was wrong." I described the extended ride and the stop by Ventura Harbor.

"Not that it matters to me anymore, but Barry told me that the medical examiner is ruling Kirkland's death as being inconclusive. It will make it easier for the cops to think it was an accident."

"You got him to tell you that?" Dinah said, totally ignoring what I said it might mean. "Wow, he must have really been trying to start things up with you again."

I laughed at the idea that telling me information about a homicide could be considered a romantic gesture. "All of it did help. By the time I got back here, I felt okay about the whole situation with Mason and was ready to shut the door on it. And then I found this." I showed her the picture of the stabbed heart with the banner attached.

"Ewww," Dinah said, recoiling. "Who? How could it have happened?"

"I don't know who," I said. "As for how, one of the French doors was open."

Dinah seemed concerned. "It's creepy to think that someone came in while we were sleeping."

I tried to reassure her that it didn't matter now that I was off the case, but she seemed fixated on who it could have been.

"We could play our Sherlock Holmes game," I said. It was something we did often. We would talk about what we knew and see what we could deduce from it. Like seeing a wet umbrella meant that the owner had been out in the rain even though he claimed to have been inside all afternoon.

"Great idea," she said.

"Let's start with believing the warning was meant for me," I said.

"Then it would mean whoever it was had to know where you were staying," Dinah said.

"There's something else more important that can be deduced from it," I said.

Dinah looked at me expectantly and waved with a flourish for me to continue. "If it was really an accident, nobody would care if I was poking around. So then it has to be . . ."

"Murder," Dinah said in a whisper.

"And it was somebody who knew I was curious about what happened to Kirkland," I said.

"Adele's crochet lesson," we both said at once.

"Adele should never have talked about your sleuthing," Dinah said, shaking her head. "What do you know about those people?"

"To start with, they were all at the events at the Rayners'." I considered what I knew about each of them. "Verona Gilroy is going through a divorce and seems at loose ends. She did say something about Kirkland advising her to check her financial statements." I thought about what I had said. "The case that Barry is working on involves a dead accountant who was a former employee of a business management firm. Maybe there's a connection." I pictured the group and who else had been there. "Ash and Bayleigh are wrapped up in opening their health spot. But there's Rory Bijorn. I think Kirkland might have said something to her as well about checking financial statements. She and Tom Kelter were squabbling about who was going to take care of their kids over the summer. I think she's upset about his new status as a hunk, too."

Dinah and I took some sips of our coffee. "They might all be too obvious," I said. "I'm sure Jerry R knows where I'm staying. He seems to know everything that's going on in Pixie. He knows that I was working for Mason. His claim is that he wanted to get the heat off of Heddy, but what if his real aim was to keep himself from being a suspect? He was Kirkland's manager. Who knows what could have been going on? Maybe Kirkland was planning to drop him. How embarrassing would that be when he was hosting Kirkland's wedding?"

I let that sit for a moment as I had a troubling thought. I didn't even want to say it, but I knew I had to. "Both Barry and Mason were suspicious of Bennett. He really doesn't seem the type, but then who knows. He could have figured out that I was working for Mason. He certainly has gained from Kirkland's death. I wouldn't be surprised if he goes from being a producer to an on-air talent. All the rom-com stuff could have been fake. He kept joking about me leaving like Cinderella and I'm pretty sure I told him about our weekend."

"Wait," Dinah said. "I have somebody else. What about Tiffany? And it has nothing to do with Kirkland. She could have found out where you were staying and decided to give you a final message to stay away from Mason."

"Thanks," I said. "I'd rather it be her than Bennett. It seemed like the kind of thing she would do. And it could have been because I showed up to deal with Mason instead of just running away. The good news is that I'm sure whoever it was will back off now that I am done working for Mason or hanging out with him."

"You know there is a package of those plastic swords in the kitchen," Dinah said. "I saw them when we made the charcuterie board."

"You mean it could have been an inside job?" I said. I was going to elaborate, but Rhoda came outside with her coffee and I abruptly stopped talking. It didn't take long before the rest of them were out there too.

"Well, ladies, this is our last full day up here," CeeCee said and then she looked at me. "Dear, did you have anything planned?"

I shrugged and admitted I had nothing.

"We could stay in and work on finishing the scarves," Rhoda said. She didn't sound very excited by the prospect.

"Not me," Elise said. "I plan to have a look around the area. I just heard from a client who is interested in buying something they can use and also rent out."

"Certainly not me either," Adele said, addressing the group. "I want to make the most of being up here. After the order for the ties I got, I thought I would go to some of the shops in town and see if they might be interested in selling them." She held up the tie as if there was any chance any of us didn't know what she was talking about. "I think they'll see that they go along with the vibe up here." Nobody said anything and I had a good idea they all had the same thought about being ready to strangle her with the tie that had haunted us the whole weekend.

"Well, then I'm going to get my spa time—a massage and a facial," CeeCee said. She took out her phone and started scrolling.

"That leaves the three of us," I said.

"Then you're not going off with Mason again?" Rhoda said. "What happened last night? Did you close in on who the killer is?"

I took a moment to come up with something to say. "I'm sorry to report that I don't really have anything to report. I think it's going to be considered an accident," I said.

"But what do you think?" CeeCee asked, looking up from her phone. I could have let it go, but it bothered me to think that someone was going to get away with murder.

"I don't think it was an accident. I think somebody killed Kirkland," I said.

"You mean it really was Heddy?" Rhoda said.

"Maybe, but there are a lot of other suspects too."

"Then why don't you do something?" Rhoda said.

"It's kind of sticky," I said. "My access is cut off." I didn't give out the details but said it was uncomfortable now that Tiffany was there. They were all sympathetic.

"Mason is a catch," Elise said. "You can't blame his girlfriend for pushing away any competition."

Adele looked at me. "Too bad you blew it with him. I'm a police wife and all, but if I was choosing between Barry Greenberg and Mason Fields, it would be Mason all the way." She reminded the group how Mason had rescued the two of us when we had been stuck on a mountain above Palm Springs.

"Don't make her feel bad," Rhoda said.

"It doesn't matter," I said. "I met someone else." It was true that Bennett might be a killer, but for the moment I wanted to get them off talking about Mason. Spending time with Mason for the last couple of days had reminded me of how much I missed him. It was like being home when I was with him.

I told them about Bennett without mentioning the part that he might have been the one to kill Kirkland. I focused on his laid-back personality and his cute ways.

"Why can't you use him as a way to get back into the middle of things," Adele said when I told them about the piece that Bennett had made about Kirkland.

I had to think fast. "It might still cause a problem with Tiffany if I was there at all," I said.

"It's a first for you, Pink," Adele said. "Giving up without finding out who did it." She shook her head in disapproval as she looked over the group.

"You have to know when to hold 'em and when to fold 'em," Dinah said. "Molly did her best."

Adele mumbled something that sounded like that my best wasn't good enough this time.

Chapter 22

"Adele has no sense about what she says," Dinah said as we got into her car. "One minute she's telling you that you are her best friend in the world and then she goes off knocking your investigative skills. Everybody knows that you can't win all the time."

"That's right," Rhoda said from the backseat. We had all gone our separate ways after breakfast. CeeCee had gotten a last-minute appointment for her spa treatments. Elise had put together a list of properties she wanted to look at. And Adele had the tie ready to show off to some local boutiques. Dinah, Rhoda and I had chosen to have lunch somewhere and go back to the farmers' market. The whole group had decided to have dinner together in town and finally experience the pink moment on our last night up there.

"But I really do hate to lose when the stakes are someone getting away with murder," I said, feeling defeated. Both Rhoda and Dinah urged me to let it go and enjoy our lunch.

Dinah had found the spot for our meal. It was a working farm with a stucco ranch-style house that had been turned into an eatery. The interior had dining areas in the assorted rooms, but we chose to eat outside. I started to let go and relax as we were led to an outdoor patio with a canopy of trees that was so dense it seemed almost like a roof. The bare wood tables gave it a rustic look.

The fresh pasta primavera was made with vegetables from their garden and was delicious. We were poring over the dessert menu trying to decide on a choice, when I saw Dinah get a troubled look. I understood why when I followed her gaze. Mason and Tiffany were being led to a table. It figured. My first thought when I saw the place was that it was just the kind of spot that he would like.

I was glad when we voted against dessert and managed to leave unseen.

There was an even bigger crowd at the farmers' market since it was Saturday. Rhoda and Dinah went off looking for Pixie mandarins to take back to their spouses. I wanted to splurge and drown my sorrows in a cup of the locally grown coffee. As I wandered through the stalls, I felt a little better. I liked the feeling of being anonymous in the crowd.

I was trying to decide if I wanted the coffee black or in a latte as I neared the coffee booth. But what I saw made me realize the idea of being anonymous was an illusion. Mason was talking to the owner and sipping a cup of the brew. He must have slipped away from Tiffany and was getting his caffeine fix. Not only was he drinking a cup but was buying a bag of the freshly roasted beans as well. I was thinking that he better hide it or Tiffany would confiscate it, when he turned in my direction. Any contact would be awkward now and I veered off to a side walkway.

I was too intent on getting out of sight to think about what was around me until I heard a yelp as I bumped into someone. "I'm so sorry," I said, turning to face the injured party. The woman was dressed in loose-fitting jeans and sneakers. A billed cap covered her hair. I was about to dismiss her as just another shopper when she said something and I recognized the voice.

I did a double take to make sure I was right. Kirkland's fiancée, Zoe, was barely recognizable without the perfect coiffed hair, tight dress, stiletto heels and perfect makeup.

"We met at Jerry R's," I said. She took a moment to process it and then nodded.

"I remember you. You were hanging out with Bennett," she said. She saw me looking at her outfit. "I couldn't stand to wear my weather-reporter clothes another minute. Don't tell Jerry R how you saw me. I'll be perfectly dressed for the memorial service." She seemed worn out and I felt for her.

"You've been through a lot," I said.

"My whole world has been turned upside down." Her voice sounded stilted, as if she was saying a rehearsed line. "It's really hard to talk about it. I'm not sure what I'm supposed to say."

I patted her arm. "Of course. I understand." I was going to tell her that I was a widow and assure her that she would get past this, but she seemed almost panicked as she edged away and disappeared in the crowd. When I turned back to check the coffee booth, Mason was gone. I bought myself a cup of the pricey brew and sat down at one of the umbrella tables. I guessed that was what it was like being in a small town. You kept running into the same people.

"Do you mind if we join you?" a woman's voice said. Meg Rush was standing next to the table holding a cardboard carrier with some drinks and something that smelled delicious. "We met at the Rayners'. I'm sorry I don't remember your name."

It was no joke about running into people you knew. I gestured to the chairs. "Sure. Sit." She had to steer her son into his chair as his eyes never left the electronic game in his hands before she took the seat next to him. "It's Molly," I said, and she nodded as she moved the food and drink in front of Harrison. She let out a sigh and took out a cup of coffee and a biscotti.

"Normally, I would fuss at him about sticking his nose in the game all the time, but after everything that's happened and what we still have to deal with, I figure anything that makes it easier for him." She took a sip of the coffee. "I had no idea they were growing coffee in California until I heard Heddy talking about her crop," she said. "I wanted to pick up some pixies to take back with us. We're going home as soon as the memorial service is over." She looked at her son. "At least, thanks to me, everything will go to him. Not that it makes up for having a father he barely knew."

"What about Zoe?" I asked, and she shook her head and pursed her lips.

"She'll still get the honeymoon trip. It's too late to cancel it." Meg took out her phone and typed something in. "I have to make sure I cancel all his subscriptions." I was surprised at how unemotional and businesslike she sounded. My expression must have given away my thoughts because she suddenly seemed to need to explain. "I've been divorced from Kirkland for a long time and by now, I just thought of him as someone whose finances I looked after. Of course, I'm sorry he's dead, but my first concern is my son."

"I understand," I said. "Have you heard anything new about the investigation?" I asked. For the moment I had forgotten that I wasn't involved anymore.

"Since Harrison is next of kin, I got the medical examiner's findings. They are claiming it's inconclusive. I guess that means it will be harder to charge Heddy with his death."

"What do you think happened?" I asked.

"I'm going with the obvious. Heddy saw somebody on her property and thought it was those aliens she's talking about and hit him with a rock. I don't know what happened after that. I'm surprised Kirkland didn't have his phone. It was always in his hand, to take photos or record something."

Harrison finally looked up from the game and took a sip of his drink, and she pushed a taco closer to him. It seemed like a good time to make my exit and I got up. "I suppose you'll be there tomorrow," she said.

I didn't want to get into an explanation of why I wouldn't and just nodded and said goodbye.

I went back into the crowd with a mission. I decided to be like the others and get some pixie mandarins to bring home. They were sweeter and easier to peel than the usual mandarins I got and just the right size for Marlowe's little hands. I was working my way back to the area with all the produce when I saw Lisa R stopped at their ranch's booth. I thought it best to avoid her and tried to disappear into the crowd, but she saw me and waved me over.

"Jerry R made me come to check on the booth." She let out a mirthless laugh. "I saw you rush off last night," she said. "Was there a problem?"

"No problem," I said. "I had somewhere I had to be."

She seemed to accept what I said and thankfully didn't ask for details. We moved away from the booth as some customers stopped and began checking it out. Lisa R watched her employees as they went to offer samples. She let out a sigh. "We have to let them be. I tried to tell Jerry R that checking on them yesterday was enough. Our employees know what to do." It seemed she was talking more to herself than me.

I wanted to say goodbye. "Again, I'm sorry about not catching the—" I didn't want to say *kleptomaniac* in case anyone heard, so just added, "thief." I gave her arm a pat. "Thank you for all your hospitality," I said.

"And thank you for the suggestions for tomorrow. It's really been hard to switch from a celebration to a memorial. Poor Zoe is getting the short shrift." She turned to me. "The tagline was so perfect— Wishing them good news and sunny skies. Luckily, I got to the baker in time and he left it off the wedding cake. Though it is printed on all the wax bags we had made."

Her comment about Zoe seemed odd and I hoped she would give more details, but there was a commotion in the ranch shop. Someone had knocked over an open bottle of olive oil. Already the thick oil had spilled over the edge of the table and was dripping on the ground. Passersby were sliding as they hit the slippery mess. "Not again," she said, rushing to grab a roll of paper towels. I offered to help, but she said they had it under control. They were setting up orange cones around the spill as I walked away.

I went looking for Dinah and Rhoda. It was time to go back.

Chapter 23

"I just want to put my feet up and spend the rest of the afternoon peacefully crocheting," Rhoda said, letting out a tired sigh. We had all been glad to load our bags of produce and other goodies into the car and head back to the house.

"I'm not so sure about that," Dinah said, pointing to the number of cars parked on the street next to the driveway. None of us said it, but we were all thinking they were connected to Adele.

We heard the din of voices as soon as we walked inside. I acted as the scout and rushed ahead into the main room. Adele had center stage and was facing away from me. With her tall build and ample shape, she seemed to tower over the others, who were all sitting. All the Hookers' works in progress had been pushed aside and the newcomers were using the space with balls of red and pink yarn along with hooks. I looked over the faces, and other than Rory Bijorn, it was a new group.

I pulled Adele aside. "What's going on?"

Adele put her hand on her hip and rolled her eyes. "It's pretty obvious, Pink. Everybody said they were going out, so I didn't think I had to tell anyone I decided to offer another crochet lesson." She glanced back at Rhoda and Dinah standing in the entrance. "By the way, it's not really my fault. I was in town and Rory begged me for a lesson for her and her daughter." I looked at the group again and saw the girl sitting next to her mother.

"The other ones heard her talking and wanted in. What was I supposed to do?" Adele said. The rest of the group was made up of two youngish women and one man. Before I could say anything, Adele had already said she would take them out onto the patio.

I gave her the okay and Adele shocked me by giving me a hug and saying I was her best friend in the world.

As Adele and her group moved outside, Rhoda and Dinah moved

into the main room. "If we ever do this again, somebody is going to have to tell Adele up front that she can't take over like this," Rhoda said. She sat down on the couch with a sigh and put her feet up. I agreed, but said we needed to deal with the current situation.

Elise came in as I was talking. She barely said hello before she started talking about the properties that she had seen. She wanted to show us all the listings and opened her laptop.

Rhoda stopped her and told her she had interrupted us. Elise sat down and took off her blazer while she made annoyed sounds.

"I know selling real estate is your reason to be now," Rhoda said. "But we are dealing with a situation here." She pointed to the doors to the patio. Elise saw the group outside and shook her head in disapproval. "Why not just tell them to leave?" she said.

"That would cause more problems than it would solve," I said. "It's not her students' fault. There's a kid out there. I didn't think of it with her group yesterday, but it would be nice to bring them cold drinks. We need to use up the stuff in the refrigerator, anyway."

We all had a soft spot for kids and it sealed the deal as soon as they realized there was one in Adele's group.

"I'll get some for us, too." Dinah offered her help and we went to the kitchen to see what we could find.

Dinah brought the drinks for our group, and I carried a tray outside with glasses of ice tea, lemonade and mixtures of the two.

I stood in the background to watch. I hated to admit it, but Adele was good at teaching crochet, particularly to Rory's daughter. Adele made it dramatic and fun. This time instead of making swatches, she was having them make the small hearts. They all started talking when they took a break for the drinks. One of the youngish women had grown up in Pixie. She knew all about the area and was a big fan of Heddy's ever since her *Sissy Sings* days. She excitedly told the others about Heddy's property being near this one. She mentioned Heddy's claims about alien visitors and then said something about what she really thought was going on. I wanted to get into the conversation, but

I heard a shriek coming from inside the house. They kept talking while I went to investigate.

CeeCee was standing in the main room holding a hand mirror. She was definitely upset about something, and when she turned in my direction, I understood what. Her face was blotchy and red. "It must have been something they used in the facial," she said in a panic.

Rhoda tried to calm her and said a cool compress would help, while Elise suggested she call the spa and ask for advice on treating it. CeeCee was too flustered to remember the name of the place but was sure she would recognize it if she heard it.

"I had no idea there were so many of these health joints up here," Elise said, looking at her screen. She started to reel off names until CeeCee recognized one.

The actress was too upset to handle making the call, so Rhoda took over. "They agreed about the cool compress and said not to wear makeup until the redness goes away," Rhoda reported.

"I can't go out in public like this," CeeCee said, on the verge of hysteria. "I so wanted to go into Ojai. There's an ethereal music concert in the park and I wanted to see pink time since it's our last night. I'd scare little children with my face like this."

"Just put on a baseball cap and nobody will notice, or care. Have you seen how the people up here dress?" Rhoda said, pointing to the group outside. "Look at Rory Bijorn." Rhoda didn't say it, but unlike CeeCee, who had only been nominated for an Academy Award, Rory had won one. She was wearing khaki cargo pants and a black T-shirt with no makeup. Her hair was pulled into a straggly ponytail. Her daughter was dressed the same.

"It seems the style here is no style. If she can go out like that, I guess I can hide under a baseball cap," CeeCee said. She seemed to have calmed a little and I chuckled to myself, thinking that at least one of us had gotten a benefit out of Adele's lesson.

• • •

The students finished and all seemed pleased that they had completed one of the small hearts. Rory's daughter had tied hers around her wrist and couldn't wait to show it to her friends.

It would have been better if Adele had been quiet, but that was never a possibility with her. She insisted on gloating about what a service she had done for the craft of crochet. She had single-handedly created new crocheters who might have turned to knitting if she hadn't been there to show them the way. She was so into herself that she didn't notice that Rhoda seemed about to explode. I had to pull Rhoda aside and convince her that fussing at Adele was a waste of time since the getaway was just about over. I promised to deal with Adele if we ever did something like this again.

CeeCee had gone back to fretting about her face and all of our attempts to reassure her were going nowhere. Elise seemed the most perturbed and I worried that she would lose it and angrily tell the actress to snap out of it. It was lucky that this was the final night. I was just trying to focus on getting through the evening ahead of us. I didn't know how much longer they would stay civil.

When it came time for us to leave, CeeCee came out wearing big sunglasses under the baseball cap, and instead of making her more invisible, they made her stand out. We tried to tell her that it was past the time of day when sunglasses were needed, but she wouldn't listen and almost tripped when she got into the backseat of Dinah's car, complaining that it was too dark to see. I rode with them, while Adele and Elise went with Rhoda.

We all met up in the parking lot where Barry and I had had our talk on the benches. The atmosphere was totally different. Downtown Ojai on a Saturday evening seemed to have the same pull as the farmers' market. The sidewalks were busy with people and it felt very festive.

Elise had found an outdoor café that featured Mexican fusion cuisine for us to have dinner. The meal was peaceful, but then there was too much commotion going on around us to have much conversation beyond talking about the menu. I ducked out at the end to buy a T-shirt for Marlowe that said *Oh Hi*. The joke that the two words sounded the same as the town's name would be lost on the toddler. But it made me laugh.

I was on my way back to the café when I heard someone call my name. Barry was standing next to the Explorer. He was dressed in his off-duty clothes and holding a cup of coffee.

"I'm glad I ran into you," he said. "I was just getting a drink for the road. I'm done here. They got a confession in the case I was working. There was no connection to Kirkland Rush. It was the guy's wife. The old story that she was mad that he had someone else."

"What about the information he had about his former employer?" I asked.

"The financial firm was investing their clients' money in run-down properties, making their celebrity clients basically slumlords," Barry said. I thought of Verona Gilroy with her perky girl-next-door persona. No wonder Kirkland had asked about seeing her financial statements. He was probably trying to see if she was a client of that firm. Being connected to slums would hardly be good for her image.

He looked up and down the street and let out his breath as he got ready to go. "It was good to see you," he said.

"Yeah," I said. "Thanks for the other night."

"I was glad to help out, though it would have been nice to know what the problem was. You can still tell me now."

"I dealt with it," I said, and he seemed disappointed.

"I guess this is it," he said, standing at the curb about to walk to the driver's side.

"Safe travels," I said.

He hesitated as if he wanted to say something else, but then he seemed to let it go. "You too," he said finally. He stepped into the street to get into the Explorer and I walked away.

The group was waiting when I got back to the café and we all walked to Libby Park. The musicians were set up in a tiled area in front of the grassy area. Some people had brought chairs and others leaned against the stucco wall that surrounded the area. We all found places to sit on the low wall.

The music might be better described as rhythmic sounds that resembled wind accompanied by a harp, chimes and bongos. An area in front of the musicians was left open and anyone who wanted to add their expressive movements was invited to use the space.

I had my fingers crossed that Adele wouldn't figure it was a good way to show off her crocheted tank-style dress with a three-dimensional red rose and join the people doing their own moves to the sounds. There were a lot of kids and then I noticed Heddy. She was wearing a tank top, stretchy capri pants and no shoes. She had a sheer scarf that she was swirling around her as she danced. As she came closer to where I was situated, I could tell that she recognized me. She stopped and the scarf fell over her shoulders.

"I had to get out," she said. "I love the ranch, but I just want to go home. My trees must miss me. Can you take me back there?"

I barely had time to register what she said before Jerry R swooped in next to her and slid his arm around her shoulder with a strong grasp. "I'm just trying to keep her safe," he said before he led her away.

I tried to dismiss it as none of my business anymore but something about her sad expression haunted me. Dinah was sitting next to me and had seen it all. She also sensed my reaction.

"You have to just let it go," she said.

I knew she was right, but it felt so unfinished. I tried to get lost in the sounds as the sun slipped lower and lower in the sky toward the famous pink moment. It didn't help when I saw Mason and Tiffany were part of the crowd. But then he had been the one to tell me about the spectacular time at sunset.

The ethereal sounds were the perfect accompaniment as everyone stopped and turned toward the Topatopa Mountains. The haze over them caught the rays of the sun and they turned glorious shades of pink along with bands of red and orange. It was magical with an aura of serene peace. And then the sun dipped lower and the show was over.

• • •

Everyone felt at loose ends when we got back to the house, and I suggested a movie. There was a selection of DVDs and they voted on *Casablanca*. I felt too keyed up by everything to concentrate on it and made them popcorn instead. I did it the old-fashioned way, putting some oil and a few kernels in a saucepan. I shook the pan now and then, waiting to hear the first pops so I could pour in enough to cover the bottom. It always felt like it took forever for those few to explode and I looked around the kitchen to occupy myself. Adele had left some red yarn on the counter and someone else had left their phone. I had this weird feeling that the universe was sending me a message as I looked at them again. The kernels finally popped and I poured in the rest and shook the pan. It sounded like fireworks as the pan filled with white puffs.

The air smelled of the popcorn and butter as I brought in the bowl. I stood around barely noticing the movie. When the film was over, they all scattered to get their things packed up and go to bed. I felt a sense of relief that for all intents and purposes the Hookers' trip was over. We had made it through with only minor skirmishes. I stayed in the main room to clean up, hoping it would get rid of my nervous energy.

By now, I was looking forward to going home and putting this whole weekend and my former side hustle behind me. But there was the elephant in the room pestering me. What really happened to Kirkland Rush was still a mystery, and from everything I had heard it was going to be left that way.

I couldn't help myself and started going over what I knew. It seemed like a lot of people had a good idea that he would sneak into Heddy's to see if the alien story was real or if she had gone over the edge. I supposed it could have been an accident. With all that undergrowth and the darkness, he could have tripped and hit his head on a rock. He could have tried to clean off the wound with the water and fallen in and passed out. Or Heddy could have seen him and thought he was one of her alien visitors and gone after him with the rock. Or someone could have followed him and used the situation to kill him. The medical examiner had not been able to tell what caused his death. Was it the blow to his head or being in hot water too long?

I moved into the main room and started gathering up the stray kernels and empty bowl. Elise had left her laptop open on the dining room table. I hesitated to touch it, considering how frantic she was about it, but it was also too easy for it to get knocked over the way it was. I inadvertently hit a key and the screen came on.

I was considering whether to just leave it or put down the top as I looked over the screen. It was the list from earlier, and I scrolled through it. I clicked on something and was astonished by what I saw. It fit like a puzzle piece with something that Adele's student had said. It all became clear as I realized what was going on. I paced up and down in front of the French doors thinking it over. And then I recognized the universe's message. Part of me said to leave it alone. Did I really want to go out there alone in the dark? But I also had the nagging feeling that this was the only chance to uncover the truth. How would I feel if I went home tomorrow and knew it was my fault that Kirkland never got his justice and a killer went free.

I didn't want to use the flashlight on my phone, worried that it might show off my location. I wanted to be as stealthy as possible. The glow-in-the-dark yarn was still hanging from the trees and all I had to do was to follow it. I caught my foot on the dry grass a few times and had to grab on to a tree branch to keep from falling. When the yarn ended, there was enough light from the moon to show off the low fence that marked the beginning of Heddy's property.

It seemed that the whole area was empty and for this last part, I needed a flashlight. I turned it on and pointed it at the ground as I carefully advanced forward.

There was one thing that held the truth about what had happened. Kirkland's phone. From everything I'd heard, he would have had it out when he went exploring. He had it at the ready to catch pictures and maybe take audio notes. I didn't know what it would show, but I was betting that it would show if he had company that night, along with information on other stories he was working on. I understood why the cops had given up looking for it. With all the brush, it was beyond looking for a needle in a haystack. And I sensed that Jerry R had encouraged them to give up the search because of what he thought it would show.

But someone had continued to look for the phone—they simply didn't know where to look. I wouldn't have either if the universe hadn't sent me that message.

I began to shine my flashlight on the ground on my side of the fence, barely noting that there was an afore-missed gate. My so-called message from the universe had reminded me that I had slipped on something the first time I had gone back there and that strand of red yarn had fallen out of my pocket, marking the spot.

I was completely focused on the ground, shining the light over the brown grass, and then I saw the bit of yarn. It only took a few steps to reach it. My heartbeat took off as I poked through the twisted dry grass and pulled out a phone. I was stunned by my own success. I tried to turn it on, but the battery was dead and there was probably a password anyway. I'd leave it to the professionals to deal with that.

I was ready to follow the yarn trail back to the house, feeling triumphant. I would leave my gig as a private private detective as a winner. It was like leaving Las Vegas with a slot machine jackpot on your way out of town.

It was a bad idea to get so full of my own success. I lost sight of what was going on around me, or more correctly, who was around me, until I felt someone grab my arm just as a bright light flooded over us. I looked back and almost choked on my breath when I saw who had grabbed my arm. The tall silver figure had buglike black eyes and a viselike grip. The light was from a craft hovering above us. My captor reached for the phone, but I was faster and I threw the phone off into the wilderness.

The figure let go and took off running in the direction the phone had gone. This was my chance to get away. I frantically looked for the glow-in-the-dark yarn to find my way back. The craft with the light was hovering above me and followed as I wove between the trees. The sound of it got louder as it seemed to be getting lower and I knew it was hunting me down. It flew right above me and then circled back. There was no doubt it was aiming to hit me and this time it would succeed. There seemed to be no way to escape and I cringed trying to duck, expecting the painful impact. But then a miracle happened. Out of nowhere there was a loud thud and the light went off as the craft fell to the ground. I looked around wondering who had come to my rescue.

Chapter 24

"It was you," I said in surprise as Mason came out of the shadows. "How?"

Before I could get any details, there was a rustle coming from between the trees and what looked like a bunch of Cyclopses rushed toward us. As soon as they got close enough, I saw they were actually uniformed officers wearing headlamps. They asked me the situation and I pointed toward Heddy's land. I got a weird look when I told them to look for a silver figure with buglike eyes.

Mason went over and kicked the fallen craft. "Not exactly from outer space. More likely a drone from Best Buy," he said.

We stayed put until the group of cops came back with two figures in silver suits.

"Okay, buddy, let's see who you really are. Take off the mask," the cop in charge said.

"There's been a misunderstanding," the taller figure said, pulling off the silver hood and revealing a very human Ash Selinger. He looked a little sweaty, but other than that seemed completely confident and maybe a little arrogant as he continued. "I know we were trespassing and it's in bad taste, all things considered. We were filming a video for YouTube. With all the rumors flying around about space visitors, we thought a video would get a lot of hits." He pointed at the fallen drone. "There's a camera in there. There's no reason to turn this into a big deal. How about we just admit that we were trespassing and pay a fine. I could bring cash directly to you."

The other silver-suited person seemed anxious to take off the full head mask. "Do you have any idea how hot these costumes are?" Bayleigh Selinger said, glancing over our little group, expecting sympathy. "Everything he said is right."

The cop was keeping a benign expression when he turned to me.

"And who are you and what are you doing here?" he said, peering at me. "I've seen you before. You were at the Rayners' the other night."

He introduced himself as Sergeant Lester Halloran.

"Molly Pink," I said. I wasn't sure of the etiquette and waited to see if he was going to offer his hand to complete the greeting. His arms stayed at his sides and I went right into explaining about the Hookers coming up for the weekend.

"Hookers?" the cop said.

"As in crochet," I said. I heard Mason chuckling at the idea that anyone would think we were the other kind of hookers. He was right about that.

The sergeant looked at me. "And then you had a part in this movie they were making?"

"They weren't making a movie. They came back to the scene of the crime. They were playing a gaslighting game with Heddy to scare her into selling her place. It's all about the hot springs. They had to have the ponds of hot water for their pricey resort. They were already promising access to them on their website. I think they were after her coffee plants, too." I wondered if I should explain how long it took to get to a first harvest, but I decided to let it go. "They must have been here doing their alien thing when Kirkland Rush snuck on the property. I'm guessing that Kirkland got more than he expected and saw the real identity of the alien visitors." I looked at the pair in the silver suits. "It was them."

"That story is nonsense," Ash said. "She thinks she's some kind of sleuth like Miss Marple. You know, looking for plots when there aren't any to make her dull life more exciting."

Mason stepped in and gave Ash a withering look. "She's a professional investigator and she works for me."

The sergeant looked at me again. This time more intently. "Not your usual PI, but then maybe that's a good thing," he added with a shrug. "Now that we have all that worked out, can we get back to what happened here?"

"Whatever," Ash said dismissively. "There's still nothing but her conjecture." Bayleigh tried to say something but Ash shushed her.

"Kirkland's phone would clear everything up," I said. I explained what I'd heard about him using it to take video notes on his phone when he was after a story.

"We looked for it," the sergeant said. "But when the ME's report came back we tabled it. Thanks, we'll have another look."

I had a hard time not smiling at the perfect setup I had been given. It was time for the big reveal. "No need for that," I said and held up the cell phone.

All of Ash's confidence faltered when he saw what I was holding. "But I saw you throw it away," he stammered.

"You saw me throw a phone, but it was my phone," I said, trying not to sound too triumphant. "This one just needs to be charged and then all will be revealed."

"Good luck getting the password," Ash said.

I hesitated for a moment and was going to let the cops deal with it, but then I glanced down at the phone in my hand and turned it over. "No problem. I guess Kirkland was forgetful. It's written on the back."

Bayleigh had stayed in the background but she finally exploded. "It was an accident," she wailed. Ash tried to shush his wife, but she kept on. "Kirkland snuck up on us while we were putting on the costumes. We panicked when we realized that he had seen us, and worse, had pictures. We couldn't let it come out that we were trying to scare Heddy into selling her place. Ash tried to get the phone, but Kirkland took off. He tripped on something and his head hit that rock." She swallowed hard. "It knocked him out. Then Ash dragged him to the hot springs and pushed him in. We left him there," she said, looking down as her voice dropped. "And we went looking for the phone. He must have flung it as he fell. We've been using the drone to look for it ever since." She looked back toward the fence and shook her head. "We never thought to look here."

"You can't use any of that," Ash said, regaining his arrogance. "You didn't read her her rights."

"That only works if she was in custody. Nobody is in handcuffs.

We're just having a conversation in the woods," Sergeant Halloran said. "But it's time to take this down to the station." He produced a paper evidence bag and took the phone.

I hoped to ride there with Mason, but the sergeant insisted I ride with him. I was relieved when he offered me the front seat.

We all met up back at the Ojai Valley PD headquarters and then were separated for more questioning. After what seemed like forever, I was allowed to leave.

The Selingers, however, stayed. Bayleigh's confession, along with what they found on Kirkland's phone, was enough to arrest them for suspicion of manslaughter. They made a last-ditch effort to get Mason to be their lawyer, but he refused. The sun was coming up when Mason and I walked out of the stucco building.

"Kudos for the reveal of the phone," Mason said when we got into his SUV. He took something out of his pocket and handed me my phone.

I was mystified. "How did you find it?"

"I kept sending texts and followed the pings," he said.

"Thank you, and thank you for whatever you did to stop the drone from buzzing me." I reached up and patted my head, grateful it was intact.

"It was a rock. I had to improvise and use what I could find."

"More of your Eagle Scout training."

"No, that's from my Little League days when I was a pitcher," he said, mimicking that he was going to throw a ball. "I'm a man of many talents. But right now we need breakfast and to talk."

Chapter 25

Now that I had my phone back, I rushed to send Dinah a text, worried that she would freak when she awoke and saw my bed empty. All I said was that I was okay and would explain when I got there.

The rest of the texts and messages were from my family, wanting to know when I was coming back and saying that we needed dog food and that the toaster was smoking. I let those be for the moment. But when I read the last text, I let out a squeal of displeasure and Mason asked what was wrong.

I told him about the bookstore remodel and my desire to keep the yarn department separate from the newly added craft area. "It didn't work out and it looks like the Hookers are going to have to share the space with whatever other craft events we put together. Maybe even a knitters' group."

"Uh-oh. Doesn't Adele have a problem with knitters?" Mason said.

"I don't even want to think about it," I said. "I'm still recovering from the whole event here." I looked over at Mason. "I don't think you ever told me how you happened to show up at just the right moment."

"It was pure luck," he said with a friendly smile. "I came by to drop off the things you left in the guest house." He pointed to the backseat and I saw the jeans and a bag with the incidentals. "I texted you and there was no answer. I went around to the back of the house and heard all the noise and saw the light from the drone. I guessed you were involved somehow. I called the cops and went to see what was going on. And then I downed that drone." He seemed pleased with himself. "I like playing the hero."

He pulled the SUV into the parking lot of the coffee shop where we had eaten at what seemed like a century ago.

It felt good to settle into one of the old-fashioned booths. I was glad to let Mason order and sipped coffee to wake up my brain. My mind was still spinning, but I remembered he had said we needed to talk.

The server set down an array of plates with eggs, potatoes, pancakes and toast and gave us each an empty one.

"You said you wanted to talk about something," I said.

"First of all, I already talked to Jerry R and told him about last night. He wanted me to tell you how grateful he is that Heddy is really off the hook." Mason looked at me directly. "You came through and made me look good. Even after you quit working for me."

"I feel better going out on a high note," I said. "And thanks for calling me a professional." I was about to help myself to the food. "Is that it?"

Mason kept looking at me. "No. There's more. This is embarrassing. I can't believe I let somebody interfere that way with my life. You would think I would have learned. Like you said, Tiffany is a lot like Jaimee." He looked down and took a deep breath before meeting my gaze. "She told me she had a conversation with you. She seemed proud of it and said it showed how she was looking after me." He shook his head regretfully. "She wouldn't tell me exactly what she said, but I gather it had something to do with your quitting." The server came back with the coffee pot, interrupting our conversation.

"Are you saying you want me to repeat what she said?" I took a sip of the fresh coffee and he nodded.

"I'm sorry it's unpleasant, but since she claimed to be speaking for me, I need to hear as close as possible to what she said," Mason said. He was sitting with his arms folded.

"I don't remember her exact words, but she said you were going to fire me because I embarrassed you by failing to find the kleptomaniac and that you regretted ever hiring me. She urged me to save face and not show up. I decided it was better to face you and resign rather than run away. Particularly after . . ." I let my voice trail off. I didn't want to dredge up the details of what I had done. I regretted it now, but I hadn't faced him directly, I'd broken off things with him on the phone.

His nod made me realize he knew what I meant. It was upsetting to repeat what she had said and I was doing my best to not show how it had upset me.

He was silent for a moment and let out a tired sigh. "I figured it was something like that, but I didn't expect it to be that bad. I'm so sorry. You have to know that none of that is true. I had no intention of letting you go, and even before you did what you just did, I thought having you work with me was a good decision. If it means anything, Tiffany went home."

"Fine. You're off the hook for what she did," I said in a flat tone. "Is that the end of what you wanted to talk about?" This was all uncomfortable and I wanted to end it.

"Not completely," Mason said. "Jerry R doesn't know about any of it and thinks you're still working for me. He and Lisa R are expecting you to come to the memorial. They wanted to do something first to thank you in person."

"I don't know. Can't they just thank you since you were my employer. The Hookers are leaving this morning. I have to see them off and check over the place. I was going to ride back with Dinah."

"I would be happy to drive you home." He paused before continuing. "I wish you would reconsider about working for me. We make a good team. Just think, you could keep your secret life. If it's money, you can have a raise."

It was a relief to hear the truth and that he wanted me to keep working for him. Still, I wasn't sure it was a good idea. This weekend had stirred up my feelings for him, making it confusing. At the same time, I regretted losing the gig.

"I'll stay for the memorial service," I said. "But I'll have to think about the future."

"I will accept that," he said. He pointed to the plates of uneaten food. "The stressful moment is over. Let's eat."

We were both starving and ate like there was no tomorrow.

When we were done, Mason drove me back to the Hookers' house and took off to check on Spike, who had been alone all night.

I wanted to make sure the Hookers got off, and since Mrs. Shedd had left me to be responsible for the weekend, it was my job to have a last look around the house to make sure everything was okay. After that, Mason would pick me up.

The house was peaceful when I walked in, probably because the group was in going-home mode. Rhoda was the only one who had finished the scarf and was showing it off before she put it away. She moved on to clearing the yarn scraps on the coffee table. Dinah was busy loading up the extra yarn into the plastic bins. Elise was on her phone. Adele was counting how many of the small hearts the group had made for her. CeeCee was just coming out of her room.

All any of them knew was that I had been out all night, was okay and would tell all when I returned. They all stopped in their tracks and wanted to hear everything.

They were all openmouthed by the end.

"I'm glad some good came out of the debacle with my face," CeeCee said after I explained how I had looked through the list of nearby spas and seen Haven listed. The directions had a map and I had realized that it bordered Heddy's property. And they listed natural hot springs as one of their amenities.

"Then I deserve some credit, too," Elise said. "I'm the one who pulled up the list." She paused a moment. "I wonder what's going to happen to Haven now," Elise said. "I ought to contact them and see if they want to sell it." Her single-mindedness always stunned me. Nobody said it, but I think we were all thinking the same thing. Elise had become a real estate version of an ambulance chaser.

It had barely registered with Adele. She was muttering about going back and facing that her marriage was in tatters until I said, "Adele, the thing that pulled it all together was something one of your students said."

Adele's head shot up. "And all of you were upset with me giving lessons. You heard Molly. It's all because of me that she solved the case." Adele stood up and took a bow.

Rhoda shushed her and wanted to know what it was that the student said. "She said she thought someone was trying to scare Heddy into selling her property." I looked over the group. "The Selingers could have piped in the hot mineral water into tubs, but it wasn't the same as having it as it came up from the ground in natural ponds."

Adele's head shot up again at the mention of the spa owners' name. "What about the ties they commissioned me to make? And the rest of it? They were going to have me as a crochet consultant and special instructor. They even wanted me to make the little hearts with the fortunes attached. They were going to be big-time clients for me." She seemed frantic as she looked over the group.

And they were the ones who did the voodoo move to the big heart, I thought to myself. I was relieved that it wasn't an inside job as Dinah and I had suspected. Or that it had been Bennett.

"Dear, be grateful that we helped you with the order for all those hearts," CeeCee said, trying to smooth things over.

Rhoda rushed to change the subject. "What about you and Mason? You spent a lot of time together. Maybe things are starting up again between you two."

"It's not like that," I said. I looked at Dinah and she gave me a nod. "You might as well know, I was working for him. Like a private private investigator."

"That's so exciting," Rhoda said.

"Was so exciting. I think I'm done with it. After this afternoon, I'm giving up being a private private investigator," I said, and explained going to Kirkland's memorial. I told Dinah that Mason was going to drive me back. I considered if I should tell them the end result of the bookstore remodel and that the yarn department had been combined with the new craft area. But why look for trouble? I let it go.

We were interrupted by a sudden ruckus as the door burst open and someone wearing boots came inside. Everyone turned toward the noise. Eric marched into the main room and looked around. He was over six feet tall with a barrel chest and dressed in jeans and a leather jacket. He was carrying a helmet under his arm. Since he was a motor officer, it wasn't surprising that he rode a motorcycle in his civilian life. He glanced at all of us and his gaze stopped on Adele. "Where's that tie?" he said. Then he saw it was sitting on the table next to her tote bag. "If that's what it takes to make you happy." He put the tie around his neck and tied it with a Windsor knot.

"And I'm not afraid to do this either," he said, picking up one of the hearts that had fallen on the floor. He stuck it onto a zipper pull on his sleeve. He looked over the rest of us. "Get it? Wear my heart on my sleeve?" He turned back to Adele. "You're it for me, babe. Let's go home."

"What about your mother?" Adele asked.

"She's moving to one of those retirement apartments."

Adele was stunned by it all. She told Eric she would meet him outside. She gave her tote bag to Dinah and asked her to take it home for her. Tears were streaming down her face. We all stared since we had never seen her cry before. And then she hugged each of us. "You guys are my buds. Thank you." She headed to the door with us trailing behind.

Adele on a motorcycle was too good to miss. Eric was already on the bike with a sidecar attached. He handed Adele a helmet and put his own on. She looked down at her long vest made of granny squares. She pulled it off and threw it at me. Eric pulled out a leather jacket from a side bag and handed it to her. She put on the jacket and helmet before hopping into the sidecar. Then she gave him a nod. "Let's ride."

He pushed his foot down on the pedal and the bike roared to life. With waves from both of them, they were gone.

Chapter 26

I hung around to see the rest of the Hookers off. Now that the weekend was done, they became sentimental about having the time together and were talking about doing it again. At the same time, they were anxious to get home. Commander had sent Dinah a photo of the bouquet of roses he had waiting for her. Hal had reservations for dinner at a romantic restaurant for the couple. CeeCee had gotten the answer she was waiting for and it was all good news. Films with older heroines were hot now and she had gotten the part she was hoping for. The movie was about a group of septuagenarians who inherit a resort on a Greek island. She was calling our weekend research.

Elise was anxious to show Logan the list of properties she had come up with for her client. It wasn't the same as winning a sales award, but it showed she was in the game.

At the last minute, Rhoda made a confession. She had gotten Hal to talk to Eric and helped work it out so Adele got her romantic ending. It had turned out that Eric had no idea what was bothering his wife.

When they were all gone, I went through the house checking for left items and doing a little picking up, though a cleaning crew was scheduled for the next day. Mason returned as I was taking a last look around the property where so much had happened. He helped me retrieve the glow-in-the-dark yarn that was still dangling from the tree branches.

"I don't know about you, but I need a nap," Mason said as we headed back to the Rayners'. I had been running on nerve and it had just run out. It sounded good to me and I gave him a thumbs-up.

In anticipation of the memorial service, a knot of newspeople were hanging out at the entrance to the ranch's driveway as we drove in and parked in front of the guest house.

We retreated to our individual rooms and I was asleep as soon as my head hit the pillow. It was amazing what a couple of hours of sleep, a shower and fresh clothes could do.

I was treated like the conquering hero when I walked into the Rayners'. Jerry R announced that Kirkland's phone had been charged and turned on. The video was choppy and cut off abruptly, but there was a clear picture of Ash and Bayleigh putting on their costumes and some audio when Ash saw Kirkland and tried to get the phone.

Heddy had come in and rushed up to me. "Nobody thinks I'm crazy anymore," she said. "And I can go home now." She promised to send coffee from her first harvest and invited me to soak in the hot springs.

The Rayners were a little more subdued, though they were clearly grateful that I had not only taken the heat off of Heddy but found out the true villains.

"I have to admit I was a little dubious about you being an investigator," Jerry R said. "But now I see that the fact that you don't look the part and have interesting methods is a huge benefit. You were very brave to confront the bad guys."

You would think that I would have grown out of blushing, but being the center of attention still got my face to turn red. "I wasn't all that brave," I said. "I was scared."

"Ah, but that's what being brave means. It's not that you aren't scared, it's that you do it anyway," Jerry R said. He turned to Mason and held up his glass. "Kudos to you for finding her."

After all the dissing I had gotten from Peter, I wished he could see the moment. But then I was sure he would find a way to be embarrassed at his mom being exciting and sort of a hero.

$$\bullet \ \bullet \ \bullet$$

Somewhere in all this, Bennett had come in with Zoe. She was dressed in a dark gray version of her weather girl dresses. He was smiling and wide-eyed when he came up to me. "Wow, and I thought you were just a pretty face. I can't wait to hear about your exploits." He looked out the window. "Got to go. My film crew awaits." He gave my arm a squeeze and rushed off.

My moment of glory was over and Lisa R collected the two Persian cats that had been wandering around. She reminded me that they were part of her rescue and asked if I would like to adopt one.

I laughed and told her about my menagerie. Jerry R was talking to Zoe about her part in the memorial service. She was uncomfortable about having to speak. I thought it was because she was so broken up about her fiancée's death, but as I overheard them, I realized it was something else entirely.

"This wasn't how it was supposed to turn out. I wish I had never agreed to go through with this charade of a marriage," she said.

"I am sorry things didn't pan out as we planned," Jerry R said. "It seemed like a good way to get a lot of attention for both of you that would translate into a boost for both of your careers. Kirkland's was sagging and we were having trouble getting yours to take off. But being an almost-widow should get you a burst of attention. I'm hoping we get an offer for a reality show or documentary. Something like behind the scenes of a weather reporter."

And then all the attention turned to the memorial service. People had already begun to arrive and were being taken to the tent that had been set up for the wedding. The interior had been changed from festive to somber. The dance band had gone all acoustic and played slowed-down renditions of their playlist as people arrived. The chairs around the tables were all set to face a podium at the end. Poster-sized photos of Kirkland had been hung around the interior.

It began with screening the piece that Bennett had made with a recap of Kirkland's life. There were speakers after that. Whatever trepidation Zoe had had didn't show when she got up to speak. She had me believing that she had adored Kirkland.

It ended with Heddy doing an a cappella version of "Somewhere Over the Rainbow." Throughout all of it, a film crew tried to be unobtrusive as they recorded it.

A reception followed. The wedding food was served buffet-style. The three-tiered cake had been revamped with a stairway going up the sides of the tiers. The top was dark blue now with stars and it had the words *Welcome to Heaven, Kirkland.*

It ended with everybody outside around the pool with the film crew capturing it all. The rose petals had been sprinkled on the surface as I had suggested and filled the air with their fragrance. And Lisa R had followed my suggestion with the waxed bags that had been meant for the slices of cake. They had been turned into lanterns with LED tea lights and were floating on the water. A drone was invisible in the darkness as it flew low over the pool and picked up one of the lanterns and carried it off as the dance band played a farewell.

As the crowd was dispersing, Bennett came up to me. "I wish I could, but I can't walk you home tonight," he said. "The crew's waiting. We have a long night of editing."

"That's okay. We all have our stuff to do." I smiled at him, relieved that he didn't know that I had thought of him as a possible murderer. "And thanks for the walks home you did do," I said with a smile. "Hanging out with you was fun."

"Yeah," he said warmly. "I hope we can pick up where we left off back in town." He held up his phone. "I'll be texting you. Feel free to do the same."

He looked around at the thinning crowd. "I don't know what the etiquette is for things like this," he said. "My BNN bosses are here and I probably should look all business." He took my hand and kissed it in a courtly manner, which somehow seemed completely appropriate. Someone called his name. "Gotta go," he said, backing away and getting lost in the crowd.

I hung around until the tent was empty and the catering people were clearing the tables. I hadn't seen Mason since people started arriving.

He caught up with me as I was about to walk back to the guest house and get ready to go home. "Jerry R wants us to come to the house before we leave." I followed him into the main house.

"Sit for a while," Jerry R said, inviting us into the living room. "We all need to decompress."

Mason nodded in agreement and we sat down on one of the couches. The living room seemed cavernous with so few occupants. Now that they weren't playing host, the couple could relax, and for Jerry R, it was a chance to stop being on and just be a person.

I was surprised how different he seemed now that he wasn't playing the part of manager. He had regrets about what happened to Kirkland, though he realized he couldn't have stopped him. There were more regrets about the set-up marriage, but this time he admitted the truth. It had all been Kirkland's idea. "I should have said no."

He talked about his other clients and how he tried to do his best for them. It had been his idea to make Tom Kelter an action star, but now it was putting a strain on his marriage and Rory Bijorn felt left behind. The best he had been able to do for Verona Gilroy was to give her a place to hang out while she decided what to do after her divorce. "At least I was able to take care of Heddy," he said with a nod toward me.

"The Selingers were new to town and they just became part of the regular crowd in our social events. I should have gotten to know them better," he said with regret.

I watched as Mason reassured Jerry R that his intentions were always good and that he wanted the best for his clients, but that they had their own minds.

None of us had really eaten during the earlier event and when the caterers brought in containers of leftovers, we all ate, sitting in the gallery and looking out at the darkness.

I saw Mason sit forward and took it as a clue that it was time to say our goodbyes and head back. Jerry R picked up on the move and instead of going along with it, pointed out how late it was.

"Why don't you stay one more night. And then you will be here for the summer solstice salute," Jerry R said, trying to be enticing. "It will be a low-key event after all this. Just the regular crowd."

"And then there's nothing until the Fourth of July barbecue," Lisa R said with a yawn.

"I am pretty beat after no sleep last night," Mason said. He looked at me for agreement and I nodded. I had been looking forward to going back, but something Jerry R said had given me an idea. It was worth it to stay away one more night.

I was so tired that I barely remembered walking to the guest house and fell asleep in my clothes. Mason was off with Jerry R the next day and I watched the crew dismantle the tent and clear up all the stuff brought for the wedding. I would have liked to let go and just relax, but I was keyed up thinking about my plan and wondering if it would work. If I could succeed at what I had been originally hired for, I could truly finish my PI career on a high note.

I didn't want to tell anyone my plan for fear that it wouldn't work, but in the end, I told Lisa R, who was glad to assist me with the setup.

The crowd was much smaller. Heddy was barefoot and wearing her usual stretchy capri pants. She arrived with avocados and bubbling enthusiasm for a new plan. She would buy Haven and run it herself, only not so pricey. After the memorial, she realized how much she missed singing to a crowd and thought she could work that into the resort. Tom Kelter and Rory Bijorn were stunned about the Selingers and still at odds with each other. Tom was going on about his workout schedule and how he had to keep in shape for his upcoming movie. He looked like he had come from the gym and wore black track pants and a white T-shirt. Rory seemed depressed and at loose ends. The dark gray cargo pants didn't help. Verona Gilroy was in her usual black clothes, though this time it was leggings and a long shirt. She seemed more cheerful than she had been the last time I saw her, and went right to the game room.

Meg Rush had been there all day. She had ended up staying over to work on straightening out more of Kirkland's affairs. Like everyone else, she was dressed down and wearing yoga pants and a loose top. As far as I could tell, Harrison had spent the whole day in the game room. Other people drifted in who I hadn't met before.

I had donated my pair of stork scissors to the cause since the kleptomaniac seemed to find them irresistible and put them in the glass case. Now all I had to do was wait and see if my plan worked.

It was a relaxed affair. Everyone ate, drank and hung out as the daylight seemed to last forever. Lisa R periodically checked the library. She kept giving me a thumbs-down, meaning the scissors were still there. As it got closer to sunset, I began to worry that it wasn't going to work. And then Lisa R came in the living room and caught my eye. She smiled as she gave me a thumbs-up.

I kept a blank expression as I moved through the guests looking for the evidence, even going into the game room. I wanted to high-five myself when I saw that my plan had worked, but instead I used my phone to surreptitiously get pictures of the evidence. Jerry R had been clear from that first night that I wasn't to confront anyone.

No one guessed that anything was up when I pulled the host aside. Lisa R came with me and explained what I had done and then I showed him what I had.

"What an idea," Jerry R said, sounding impressed. Just to be sure, the three of us went back into the party and he checked out the guests. There was no question of who it was.

Mason noticed our odd behavior and came over to see what was up.

"It looks like your gal scored again," Jerry R said. He had me show the pictures on my phone. "Verona is the one," he said, keeping his voice low. She's in the game room. I'll take it from here."

"I don't know what I am looking at in those photos," Mason said. "What did you do?"

"With Lisa R's help we set up the display case with my stork scissors. Then we stationed two of the white Persian cats in the library with the doors shut."

Mason's face lit with understanding as he looked at the photos again. "The cats must have been happy for the company and swirled around her ankles, leaving a souvenir of their long white fur." He was grinning as he hugged me.

"And now I can go home truly a winner," I said.

We all went outside to watch the pink moment on the longest day of the year. It seemed extra magical this time as the mountains glowed pink and the sky was a riot of pastels.

It was dark when Mason, Spike and I drove out of Pixie on our way back home.

I was still thinking about the kleptomaniac being Verona. I wasn't supposed to get personally involved, but I couldn't help it. I felt bad for her, though I was sure Jerry R would get her some help. "I realized how I screwed up before," I said. "It had only seemed like everyone was gone. It was my mistake not to check the game room. Verona must have still been in there when I left."

"You can't still want to quit working for me," Mason said. "Jerry R kept telling me I better not let you go. What's it going to take to keep you?"

I decided that I needed to be honest and tell him the real reason I was hesitating.

"You seem to have it down about letting go of whatever we had. You can be indifferent, but I don't think I can be," I said.

"Oh." He glanced over at me as if he was collecting his thoughts. "About that. Maybe I wasn't a hundred percent honest," he said. "I kept telling myself I could just look at you as someone who worked for me. I thought if I told it to myself enough times it would be true." He shrugged. "But it isn't." There was a pause and I thought he was going to agree that under the circumstances it was best to end our working arrangement, but instead he let out a sigh. "It seems a shame to let go of something that seems to work so well. I'm sure we can figure something out," he said. He pointed to the dog sleeping in my lap. "Even Spike agrees."

"We could see how it goes after another case," I offered.

"Deal," he said with no hesitation. "I'd shake on it, but I need my hands on the wheel."

The traffic was light and we made it home quickly. When we pulled into my driveway, the lights were on and I could see people in my living room. "I'll probably have to tell them I'm working for you. So they don't think it's something else," I said. "I did tell the Hookers I was working for you, but they think it's done." I handed Spike off to him and opened the door to get out.

"Should I come in?" he asked, looking at the activity going on in my living room.

"You might as well. You know, they all love you."

He grinned. "They obviously have good taste."

He brought Spike in with him and my herd of animals folded him into the group. The She La Las stopped rehearsing to greet him. His face lit up when Marlowe toddled over to him. I heard my father telling him there was Thai food in the kitchen. Peter and Samuel went up to him and did some kind of silly handshakes. They barely noticed me as I took my suitcase into the bedroom and began to unpack. I took out the purple velvet bag and thought about opening it. The guy who gave it to me had said when I wished for someone or something I wanted, whatever was in the bag would make it happen.

I paused as I thought it over. I wasn't sure what or who I wanted to wish for. I smiled to myself. It was better to let it happen on its own.

The Hookers' Weekend Scarf

The Rayner Ranch Chocolate Olive Oil Loaf Cake

The Hookers' Weekend Scarf

This is a fun, colorful scarf inspired by a certain TV female detective known for her colorful, offbeat wardrobe. It is made up of 12 granny squares with four rounds of stitches. The last round is done in an off-white, but the three rounds inside can be all one color or a varied combination of colors.

The yarn is a cotton yarn like Peaches 8 Creme (100% cotton, worsted weight, 120 yds/109 m). How many colors is up to you. The Hookers mixed 5 different colors for the center portion, with off-white on the fourth round of all the squares.

The instructions explain how to end a round if a new color is being added or how to continue if the color is staying the same. If a new color is being added, the round is fastened off and the new color is added with a slip stitch in any corner. If the color is being continued, the yarn is moved to the closest corner with several slip stitches.

It's a good idea to lay out the squares before they are put together.

H – 8 (5mm)
Yarn: one skein of each color, 2 skeins of off-white
Tapestry needle for weaving in the ends

Stitches used:
Chain — ch
Slip stitch — sl st
Double crochet — dc

Squares are approx. 5x5 inches
Finished scarf approx. 60 inches

The Square
Make 12

Ch 5 and join with a sl st

Rnd 1: Ch 3 (counts as dc), 2 dc in ring, ch 2, 3 dc in ring, ch 2, 3dc in ring, ch2, 3dc in ring. Join with sl st in the top of the beg ch-3. Fasten off if the color is going to change. Add new color with a slp st in any corner. If the color is continuing into the next round, use several sl sts to move yarn to the next corner.

Rnd 2: Ch 3 (counts as dc), 2dc, ch 2, 3 dc, ch1, 3dc, ch2,3dc, ch 1, 3dc, ch2, 3dc, ch1, 3dc, ch2, 3dc, ch1. Join with sl st to top of ch 3. Either fasten off and add new color, or move yarn with sl st to the next corner.

Rnd 3: Ch3 (counts as dc), 2dc, ch2, 3dc, ch1, 3 dc, ch 1, 3dc, ch 2, 3dc, ch 1, 3dc, ch1, 3dc,ch 2, 3 dc, ch 1, 3dc, ch 1, 3dc, ch2, 3dc, ch1. Join with sl st to top of ch 3. Fasten off and add off-white yarn with sl st in a corner.

Rnd 4: Ch3 (counts as dc), 2dc, ch2, 3dc, ch1, 3dc, ch1, 3dc,ch 1, 3dc, ch2, 3dc, ch1, 3dc, ch1, 3dc, ch1, 3dc, ch2, 3dc,ch1, 3dc,ch1,3dc, ch 1, 3dc, ch2, 3dc, ch1, 3dc, ch1, 3dc,ch 1. Join with sl st to top of ch 3. Fasten off. Weave in ends.

Join Squares:

Hold one side edge of two squares together, matching sts and corner-spaces. Working in front loops only of both squares, join yarn with sl st in corner ch-2 sp at matching side edges. Sl st in each st across, sl st in corner ch-2 sp. Fasten off and weave end ends. Repeat to join all the squares in a strip.

Recipe

The Rayner Ranch Chocolate Olive Oil Loaf Cake

The Rayner Ranch was famous for this cake and it was a mainstay at every party or get-together. The olive oil adds a subtle fruity taste to the moist cake.

1½ cups all-purpose flour
¾ cup unsweetened cocoa powder
1 cup sugar
½ cup light brown sugar, packed
1½ teaspoons baking powder
½ teaspoon baking soda
½ teaspoon salt
2 large eggs
½ cup extra virgin olive oil
1 tablespoon vanilla extract
1 cup boiling water
Powdered sugar for garnish

Preheat oven to 350 degrees F. Grease a 4.5 x 8.5 loaf pan, or line with parchment paper.

Combine the flour, cocoa, sugars, baking powder, baking soda and salt in a large mixing bowl. The Rayners always use a bowl with a handle as it is easier to pour the batter into the pan.

Mix together the eggs, olive oil and vanilla in another bowl or large measuring cup. Pour into dry ingredients and mix until there are no streaks of the dry ingredients. The batter will be lumpy.

Pour in about 1/3 cup of the boiling water and mix into the batter. Add the rest of the water and mix until it's smooth. The batter will seem liquidy. Pour in the prepared pan.

Bake for approx. 60 minutes. When a toothpick comes out clean, it's done.

Cool pan on a rack until cool enough to handle. Remove from pan and finish cooling on rack. Sift powdered sugar on cooled cake as a garnish.

Slice and enjoy!

About the Author

Betty Hechtman is the national bestselling author of the Crochet Mysteries, the Yarn Retreat Mysteries, the Writer for Hire Mysteries and the Crochet and Crumpet Mysteries. Handicraft and writing are her passions and she is thrilled to be able to combine them in all her series.

Betty grew up on the South Side of Chicago and has a degree in Fine Art. Since college, she has studied everything from improv comedy to magic. She has written newspaper and magazine pieces, short stories, screenplays and a middle-grade mystery, *Stolen Treasure*. She lives with her family and stash of yarn in Southern California.

See BettyHechtman.com for more information and excerpts from all her books. She blogs on Fridays at Killerhobbies.blogspot.com, and you can join her on Facebook at BettyHechtmanAuthor.

www.ingramcontent.com/pod-product-compliance
Ingram Content Group UK Ltd.
Pitfield, Milton Keynes, MK11 3LW, UK
UKHW041915010425
5247UKWH00004B/309